MW00980204

DRAGONS IN FLIGHT

First Printing, February 2014
Revised edition, March 2015

Dragons In Flight is a work of fiction. Names, places, and incidents are either products of the author's mind or used fictitiously.

ISBN: 978-0-9911965-0-0

DRAGONS
IN
FLIGHT

LEE FRENCH

BOOK 3 OF THE MAZE BESET TRILOGY

ACKNOWLEDGMENTS

I wish to thank the usual suspects for their continued encouragement as I struggled with finding the right way to end Bobby's story. Erik, Gwen, and Bob in particular deserve chocolates and my undying affection and gratitude.

Or is this the end of Bobby's story?

PROLOGUE

WILL

This moment needed to last as long as possible. Will couldn't help but let a few tears free, with his arms around Jasmine and his face buried in her neck. Even if they were in a helicopter piled with the sedated bodies of everyone he'd come to trust, he had her. Finally, after so long without her, they were together again and he could smell her scent. He had no idea what was going on. That didn't matter right now.

"Will, you're squeezing too hard," Jasmine shouted over the noise of the helicopter.

As little as he wanted to loosen his grip, he did, though he still held her close. "I missed you." He didn't really care if she heard it or not, but her ears were sharp, and the way she rubbed her cheek on his told him she probably did.

The ride felt excruciatingly long and unbelievably short at the same time. As soon as it landed, he'd have to let go so she could walk. With luck, they'd be able to find quiet and have time to talk. When the helicopter touched down and he was ushered out with Jasmine, the gun pointed at him made that hope seem foolish. He realized they probably would rather he not spoil whatever fiction made Jasmine work for them.

Before anyone could rip them apart, Jasmine stopped and wrapped herself around him, kissing him again with joy and lust and longing. It might be the last time he saw her for a while, so he returned the embrace with everything he had. For a few minutes, he forgot where he was and how he got there and why.

As such things always must, it ended. Someone tapped him on the shoulder. "C'mon, we gotta get you in for a debrief."

Will stared into Jasmine's eyes, the part of her he'd been initially attracted to years ago when she brought Walnut, an injured wild squirrel, into his practice. The rest of her, from mind to toe, was a delight, and she kept him sane and alive, but her eyes—icy blue and so exotic—made him ask her out the first time. He put a light kiss on the tip of her nose, still oblivious to nearly everything going on around them.

"No, really. Let's go, loverboy." The soldier stepped behind Jasmine where Will could see him easily and gave him an unamused, impatient glare.

Granted, that guy had a really big gun, but he had a squirrel-girl. "I'm not going anywhere without her."

Jasmine smiled up at him brightly and squeezed him. "No, never again. No more being apart."

The soldier, a square-jawed muscle man, glared at Will, brown eyes hard and unfriendly. "That's not how this is going to work. Boss says you come alone, so you come alone. Milani can grab a bunk and wait for you."

Will clenched his jaw. "No, I'm not playing that way. If you want to haul me off at gunpoint, then Jasmine," he turned his gaze back to her, giving her a look he hoped she would understand, "is going to run for it, and you'll never see her again." The guy had orders. Will knew that. He didn't care. "Tell you what, though. If you let it go until morning, I'll come willingly and tell them whatever they want to know without a fuss."

The soldier growled in the back of his throat, eyes narrowed and mouth a thin line. "I'll see if I can get authorization for that," he grunted. A gesture got some other soldier to hold a gun on them both, and he trotted away.

Jasmine wanted to be hugged more, so he pulled her close again and held her there. He shut his eyes against the sight of people he knew and cared about being carried past, unconscious on stretchers. He had no superpowers, unless being a licensed veterinarian counted. What could he possibly hope to do about all of this? If he got a chance to help them, he'd do it. Jasmine could only do so much too.

"Nope, your offer was refused. Let's go." Hands grabbed him and dragged him away.

"Jasmine, run!" Hands grabbed him and dragged him away. He opened his eyes to see Jasmine blinking in shock. "Jasmine, run!" He saw her blink one more time, then she shrank down into her squirrel shape and took off faster than the eye could track. The men around him swore. Several fired guns at her. All of them missed.

"I ought to shoot you right now for that." The soldier pressed the barrel of a pistol to his temple and cocked it. "Give me one good reason why I shouldn't."

Will had never been seriously threatened with a gun before. The feel of the metal on his flesh scrambled his brains with panic. "I warned you," he whimpered. One thought sustained him: Jasmine got away. If he couldn't stop hyperventilating, though, nothing else would matter.

"Might as well take me in to be questioned at this point, or duping Jasmine was all for nothing. It isn't like she won't know it if you kill me." Hopefully, the quavering of his voice wouldn't undermine the message.

The soldier restraining him coughed. "Sergeant, we should just take him in. Those are the orders."

Sergeant grunted in the back of his throat and flared his nostrils. His jaws flexed.

Will screwed his eyes shut and cringed away from the gun. If he had to die right here, right now, at least he knew Jasmine was safe. Thoughts about how she would manage without him flooded his mind. She'd been fine before he met her but did so much better with him than without. He imagined her weeping over his grave and consoling herself by binge eating mixed nuts.

An eternity later, the gun left his temple, and Sergeant clicked the safety on. "Get him out of here," he snarled.

"Oh, thank God." Will sucked in a lungful of air, grateful for whatever made this man not kill him.

"We'll see how you feel in an hour."

Chapter 1

Bobby

He wriggled down a tight, dark, slimy tunnel with squishy sides. It meant he couldn't go as fast as he wanted and couldn't fly. That mattered because dragons had wings. It didn't matter though, because he had a mission, and he'd be there soon. Another few inches and he reached it.

Blowing fire at the tunnel floor made it weak, and he punched his sharp claws and face through it, then launched himself forward. More fire made the gunk he found shrivel up. Soon, he punched out into open air and could finally fly.

He turned to see what he'd ripped his way out of to find a flat chest with a faded red shirt covering it, the gory hole spraying blood up at him. The girl had dusky skin and big brown eyes, wide with shock. She couldn't be more than five years old and clutched a fuzzy brown bear in one hand. Her hair was swept up out of her face in twin pigtails.

While he watched impassively, she fell to the ground in slow motion, reaching out her hand to touch him. Her eyes went rigid and glassy, yet they still stared at him with silent damnation. "Why did you kill me?" Her mouth didn't move; the words came out of nowhere.

"I don't know." Bobby's voice was cold, wrong. "I just did."

"I died for nothing?"

"Yeah." He looked around and saw more of his dragons bursting out of the chests of more children. They surrounded him, a circle of babies and toddlers and kids. All of their dead eyes stared at him and he felt nothing. The dragons came together, burning the blood and gore off each other's bodies. These were just foreign kids; they didn't matter.

One little white boy stood in the middle of all the carnage, looking around with his icy blue eyes. "What happened?"

Bobby the dragon flew toward Sebastian. The boy didn't need to see this kind of thing. Before he could reach the spot, Lily stepped out of nowhere and grabbed Sebastian up. "Stay away from us, Bobby." He knew that hate-filled glare too well.

"Wait, it was an accident!"

"Everything is always an accident or a mistake with you, Bobby. We won't be your next mistakes."

"Come on, hurry up and wake up." The voice didn't fit her this time. It belonged to someone male that he vaguely recognized. All of a sudden, a bright light flared in his face and something patted his cheek.

He tried to pull his claws up or turn his neck. Everything refused to obey him. "What in heckbiscuits?" His speech came out slurred, sounding like himself. No more of that cold, flat stuff.

"We don't have time for this. They said you have some kind of super-metabolism."

Bobby groaned and blinked repeatedly. Though he tried to roll to his side, something held him in place. In reaction to that, he struggled to get free, to no avail.

"Quit it. You're tied down. All I want is answers."

"Turn down the lights or something. I can't see nothing."

Something got between him and the source of the light. He blinked a few more times to see icy blue eyes looking down at him. Two pairs. Both belonged to men about the same age as he, so nineteen or maybe a year or two older. One was taller than the other and in better shape, and he had short, light brown hair in a messy-on-purpose sort of style. The other one had shorter red hair and lots of freckles. Brown Hair looked angry, specifically at Bobby. "Where's Elena?"

Bobby wished he could rub his eyes. Instead, he kept blinking. "Who? I don't know no Elena."

"Don't lie." Brown Hair turned to Redhead. "Is he lying?"

"I have no idea." Redhead shrugged. "I told you I couldn't read him."

He didn't understand any of this. They were talking gibberish or something. "Read me? What in heckbiscuits is that s'posed to mean? I ain't lying, I ain't never met no—" He frowned. Actually, now he thought about it, that name did sound familiar. Sort of. "Wait. She about five and a half feet tall, long hair, nice rack, don't speak no English, Mexican-looking?"

Brown Hair's nostrils flared with annoyance, and his eyes narrowed. "Spanish. She's from Spain. And yes, that's her. It's nice to know you can't be bothered to remember names. Now, what have you done with her?"

"Whoa, wait a minute." If he could put up his hands to ward the guy off, Bobby would. "I ain't done nothing to, with, over, or under her. I met her is all." This didn't make any sense. "Why don't you just ask your buddy Privek? He knows where she is."

"I don't think he's lying," Redhead said. "It's hard to tell, but I don't think he's lying."

Brown Hair reached up and ran a hand through that messy hair in frustration. He paced out of and back into Bobby's sight. "He said you took her, you and Cant."

"Stephen didn't do...well, it weren't like he—" Bobby frowned and struggled fruitlessly against his bindings again. He couldn't lie there and not want to be free. "What I mean is, we didn't grab her or nothing. She was working for Privek when we met her."

"What?" Brown Hair hurried back to Bobby's side and looked down at him with a face full of disbelief. "What do you mean? Why would she be working for him?"

"That there's a question I'd like to ask you, turns out. On account ain't nothing good never happened around him."

Redhead frowned down at Bobby. "You're not getting out. The drug is still in your system and the bindings are secure. But, more importantly, I'm a telepath. If Privek was jerking us around, I'd know."

A telepath? Bobby stopped squirming and looked up at Redhead. He knew what that meant. The guy could rifle through a body's head and read everything there. "He had a guy killed and framed me for it. He had me trussed up in a lab and experimented on. He had me shot, he sent goons after me, he's been abducting everybody like us across the country, and you think he's an okay guy? Where in heckbiscuits your head get shoved up?"

"Hang on," Brown Hair said.

Bobby cut him off. He knew getting cranky didn't help anything from his perspective, but he was the one tied up on the damned slab. "Look, either you're gonna let me go and we're gonna figure this stuff out together, or you're gonna throw me back under whatever rock I done got shoved. Make up your damned mind and get to it already."

"Fat chance," Brown Hair snorted. "We've seen what you can do.

We'd have to be stupid to just let you go."

Scowling, Bobby could easily imagine what kinds of things Privek showed them and told them. "Lemme guess. I'm dangerous and gotta be contained or whatever until I can be talked into sense or something? Privek show you stuff from Hill?" Redhead nodded. Brown Hair watched him, his expression slowly changing from skeptical to thoughtful. "He bother telling you why all that happened?"

Redhead jumped in to explain with all the eagerness of a brown-nosing pupil. "You killed people, they managed to detain you, and you broke out."

Bobby laughed. He couldn't help it. As much as he expected it, the answer still surprised him. They both watched him, Redhead with some alarm, and Brown Hair getting more calculating. "I kinda figured he'd leave out details and all. That's the only way to explain you lot working for him. Them two men I done killed, they were trying to abduct Lily and her boy. I didn't even mean to kill 'em. That were an accident. One of 'em tased me afore I did anything to them, and the dragons got mighty angry about that.

"They managed to get the drop on me, sure, and two girls too. Took us all to some house, pumped me full up of these drugs. When I woke up, they wanted me to talk, so they started—" Just thinking about that made him angry, really angry. "Let's just say it was all guys in them suits, and they were using a female prisoner against me and leave it at that." Honestly, he didn't know if they would've actually raped Ai without Anita intervening, but he was mightily glad he didn't have to find out.

"The other girl managed to get free, and them two escaped, but I didn't. I got shot. They took me to Hill for medical attention. All that mayhem there was the rest of us doing what best they could trying to rescue me from their custody. Killed a guy there, yeah, but only because he was trying to kill me first."

Redhead blinked and looked up at Brown Hair. "I could actually tell he was being honest with all of that. It's hard to explain, but he's not lying."

Brown Hair nodded to show he understood. "What about Afghanistan? I saw pictures. They were a lot more...disturbing."

It would be nice if he could turn away and look at something else. Bobby settled for shutting his eyes. The girl from his dream stared back at him. "I...ain't rightly proud of what all I done there. Some of it weren't a'purpose or even needful. All I got to say in defense is it were mostly what Privek told me to. Stephen and I was trying to get him to trust us so we could find Jasmine and the rest of you to break you outta wherever he had you stashed. Weren't no reason to think he weren't doing to you what he done to me, Jayce, Alice, and Ai. I got stains on me, sure as heckbiscuits, but it ain't on account I'm just a rabid dog or nothing."

"What's a 'heckbiscuit'?" Redhead squinted at him.

Bobby shrugged and looked up at Redhead again. He tried to, anyway. "Something Momma says. Ain't polite to use stronger language 'round folks you don't know."

"What will you do if we let you go?" Brown Hair seemed to be taking all of this at face value, which was good because he would obviously be the one who to the decision.

He didn't even have to think about it to answer that question. Bobby locked his gaze on Brown Hair, who didn't flinch away from the intensity. "Bust as many out of here as wants to come, go back to the farmhouse, and get as many as I can to go public so they can't do this crap to us again."

Brown Hair grimaced in distaste. "I don't want to be public. With what I can do, I don't ever want people to know about it without my telling them on purpose."

"I can respect that, but it ain't gonna work for us all to keep quiet." Bobby heaved a sigh. "I don't especially want to be DragonBoy or whatever, but if that's what I gotta do to keep anyone from being able to use Sebastian for a test subject, then I'll be the first one in line. I'll answer every stupid question I gotta. I'll go on TV and make a damned fool outta myself. Ain't right what I saw, taking a boy from his momma like that. Didn't you hear him screaming? 'Cause I sure did."

Redhead's eyes went wide. Brown Hair took a step back, looking like he wanted to think. "How did you hear that?" Redhead asked. "You were the first one down."

"I got one dragon off and tried to warn Stephen, but it didn't work. Something smashed it when they shot him."

Redhead looked up at Brown Hair, who Bobby couldn't see anymore. "I think—" He cut himself off, probably in response to a gesture by Brown Hair, and looked chastised. They stood in silence for maybe half a minute.

Brown Hair came back into view, moving so he could look Bobby in the eyes, face to face. "We're going to let you out, and we'll even help you free everyone else, but," he raised a finger in warning, "you have to prove it first. Privek has been nothing but professional with me and has repeatedly asserted you're a dangerous maniac. Paul has never sensed any duplicity from him. Your assertions are believable, but you need to prove them."

Man, this guy used a lot of big words. Bobby had to actually think to understand what the guy said. "What's 'duplicity' mean?"

Redhead got an amused half grin. "I've spoken with him several times, and I've never sensed him lying to me. If what you're saying is true, I should have picked up something, something to tip me off he was omitting details or plain lying. But I never have. How someone might do that, I have no idea."

"But, in spite of that," Brown Hair smirked, "you seem more reasonable than he gave you credit for, and I know you rescued several soldiers in Afghanistan when you didn't need to. So, we're going to give you the benefit of the doubt. Just you, though. Everyone else stays here until we're sure. Just in case you're thinking about killing us to eliminate us as an obstacle, I have some more of the drug that makes you unable to use your powers."

Bobby narrowed his eyes at Brown Hair, mildly annoyed by the threat and the implication. "How d'you know about them soldiers?" It seemed like something Privek would want kept as quiet as possible.

"I healed them." Brown Hair bent to the task of undoing the straps.

"Huh." The guy could heal. That was pretty handy. Well, not for him. Bobby didn't need that, but not many of them could heal themselves. "Are you sure it ain't okay to grab one other person?" He turned his head, and that felt like Heaven.

"I think it's in our best interest to only have one of you to keep track of. Besides, it's going to be hard enough to get you out quietly."

Oh, his arms, yes, and his chest. Finally, he could sit up. His head still felt a little woozy, probably from the drugs, but freedom was heavenly. "How long I been trussed up?"

"A couple of days." Brown Hair stood back and let Bobby finish undoing the restraints himself.

Clumsy hands fumbled over the straps, bringing back the memory of Anita leaving him behind, but this wasn't that, and these guys weren't she. When it became clear he needed help with the releases, Redhead stepped up and clicked them open for him. "Where are we? Like, what state, I mean."

"We're in Washington, DC."

"You guys got names? Everyone calls me Bobby." He needed help to get down to the floor too, and his legs were unsteady. Redhead yanked a tube out of his arm.

"Liam," Brown Hair said, then he pointed at Redhead. "This is Paul. We'll see if it's actually nice to meet you or not."

Bobby snorted. "Your girl was in Virginia last I knew. Was paying attention when we got close, figured we'd want to go back there again." He gave a shot at popping off a dragon. It didn't work. "I guess we'll need a car or something. How we getting outta here?"

This room reminded him of a TV show morgue. It had a bank of drawers the right size and looked sterile and easy to clean. The bed he just got up from was a sliding cot. Paul shoved it back into its drawer. This bank had nine drawers, which wasn't nearly enough to house everyone. Maybe only the ones they were really scared of wound up in here. He'd give a lot to be able to check who was in them but didn't think Paul and Liam would just stand by and let him do it.

"Leave it to me," Paul said with steely determination. He went for the door.

Behind his back, Liam grinned like Paul was possibly the most amusing thing he'd ever seen. "Lean on me. I'll help you out." The guy stood at least four or five inches taller than Bobby, definitely over six feet. Paul was about his own height, five foot nine. All three of them had a similar compact build, not broad-shouldered or hulking. Of the three, Bobby had the most muscle, but Liam was no slouch. Paul probably never did any kind of hard work in his life with anything but his brain. "We'll have to take your car," he added to Paul. "Mine doesn't have a backseat."

One arm over Liam's shoulders, Bobby looked around, taking in details. They left the small room. The place felt very institutional with cement walls painted white and some kind of stone flooring in red flecked gray, fluorescent panel lighting overhead. A guard sat at a desk just outside the room, but the man ignored the trio completely for some reason, his eyes glued firmly to some papers in front of him.

Much to his surprise, they took the elevator at the end of the hall. An escape seemed to Bobby to be a window or stairwell thing. According to the row of buttons, they were in the second and lowest basement of a building with seven floors above ground. Paul actually looked nervous and stressed now—his eyes darted around as if he could see through the ceiling, and this did nothing to inspire confidence.

"You guys sure about this exit plan?"

Liam coughed lightly. "Let's not distract the telepath while he uses his mind to clear a path for us."

"Ain't that creepy as heckbiscuits."

"A little, yes."

Bobby nodded and thought of something he wanted to know. "Can I ask you, how'd those guys turn out after you healed 'em? The ones that were really messed up."

Liam frowned and looked down. "There's only so much I can do."

"Meaning what?" Bobby wasn't harsh with the statement. He just wanted to know. "Look, I done seen 'em beforehand. One of 'em didn't want to live, another one died on the way to you. I'm just wondering how the ones what survived are doing. I mean, you said you saw pictures of what happened out there. It's on account of what got done to them more'n anything else."

Huffing out another breath that spoke of discomfort with the subject, Liam nodded. "I can't replace lost parts. As for the rest," he said with a cringe, "we had to cause some damage to heal what was wrong. Each of them had something that healed up horribly in the time they were there. None of them walked away whole again, but they're all in much better shape than modern medicine could have done."

That was both a terrible thing to know and a great relief. "I'm glad to hear that. None of those guys deserved to live crippled up like they been made. Heckbiscuits, nobody does."

Liam glanced at him, measuring and weighing. "You're a dangerous man, Bobby." The elevator doors opened on the ground floor, and they walked out into a nearly empty lobby. He didn't give Bobby a chance to ask what he meant by that. "Keep quiet until we get to the car."

It made no sense to Bobby at all, given he only wore his pajama pants and still needed the help Liam provided, but no one even gave them a second glance. The guards here—actual uniformed police officers of some variety—looked, then their eyes slid right over the trio and ignored them. Paul led them boldly through the front door and into sunlight too bright for Bobby's mood. He didn't like leaving all the others behind. How he would explain that he did it without everyone assuming he'd gotten back up on the Head Cowboy horse?

They reached the car, a little four-door piece of crap. At a guess, it probably had more years on it than any of them. As soon as Paul shifted his attention away from the building to the car, he froze in the act of pulling out his keys. "Guys, there's...some...thing in the car already."

Bobby looked up and saw a person sitting in the back seat. Liam must have been mostly watching the ground as they went too, because he stopped, just as surprised. The woman in the car turned her head right then, and Bobby recognized her. "Oh, it's Kaitlin. No worries then. She's one of us."

"Kaitlin? Kaitlin Tremont? What's she doing in my car?"

"Obviously," Liam muttered so Paul wouldn't hear, "it's because she has no taste."

Bobby snorted and lurched to make Liam get going. "She sees the future and stuff. Creepy, a little cranky, but harmless." Before he could reach the car and knock on the window, she saw him and waved with a mildly amused smile. Of course, the doors weren't locked. Paul probably forgot to do it, since she didn't have any special car-boosting skills he knew of. Then again, he didn't really know Kaitlin all that well. Maybe she could break into one with her eyes closed. Didn't seem likely, but it was possible. He reached out and opened the back door while Paul fumbled with his keys.

"Don't panic," Kaitlin said with a grin. She wore red, black, and gray in the form of a hoodie, miniskirt, leggings, and chucks, and sat there calmly with an orange and pink striped backpack on her lap, like this wasn't a clever, daring escape from that giant, unmarked institutional building.

Bobby smirked and tipped an imaginary hat to her as he bent to get into the back seat with her. She scooted over so he could. "Kaitlin, what're you—" Stupid question. "Never mind. I'm real glad to see you got outta the farm alright. This here's Liam." He jabbed a thumb at his rescuer.

"There's something in the car," Paul announced again, this time with an edge of panic to his voice.

"That's Paul." Bobby leaned back out and glared at the other guy. "She ain't a 'something.' She's a 'someone.' " He wasn't inclined to explain anything else right now and just wanted to get out of here.

"Where are we going?" She watched Paul and Liam stand there beside the car and have a whispered conversation.

"If'n I can get Liam his girl back from wherever Privek's got her stashed, them two're gonna help get to the bottom of all this and get us all free."

"Ah." Leaning forward over Bobby's lap, she stuck her head out through the door. "Gentlemen, Agent Privek is coming back from lunch in about five minutes. If you want to conveniently miss him, we should get going."

This pronouncement made both men stare at her. Bobby sat back with a bemused smirk and watched them take a few seconds to come to some kind of realization, then hurry to get into the car. Both kept glancing back at her without saying anything.

Paul navigated them away from the building. When they stopped at a red light, he turned around and looked her over with narrowed eyes. "Your mind is weird."

She shrugged. "So is your nose, but I wasn't going to say anything. Because it would be rude."

Paul's mouth opened and shut twice, then he faced forward, staring out the front windshield and sounded sulky. "I meant it isn't like a normal person's mind."

"Same goes for your nose," Kaitlin retorted.

"You know, they're actually helping. You ain't gotta be difficult."

Liam, who ignored the exchange up to then, turned around and said pleasantly, "What does that mean that you can see the future?"

"Precognition, the real deal." Kaitlin shrugged again. "I make a killing on the stock market. I also wind up in the strangest places, sent there by stuff I see. It's a double-edged sort of thing. I knew you were going to haul Bobby out and take this car and that it would be unlocked already. So, here I am."

Liam nodded, his mouth drawing down into that same thoughtful, calculating quirk as before. It struck Bobby as funny how this wasn't the first time he sat in a car with three others of his kind, escaping Privek and his Suits, off to do whatever it took to get the others to safety. He'd give a lot to have Jayce, Alice, and Ai—or Stephen and Matthew—here with him instead. He knew them and trusted them. These three would have to do.

"Which part of Virginia?" Paul pointed at a sign with too many numbers and unfamiliar names for Bobby to know how to direct him.

"Southeast of Culpeper on Route 3." Bobby watched Liam pull out his phone and tap on it to get a map. It looked like a fancy one, with all the bells and whistles. His clothes were nice too, though Bobby wasn't much of a judge of that kind of thing: slacks and a crisp shirt, a slick watch, nice shoes. Paul, on the other hand, wore jeans and some band's t-shirt with a soft, plaid, button-down shirt hanging open over it. They got to keep all their own stuff. Must be nice.

"I don't want to be a pain, but is there any way I could get some clothes?"

Kaitlin shoved her backpack at him. "I brought some of your stuff from the farmhouse."

"Oh, thanks." Bobby opened up the pack and fished around in it.

"You were at the farmhouse?" Paul frowned and glanced back. "How come we didn't catch you? Wait, how come I didn't notice your mind there?"

Exaggerating her enunciation and drawing it out like she was saying it for a stupid person, Kaitlin said, "Pre-cog-ni-tion."

"Why is the car making that noise?" Liam looked over at Paul, probably referring to how the engine knocked. It might have been a question only asked to distract him from that discussion.

Paul blushed. "It's an old car. It does that sometimes."

"What d'you drive, Liam?" Bless Kaitlin. She'd brought him jeans and a t-shirt.

"Something newer than this," he answered smoothly.

Kaitlin rolled her eyes. "Instead of talking about cars, why don't you all just pull down your pants and compare already?"

Cracking into a broad grin, Bobby chuckled. "Yeah, yeah. We're all on the same team here. Ain't no reason to get touchy about nothing. Any chance that noise is any different than it ought to be, Paul? 'Cause I'm pretty sure one of you eleven folks climbed into the car while we was at White Sands, and that's how you found the farmhouse."

Paul gulping audibly and Liam shifting in his seat confirmed that theory. "Maybe we should stop to check. It might be bugged."

Liam shrugged. "In which case we're already screwed and they already know where we're going. Stopping now to check would only delay us further and give them more time to prepare."

"When you know there's a trap, charge in to take 'em off guard. My kinda tactical approach."

"Look," Liam turned around, annoyance on his face loud and clear. "I gather this is all very entertaining to you, but Elena is my— She's—" He made a frustrated noise and turned back around. "She's very important to me."

Taken aback, Bobby blinked a few times. "Ease back I don't mean nothing by it. I get it. You're in love with the girl, it's cool. We're gonna rescue her." He knew a thing or two about being willing to do whatever it took for a woman.

Liam rubbed his face and didn't answer. Kaitlin watched Bobby, her expression thoughtful. "While you were gone, people talked about you a lot more than they normally do. No one really thinks very highly of your brains. They all figured Stephen talked you into taking off. But he didn't, did he? It was your idea to go ride on the fancy white horse, wearing the white hat. You were expecting to come back a big damned hero."

Bobby sighed and looked out his window, not wanting to admit the truth in front of Liam and Paul. Not out loud, anyway. "It don't matter." Tony had figured the same thing out, and he hadn't liked it then, either.

"Uh-huh." Kaitlin crossed her arms and stopped watching him. "I could have told you it was going to be a disaster."

"Yeah, well, I can tell you it woulda been stuck in committee for a month," he snapped. There was no reason to get testy with her, though. She had every right to be annoyed and prod him. "Look, yeah, I know. All this is my fault, okay? I get that. Been said, don't need a refresher."

She snorted. "It's not your fault, Bobby. That's like saying it was Tarkin's fault Alderaan got blown up. Technically true, but Palpatine was really to blame for that."

"What?" Bobby had no idea what she was talking about. Those names meant nothing to him. Actually, that last one maybe sounded a little familiar, but he couldn't place it.

Kaitlin rolled her eyes. "Never mind. I'm just saying that everything's connected. You can take responsibility for your choices, but it's not really your fault we're all in this situation. Liam, why are you working for Privek?"

Liam slumped against his seat. "We were at the airport, going through customs. Homeland Security was giving me a hard time. They separated us. When I got it straightened out, she was just gone. Elena, I mean. She disappeared. They had no idea where she went or when, and when I got them to check the security footage, there was nothing to see. Privek showed up, said he was leading a special task force to deal with us. He said he'd help me find her if I work for him. I tried to just pay him off, but he didn't want money, he wanted me to use my...ability for him."

Kaitlin nodded like that matched her expectations. "See? Privek. So, he takes Elena and says these dangerous mutants or whatever stole her, and if you work for them, he'll get 'his people' to find her. Classic bad guy tactic."

Even though he didn't quite follow the logic, Bobby shrugged. "I guess we should just be grateful they only managed to get eleven of us."

"Why do you keep saying eleven?" Paul looked at him in the rearview mirror, genuinely confused. "There's only ten of us on our side."

Bobby took a long, slow blink,and stared back at Paul through the mirror. "What d'you mean there's only ten? We checked every name on the list, and Privek got ten, plus Jasmine." He'd read that stupid list so many times he had it partially memorized. It was in alphabetical order by their last names, though he could only recite the first names down pat. "Brian, Kevin, Raymond, Dianna, William, Chelsea, Kanik, Paul, and Maisie. Them's all the ones what got took before we found 'em. Jasmine got took later."

"William is me. I go by 'Liam,' but I don't know any Kanik."

"Yeah, I'm obviously Paul, and I recognize the other names, but not Kanik."

Bobby looked at Kaitlin, who he figured had to be thinking something smarter than he. "Ain't that a broke pickle."

"Whatever that means," Kaitlin said, then she shook her head. "This Kanik guy is maybe someone we should be interested in talking to."

Liam asked, "Where did you get the list? We never saw one. Privek just had all your names somehow."

"It were in the place we done broke outta that first time. Privek said mistakes were made. Stephen and me kinda figured he meant that they didn't expect me to wake up like that, so they weren't set up for us yet. Ai picked it up on the way out. Though, in fairness, Stephen also has an alternate theory that we was supposed to break out and that list was planted all over the place to make sure we got it. I just can't figure that angle out, on account it don't go square with everything that happened."

"I remember him saying that," Paul said thoughtfully.

"How in heckbiscuits d'you 'remember' that?"

Sheepish and blushing again, Paul hunched down as much as driving would allow him to. "I was there when you met with him. In the next office over. Privek wanted me to read your thoughts. Only, I couldn't. Because you're too... I pick up each of your dragons as a separate little mind, and they're all too tight and close to pick anything out. The only time I seem to be able to get anything from you, other than a highly confusing mess I can't really read, is when all the dragons seem to be thinking the same thing. I guess that doesn't happen much."

"Wait, right now? I'm a bundle of dragon minds right now?"

"Yeah. It's like you're made of bees. There might be a central, core part, but I can't see it."

Bobby had thought the dragons didn't really exist unless he wanted them to. To find out they were really always there, just out of sight, shocked him so much it hit almost as a physical body blow. And he thought it was hard to explain his superpower before. Now, he didn't even understand it. Was he really just a weird hive mind effect? How did this make sense, given he wasn't made of dragons until he broke apart that first time? Or was he always this way, just with no instinct to guide him to let them loose?

"Stephen doesn't exist to my mind," Paul admitted. "And Kaitlin, you're...disturbing. Your mind is running backward and forward at the same time with an echo in both directions and feels like it wants to burst out of you and eat me."

"Nice to know you can't read me," Kaitlin said cheerfully.

"I can, it's just difficult and unpleasant."

Bobby still sat there, stunned, while the conversation moved on around him. The drugs had to be out of his system by now, and he popped a dragon off his thumb. It sat on his palm, looking up at him as he looked down at it. Was it he or was he it? Was there any way to tell? Did it matter? Knowing that wouldn't bring back those kids he'd killed. Knowing that wouldn't get Sebastian out of whatever they were doing to him. Knowing that wouldn't fix what went wrong between him and Lily.

"I'm you and you're me," he told the little dragon softly. It nodded and chirped. The small, silver critter walked across his hand to rub its head on his thumb affectionately. "Hey," he said, louder and to Paul. "If'n you see a place, I need to eat soon. Ain't picky. A junkyard'd be good too. Drag-ons gotta eat separate."

"Yeah, I'm a little peckish too," Paul said with a nod. "I'll keep an eye open for something."

"That makes no sense," Liam said. "Why do they need to eat sepa-rately?"

"I dunno. I almost done drowned on account of it once, though, so the 'why' ain't nearly so important to me as the fact of it. They gotta eat, but it ain't urgent right now. Just can't let it go too long."

"It still makes no sense. When you eat, they should be fed, and the reverse."

Kaitlin laughed. "Yeah, because any of this makes sense. Don't even get me started about how what I can do jives with free will. You can't possibly tell me that out of all of us, Bobby's the only one that defies logic for you."

The car went quiet. Bobby stared at his dragon and didn't know what to think. Mostly, he didn't want to think at all. Sure, he spent some time trying to figure out what his mind really was, but that had more to do with knowing his limits, not understanding how it actually worked. In truth, he didn't want to know how it worked. On some level, he worried that the second he understood it, all of it would stop working, even though he knew that was stupid. He wasn't Wile E. Coyote.

After a while, he decided to find out what the other side actually knew. "You guys all know where we come from?"

Liam and Paul shared a look. Liam shrugged. "We have theories. You?"

"Ayup, we got a theory. Starts with 'half' and ends with 'alien.' "

Kaitlin snorted. "It's not like Privek doesn't already know we know things. We think the government has or had an alien locked up someplace and spliced her DNA with human to make us, probably by harvesting her eggs and using human sperm. Presto, test tube babies. Someone is still working on how the alien got here."

Both men reacted. Liam seemed to know how to keep himself more or less under wraps, but Paul had no such skill, and Bobby could tell before he opened his mouth that he couldn't believe what she'd said. "How did you figure all that out?"

Kaitlin snorted and said, again very slowly and with exaggerated pro-nunciation, "Precognition."

Bobby laughed, hard. He hadn't had much cause to in a while, and it felt good. "I know Privek thinks I'm stupid. That's fine. But I ain't. None of us is."

"Privek did lead us to believe you aren't," Liam paused and spoke delicately, "precisely *talented* mentally."

"Yeah, I bet." Bobby stared out the window, trying not to take offense at that. He and Stephen had wanted to be underestimated. It just kind of burned to know people talked about him that way. Time to change the subject again so he could stop thinking about it. "Why you on Privek's team, Paul?"

The telepath blushed. "Agents showed up on my doorstep, saying my country needed me. I guess...I don't know. It was stupid. My dad is a cop. He was actually proud of me for something for the first time."

Since he looked embarrassed, Bobby just nodded. "That there's some powerful motivation."

Liam scowled. "If Privek took Elena specifically to manipulate me, he will regret it."

"I'm in," Bobby said cheerfully. "I'll hold him down. You open up a can of whupass."

Paul gripped the steering wheel until his knuckles turned white. "I just don't understand how he fooled me. That's not supposed to be possible."

"I fooled you by wrapping my head in tinfoil." Kaitlin shrugged. "At least, I assume that's why I did it. Maybe he's actually got some superpower or something."

That quieted the car again. Bobby could only guess what Paul and Liam might be thinking about it. For himself, he squirmed a bit about how much he and Kaitlin had shared compared to how little they got in return from Paul and Liam. But then, he figured they didn't have a lot of trust here and had to start someplace. Somebody had to give first, and he didn't mind being the one to do it, especially if it meant they'd hold up their end of the deal.

Not long after, Liam turned on the radio and found a station playing inoffensive jazz. An hour later, they'd passed Culpeper and Bobby perked up, paying attention to where they were. "Seems like a bad idea to just drive right up to the front door and park in plain sight," he said as he noticed a familiar sign. "I suggest driving past and finding a place to park off the road what ain't too far away."

"Good plan," Liam nodded.

Kaitlin shrugged. "I'll wait in the car."

Looking her over, Bobby lifted an eyebrow. "That ain't 'cause you know something bad's gonna happen, right?"

She gave him a very fake innocent look. "Nope." Her face dropped into a more serious cast. "You don't need me to do this. I'll only be in the way and don't have anything like the skills needed to break into a place and infiltrate security and whatever else you're going to have to do. Besides, if Paul leaves the keys, I can bring the car around for a quick getaway."

"If anyone's gonna be able to do the whole quick getaway thing, I expect it's you," Bobby nodded. "Assuming that's okay with Paul?"

Paul gulped. "Maybe I should stay with the car too."

Liam gave Paul a flat look. "How are we supposed to get in without your help? Should I heal them as a distraction?"

"I just—" Paul made a frustrated noise in the back of his throat.

Bobby laughed. "You don't trust Kaitlin not to drive away and leave you both stranded with rattlers."

"All three of us," Liam corrected.

"Naw," Bobby shrugged, "I ain't that easy to leave nowhere, seeing as how I can, ya know, fly. I ain't worried." He pointed out the window at a wall of shrubbery. "That's it. I swear on my Daddy's grave."

Kaitlin reached over and put her hand on Bobby's arm, her eyes unfocused. Paul squeaked. The car swerved and went into the ditch on the side of the road. Bobby burst into the swarm on impact and surrounded Kaitlin to protect her as the car flipped over and rolled a few times before landing upside-down in the field across the road from the target house. His intervention kept her conscious.

As soon as the car stopped moving, Bobby re-formed and yanked the back door open, then hauled her out. "You okay?" He grabbed her by the shoulders and made her look at him.

She mumbled some swearwords then shook her head to clear it. "More or less. What the hell happened?"

"I dunno. C'mon, we gotta get 'em out before anything blows up." How he wished for Jayce or Stephen, because either of them could rip the doors off. Both Paul and Liam had been knocked out cold. At least this beat-up old piece of crap was made more of metal than plastic. It didn't look like either managed to get seriously hurt or would need to be wrenched out. Both still wore their seatbelts and probably had their bells rung.

"I didn't even see that coming," Kaitlin grumbled. She crawled to Paul's door and yanked on it. The door groaned and refused to budge.

Bobby tried Liam's door with the same result. "Just worry about getting them out." He scowled at the car then remembered he had a small army of tiny claws at his disposal. Letting off a handful, he had the dragons zoom inside and cut the belts so both men thumped onto the ceiling of the car. From there, he and Kaitlin hauled them out through the broken windows.

"Someone heard that. They had to," Kaitlin said as she pushed one of Paul's eyelids up and peered at his eye. "We've got to get them away from here before anyone shows up."

"Are you people okay?"

"Too late," Bobby muttered as he looked Liam over for serious injuries. They were both incredibly lucky because they must have hit that ditch at fifty miles an hour. Someone crunching through the leaves made him turn to see the owner of those feet. And stare.

"Sergeant Riker?"

The soldier stopped and stood there, staring stupidly for a full second before hurrying over to put a knee down beside Liam. "What are you guys doing here? I figured you would've stayed in the Sandbox."

The last time Bobby saw Riker, he had injuries to his feet that meant he'd likely never walk right again, yet here he was with no sign of any kind of lingering debilitation at all. He even still wore military gear: jungle BDUs. Riker looked over Liam, showing full recognition. Liam had said he healed soldiers. At the time, Bobby thought he only meant the really messed up ones in that warehouse. It hadn't crossed his mind that guys with lesser wounds might have gotten the benefit of his ability.

"I...uh...long damned story, man."

"Yeah, same here. This guy," he patted Liam on the chest, "fixed me up right. I got shunted to this duty as a sort of reward, I guess, and to keep me quiet. All five of us are here, doing the most boring guard duty rotation imaginable. What are you up to?"

Bobby had a choice. He could be honest, or he could lie and try to play Riker. Which wasn't really a choice at all. "Looking to break into the facility you're guarding to relieve your new boss of something he stole away: Liam's girlfriend. Don't expect we got a whole ton of time to explain, so the short version is like this. There's a guy named Privek what's running all this, in charge of us with these superpowers, and he's been lying to us and using us against each other. We're looking to expose him and get some justice. Right this minute, I need to prove all that to these two, which is why we came for his girlfriend."

Riker frowned and nodded. "I have no way to evaluate that information, but you saved my life and what was left of my squad, and Liam healed me up better than doctors could've done. There's no one named Privek here that I know of, but if his girlfriend is here, let's get her out."

Relieved by his response, Bobby gave him a grim smile. "You got any ideas, Sergeant?"

The sergeant stood up and scratched at his clean-shaven chin. "I don't think it'd be a good idea for me to do your dirty work for you, but I can look the other way and report this as nothing."

"That'll do," Bobby nodded with a grim smile. He offered his hand to Riker, who shook it firmly. "I hope there's a chance to have out the long version of the story."

"Yeah, me too. Good luck." The soldier got a lopsided grin. "I didn't see anything. The noise must have been animals."

With a bemused snort, Bobby tipped an imaginary hat and broke apart into dragons. As the swarm streaked away, he heard Riker say, "Still a trip to see that." Kaitlin said something in return that he couldn't hear. His attention shifted to the simple task of getting into the house. Like most buildings, big or small, this one had vents, and he sent the swarm in through one. From there, they flew around in the ductwork and stopped where they could see in. The ground floor remained as he remembered it: furnished like a house and barely used.

He remembered sitting in that room over there, watching Stephen drink Elena's blood. Stupid vampire. Damn fool would be free if he'd just given Bobby the benefit of the doubt instead of assuming he was playing a dumb joke. As if he would've done that after everything they went through together.

His dragons wanted him to focus on the job and get it done and made that clear to him. The sooner they got Elena out, the sooner they could get to other, more important things. That stupid vampire was counting on him, not to mention all the others.

Bobby threw himself into one of the dragons and found a door he thought would lead to the basement. It was in the kitchen, which they must use as a kind of break room. A coffee maker percolated away on the counter, dirty dishes sat in the sink, and the dishwasher ran. Would anyone notice if he dropped his whole body in here and swiped something to eat? Better question: was it worth it to risk being seen here just to fill his belly?

Thinking about it that way sent him to the door, where he landed on the deadbolt that locked from the other side. A keypad on the wall next to it had a card-swiping thing, so he needed someone else to open the door for him. The downstairs probably had ventilation. Finding its access would just take time.

Screw it, he needed to eat. Dragons poured into the room. He reformed and went for the fridge with one hand missing and a rumbling belly. The other two dozen dragons spread out through the ductwork to find the right access point. Most of what he found in the fridge was in bags or reusable containers, lunches for the people here. If every person working here brought one of these things, then there were twenty. Hopefully, that included Riker and his men, so there would only be fifteen or so. He could evade that many people.

Nothing else in the fridge would feed him; ketchup and pickle relish sounded gross by themselves. He shut the door and scanned the room, noticing a bowl of fruit. Just as he stuffed a bite of banana in his mouth, the mysterious locked door beeped, the little light with the keypad flashed green, and it opened. Of course. Bobby made a start to flee for a hiding spot, but he didn't have enough time before the door opened all the way and an older woman with a severe bun stood there, looking at him with suspicion and confusion.

Jeans and a t-shirt probably didn't measure up to the dress code around here, given she wore a navy skirt suit with matching pumps. Add to that what must be a comical expression of surprise on his face, his icy blue eyes, and his missing hand...she had plenty of reasons to be suspicious and confused.

Bobby really did want to eat the banana. He wanted more for Privek not to know he'd been here. Dropping the fruit, he rushed her before the door could shut and clamped his one hand over her mouth. Her back and head thumped against the door frame, and she squeaked without trying to bite or kick him.

"I ain't gonna hurt ya," he whispered into her ear, "if'n you don't give me a reason to." It worried him a bit that he couldn't be sure how much he meant those words. He saw her eyes go wide and scared, which made him feel a little dirty on the inside. He'd killed people indiscriminately and had more or less come to terms with that. It still bothered him to rough up some random woman. A real man didn't treat women like this.

She nodded and put her hands up in surrender. What did she do here? No idea. Could be nothing more than a pencil pusher, could be in charge of the place.

Swallowing back bile from his own behavior, Bobby nodded back. If only Stephen was here, he could do his vampire thing and get what they needed from her that way instead. "I'm gonna pull my hand away on account I got some questions. You scream or shout for help and I'll kill you, we clear?" Would he really do that? No. Yes. Maybe. Hopefully not.

Again, she nodded and looked like she took that threat very serious-ly. When he pulled his hand away, moving his arm to keep her restrained, she sniffled. "Please don't hurt me," she whispered.

"There a girl named Elena here?" He remembered her introducing herself with that name, so he figured she must be using it with her cowork-ers. To be on the safe side, he rattled off a description of her.

The woman shook her head. "No, she was transferred two days ago."

Of course she was. Bobby bit back a few unfriendly words. "Where to?" The woman swallowed nervously, so he added, "It's important. Her family thinks she been kidnapped."

She blinked several times in surprise. "Oh. Um, I could...maybe find out?"

One of Bobby's eyebrows lurched up. "You think I'm gonna trust you to go back down there and not tell folks there's a guy up here what ain't supposed to be? I may not be a genius or nothing, but I ain't stupid, lady. Just tell me all the places she might be. You gotta know that, right?"

Nodding again, she took a deep breath. "White Sands, Groom Lake, or Adelphi. If there are any other facilities where she might be, I don't know about them."

"What about the one in DC?" Wouldn't it be funny if Liam had walked past her five times a day without realizing it? No, not really.

"No, she doesn't speak enough English. She has to be someplace where no one will ask questions."

That made sense to Bobby. "You know why she was here? Or why she was transferred?"

"Something about her boyfriend? Not really. Work here for a little while and you learn not to ask questions."

Bobby snorted, amused by that. "Sure. What you don't know is what you can't object to." The little growl on the edge of those words made the woman go still as her heartbeat raced. "You listen and listen good," he told her with quiet intensity in his voice. "I don't know what you think is going on here, but it ain't all it seems. Maybe you're doing some good, I don't know, but from where I'm standing, you're doing stuff where the ends justify the means, and that ain't never nothing good." If saying that made him an immense hypocrite, he could live with believing Privek had forced his hand.

"Point is," he continued, trying to be as dangerous looking and sounding as he could manage, "I aim to cause some ruckus for your bosses on account they done caused harm to a bunch of folks I care about, and if you tell them I was here and what I wanted to know, it's gonna make things harder for me. What d'you think I ought to do about that?"

She gulped. "I don't feel well all of a sudden," she said breathlessly, eyes even wider than before. "I think I might go home and sleep it off. Maybe I'll call in tomorrow too."

Pleasantly surprised by her answer, Bobby nodded. He also understood: he had until the morning after tomorrow for sure, but past that, all bets were off. "Sounds like a plan to me." Letting go of her, he backed off. "I hope you ain't hurt." He scooped up the banana because he didn't want to swarm in front of her. If she never saw him use his superpower, she couldn't tell Privek which one accosted her. Might as well finish the fruit he'd already peeled. And take an apple and an orange.

"No," she said meekly as she reached up to rub her head.

"Well, go on and git." He waved her off with his one banana-filled hand, trying not to call attention to how the other arm ended abruptly at the wrist.

She turned and scurried away, the sounds of her shoes moving swiftly down the hall, punctuated by a door opening and shutting. As soon as it banged closed, he flowed into the swarm and got them to carry the fruit outside, where they met up with the rest of the dragons. From overhead, he saw Riker standing at what must be his post, watching the woman get into her car. Bobby stayed high enough to not attract attention and slipped over to re-form on the ground next to Kaitlin.

The other two men had awakened. Paul looked perfectly fine, though annoyed. Kaitlin sat without a scrape on her, her whole body turned away from Paul. Liam, on the other hand, held his head gingerly and had several cuts and bruises.

"Ain't you a healer?" Bobby started munching on the apple the second he had a hand and mouth to facilitate it.

"I can't heal myself," Liam groaned, "only other people."

"Dang, that sucks."

"I was already aware of that, thank you. Since we're pointing out the obvious, you don't have Elena."

Bobby sighed as he finished his bite of apple. "Well, she ain't here. I got three possible places she might be and only today and tomorrow afore somebody probably realizes I been here. If'n we had more help, it'd be easier to get 'er done in that span."

"Forget it," Paul grumbled. "Not a chance we're letting anyone else free after Kaitlin made me crash the car."

"It's not my fault," Kaitlin snapped, "that you can't focus well enough to drive straight when my power goes active. Thanks to you, I didn't even get anything out of it."

"Great." Bobby stared off at something else, not really paying attention to the bickering. His mind moved on other things. Like how to get where they needed to go and do what they needed to do. "Is the car dead?"

"Yes. Kaitlin killed my car."

Kaitlin reached over and smacked Paul in the arm. "Whatever. It was already making a funny noise and probably older than you. Quit whining. The bigger problem is we have no transportation and a time limit. Why do we only have that long?"

Bobby shrugged, unwilling to get into it. "Life's like that. I can get me gone no problem. You lot are gonna have to walk until you find something." He crunched into the apple again and had another thought. "Or maybe see if Riker will give you a ride or something. Your phone," he said to Liam, "has bells and whistles, don't it? The places I got to try are White Sands, Groom Lake, and Adelphi. I know where the first one is. I been there. The other two, I got no idea."

Liam tapped on his phone. "Groom Lake is a military base in southern Nevada, also known as Area 51. Adelphi has too many options."

"Area 51 is real?" Paul peered at Liam, echoing Bobby's skepticism.

"Apparently." Offering his phone so Paul could see for himself, Liam went back to nursing what must be a headache of serious proportions.

"Where's White Sands?" Paul looked the map over, holding it so Kaitlin could see too.

"New Mexico. Which ain't far from Nevada. You all could work the Adelphi angle while I get myself out west and check those places out."

"I don't think so," Liam growled. "You're not leaving my sight again."

Bobby huffed. "I came back, didn't I?"

"Doesn't matter. If you're going, so am I."

"You can't leave me alone with this." Paul indicated Kaitlin with a little jerk of his head.

Kaitlin rolled her eyes again. "Like I want to spend my time with you, either."

His hands too full to rub his face, Bobby sighed. "Look, I can fly. Can any of you? We don't got time to wait for whatever you can do to get a ride to someplace worth being. I coulda just took off and left you here, but I didn't. I came over to tell you what's up. I ain't your enemy. We're on the same side. All I want is all of us free and not being used against our will. Ain't no more complicated than that. Everything I done's been about that, whether it seemed like it or not."

Kaitlin got to her feet and picked up her bag from where it lay on the ground behind her. "You guys can keep me as a hostage against his word if that's what it takes."

"All it will take is one stupid phone call," Liam said irritably, taking his phone back from Paul, "and we'll be on our way as soon as a tow truck can get here."

Bobby lifted an eyebrow, wondering if he was the only one feeling like a healthy dose of paranoia would a good idea. "You planning on using your name and all, let Privek know you been here? I'm sure he won't notice, won't read nothing into it. Ain't nothing wrong with you going for a joyride and needing a tow truck out near Culpeper, where there just happens to be a facility Elena was in until two days ago."

"I hate you." Liam grumbled it with no real heat and stuffed his phone into his pocket.

Poor guy had to be in a lot of pain. Bobby sighed. "Yeah, yeah." He waved that off and fixed Liam with a dead serious look. "We'll find her, man, I promise, and you'll get her back. Don't know how, but I got this far. Ain't gonna give up now."

CHAPTER 2

LIAM

"So, there he goes. We're never going to see him again." Liam rubbed his aching head as he got to his feet with Paul's help.

"If there's any one person you can trust to stick to the mission of 'rescue the girl,' it's Bobby." Kaitlin smirked and led the way back to the road, peering down the direction they'd come from.

"What are you looking for?" Liam had so many bumps and scrapes that he felt like a walking ache from head to toe. Some of it had healed when he took on Paul's injuries, but not much. His power sucked.

Kaitlin waved at someone and walked down the road in the other direction. "Traffic, duh."

"Why are we going this way? Culpeper is back that way."

Paul still scowled at her. "She saw something just now. I can tell."

Kaitlin pursed her lips and waited a second or so before answering. "Yeah. I saw Riker, pointing this way. Across the road."

"But your mind went wonky for a second," Paul insisted. "What did you actually see?"

"Why, did it make you want to crash your legs?"

Paul growled under his breath. "If you hadn't killed my car, we wouldn't be in this situation."

"If you had the balls to handle the unexpected, your car would be fine."

These two might kill each other, unless he killed them both first. Liam took a deep breath to push aside all the pain so he could try to make some peace or at least shut them up for five minutes. "It doesn't matter. What we need is to get back to DC as soon as possible. Someone's going to notice Bobby's missing at some point, and if we're not accounted for, we're going to be the prime suspects. Did you see anything that will help us get there?"

"Yes." Kaitlin looked both ways before jogging across the road, beckoning them to follow. The driveway she went up belonged to the next property over. He followed her and so did Paul, figuring that getting anything more would to be similar to trying to get his mother to eat at a greasy spoon diner: close enough to impossible as to not be worth the effort.

She led them a short way past a gap in the wall of trees and shrubs to absolutely nothing, where they stopped and looked around. "Something is going to happen here, right?" Liam was starting to think he'd entrusted his fate to a lunatic.

This time, she skipped the sarcastic reply and only nodded. She stood there serenely, like everything was right with the world,and everything she expected to happen was happening. Liam couldn't see any reason not to, so he sat down and put his head in his hands, wishing the precog had the foresight to bring a bottle of aspirin. Seriously, if she knew so much, how come she didn't see that? She brought clothes for Bobby, after all. He also wished he could get his head to stop playing light jazz in the background, which it had been doing for a few minutes now.

"Liam, can you stop...thinking so much?" Paul stood with his hands crossed and a grumpy frown on his face.

"Given the alternative of being a blank, drooling moron, no, I don't think I can." He heard Kaitlin snort. "I think you need to work on your shielding. The crash must have jarred your concentration more than you think. I can hear music."

Paul blushed bright red and mumbled an embarrassed apology. Putting his hands on his head, he paced several steps away then turned and came back.

After a minute of merciful quiet passed, a blue sedan pulled in and Riker leaned out the window. Bewildered by this turn of events, Liam stared stupidly as Kaitlin took the passenger seat, leaving the back for him and Paul.

Riker gave him an expectant look, which shook Liam awake. He got to his feet, hurried over, and got in. Mindful that his ability didn't really protect him from anything, he put his seatbelt on.

"What're you doing?"

"Helping." Riker backed the car out, choosing the direction Kaitlin pointed him in, away from Culpeper. "This is bullshit duty and I know it. So does the rest of my team. We know something's going on and trust Bobby. Even if this means we get branded as traitors, we want to do what's right, not what we're told. Where are we going?"

"That way," Kaitlin said, pointing straight ahead.

Liam glanced back and saw another car falling into line behind them. The driver gave him a perfunctory wave. He waved back out of habit and settled into his seat, facing forward. Bobby was more dangerous than he thought. Not because he killed people—Riker did that for a living—because he was so damned likeable and believable. He had that harmless good guy routine down pat, so sincere Liam thought the guy believed himself. "This is getting out of control."

"You healed me," Riker reminded him amiably. "I was given an option to either keep my mouth shut about that or be charged with treason. Bobby and Stephen asked me politely to keep my mouth shut about them and what they did to free us. Guess which one I trust more."

Now he stood firmly on the other side. There wouldn't be any going back. He wanted proof and hadn't gotten it yet. He still switched sides anyway. Heaving a sigh, he rubbed his eyes. They ached as much as everything else. More than anything, he wanted Elena. He never knew how badly he needed someone until he had her, and then she was gone, disappeared so abruptly he worried he'd dreamed her up. For all he knew, he'd sent Bobby off on a wild goose chase, searching for a figment of his imagination, one that laughed and danced and made him willing to do nearly anything to get her back.

"We should go back." Even the stupid tree-lined road made him think of Elena, mostly because he wanted to watch her watching it. She'd love this, all the vibrant life streaming past. Who knew what she'd see in it that he didn't. "To the facility in DC, I mean. And by 'we,' I mean Paul and I."

Paul made a small noise of discomfort beside him and pressed the heel of his hand to his forehead. Liam snapped his head to Kaitlin and watched tension seize her shoulders. Paul was a precognitive vision detector, apparently.

"No," Kaitlin said as she relaxed, "we don't want to go there. We need to go someplace else. Riker, does Adelphi ring any bells for you?"

"That's where the Army Research Lab is based. A couple of the cars that come and go from this site have parking stickers for it."

"That must be it, then." Kaitlin turned around in her seat and fixed

Liam with a square look. "She's there. I know it."

Dear God, he thought, let it be true and a lie. "What—" His voice cracked enough that he had to cough to clear his throat and start over again. "Is she okay?"

"She's alive. I can say that much for sure. Her condition—" Kaitlin pursed her lips. "What I see, it's going to happen unless we change something, but there's no way to know if we're actually changing something or doing what will make the thing happen, not unless I can see a cause-effect chain with a link I can break. Like, I saw a car crash for Lisa once, so I told her not to get in the car, but I couldn't have said whether it mattered if she got in the car and chose a different destination, or left an hour later, or anything like that. All I could see was that if she got in the car, she was going to die."

Liam nodded. He tried not to think about the ramifications of someone having that kind of ability, because he wasn't interested in examining his beliefs and feelings about religion and predestination and the rest of it right now. Elena made him want to believe in God wholeheartedly, if only so he had someone to properly thank for nudging her into his life. "Just tell me. I need to know."

Kaitlin left a long pause—long enough to make him want to grab her and shake until the words fell out—before she said, "She's working for them, using a computer a lot. She's about to stumble across something she doesn't understand and take it to her boss. Whatever it is, he tries to get her to just ignore it, but she won't, because it has your name in it. He—" She turned away, settled back in her seat properly again. "It all goes downhill from there. In a bad way. But they aren't going to kill her."

Someone seized his heart and squeezed, trying to crush it. "Okay," Liam heard himself say in a strangely distant voice. Part of him panicked.

The rest tried to think of a way to get around whatever awful thing Kaitlin had seen happening to her. "Then we should hurry. I can call someone, get reinforcements or other help."

"Who're you going to call? The Ghostbusters?" Kaitlin snorted to further express her disdain for his idea. "We've got Riker and his guys. They can get us into the facility. Paul can do his thing. I'd rather not go in, but the alternative is standing around by myself, which probably isn't a good idea."

Paul put a hand on Liam's shoulder. "We'll get her out," he said softly. "We'll be in time. I'll do whatever we need to make sure it happens." Turning to Riker, he said, "Put the pedal to the metal. I'll handle any cops that take an interest."

He'd do anything to get her free—anything at all. If the rest of these people wanted to get dragged down with him, that was their choice. He wouldn't force them. He wouldn't turn them away or try to run off without them, either. Seriously, he was about to break into a military research facility. He needed all the help he could get.

Chapter 3

Bobby

Bobby headed for White Sands, Liam's phone number on a slip of paper in his pocket. His gut said Groom Lake was more likely, but the Missile Range had unfinished business of a sort, and he wanted to finish it. It was dark when he flew over the main clump of buildings at White Sands. The place had enough streetlights that the dragons could see just fine where to go, and they dove into the ventilation system. Just because he didn't have much ability with a computer didn't mean he couldn't find anything. This entire place would be checked over, inside and out, and nothing was going to stop him. If Elena was here, he'd find her.

The swarm spread out as it had in those small towns in Afghanistan. Freaky nightmares aside, that felt like it happened a lifetime ago, even though only about two weeks had passed. Here, no space would be left unexplored with them on the job, and Bobby waited for them to get it done. The only things he cared about right now were finding Elena and not being noticed, though he did make a point to be really clear about how no one should be attacked or killed.

While they worked, he floated in the middle, trying not to let either the dead stares of those kids or Sebastian's wailing replay in his head. The first one he couldn't do anything about except deal with it. As for the second… He should have pushed harder for him and his momma to get freed, though he could well imagine they'd be under more intense security than he. After all, he'd only been a thorn in Privek's side. Lily had proved they could pass the eyes—and maybe their superpowers—on to children.

At least this time he'd been awakened on purpose by someone without a grand plan beyond finding a girl. If Privek had set this up somehow, he'd done it to mess with Liam and Paul, not him. To heckbiscuits with Privek. No way he gave everyone at that house in Virginia instructions on how to deal with that kind of questioning just in case someone showed up and asked about Elena. Actually, now he thought about that, it *was* possible. Sounded like an awful lot of excessive paranoia, though. Privek hadn't displayed that before. Instead, he'd carried out plans and reacted.

His dragons found a lot of sleeping people, but none of them were pretty Spaniards. None of the awake people were Elena, either. The foray didn't take long, and he sent the swarm out to check on the outbuildings, several structures scattered about the rest of the base. Each of them was set up with a fair amount of security and intended for a different project. He knew this from his last visit.

For the sake of being thorough, he sent them through both the Maze Beset buildings, knowing he'd find one empty. The other one not only had been where they'd met Mike but also housed a project trying to recreate some kind of space-time thingumbobbadoodle. Stephen and Sam understood it better than he did. Actually, probably everyone understood it better than he did.

Speaking of that Mike guy, one dragon found him. He sat in the break room with a sandwich, reading a book with no one else around. Guy must not have any friends. Maybe that was why he had been willing to fol-

low Sam out instead of calling security to haul her off. Bobby figured introducing himself ranked low on the list of Intelligent Things To Do. Mike
might know something, though, or hear something later and be willing to
pass it along.

Bobby jumped into the dragon and landed it on the table. Engrossed
in his book, Mike failed to notice it. He had the dragon tap a claw on the
table then chirp.

"What's..." Mike lowered his book. "Oh my God. Um, Sam? Are
you here?" His eyes darted all around expectantly.

The swarm converged on the room while Mike watched, his mouth
falling into an 'o' shape. Bobby re-formed and held up his hand in greeting,
pointedly not smirking. The one dragon flew to him and merged onto the
end of his thumb. "Hi there. Sam ain't here." Since Mike obviously
thought of her, he decided to follow that bone. "She's in trouble, actually,
which is why I'm here. I need your help."

Mike hesitated for only one second before he grabbed his book firmly and stood up straight and tall. Bobby got the feeling he'd march off to
storm Fort Knox if he thought he'd find Sam trapped inside. The reaction
seemed over the top, but who was he to judge what a guy would do for a
girl after only meeting her once? "What happened? What can I do?"

"Can we talk private-like in here without worrying about nobody
coming in?"

Mike scanned the room, as if he had to check for other people.
"Yeah, everyone's gone for the day. I'm just running some test routines."

"Great." Bobby gestured, and Mike sat down again with him. "My
name's Bobby. I'm made of tiny little dragons. Sam's got a special ability
too. There's thirty-five of us in all, and there's somebody trying to mess
with us. Doing a pretty good job of it, I'd say. Sam and bunch of the others

are locked up right now, and I'm working on getting 'em free. In order to do that, I gotta understand what all's going on."

He had Mike's rapt attention. "Were you all born like this?"

"That there is a pickle of a question. Suffice to say that we all been developing these abilities all sudden-like over the past few months. Don't rightly know why now. Don't much matter, neither. I gotta figure out the future, not the past. They're up to something, and I want to know what. You got any real idea what they're working on here?"

"Well, actually, I didn't know much until a couple of days ago." Mike stroked his chin thoughtfully. "The day before yesterday, there was a boom and the whole building rocked like an earthquake happened, then everyone was really excited. I really only work with data, inputs and outputs and manipulating it to do what they want. It wasn't ever necessary for me to understand the whole picture. Some of the project leads here were *so* excited by what happened that they started babbling about it. They've been trying to create a wormhole."

From the way Mike looked at him, Bobby got the impression this was a big deal, or at least interesting. His idea of wormholes involved worms making them in the dirt. This probably related to the stuff Hanami-di told them about. He didn't understand any of it then, either. "And that means...?"

"Okay." Taking Bobby's response in stride, Mike held up his book with one hand and fished his keys out of his pocket with the other. "Imagine the book is Earth and the keys are some other planet in the universe someplace." Mike took his keys to the counter and left them there then returned with the book. "They're really far apart from each other. The distance is outside a human being's ability to actually comprehend. If you were to try to drive the distance in a car, it would take thousands of years."

"That's a long damned time."

"Yeah. Now, suppose you could somehow create a conduit between the book and the keys so that when something is put into it, it comes out the other end in just a few minutes. That would be pretty incredible, wouldn't it?"

"We're still talking about that thousands-of-years thing with the Earth and the other planet, right?"

Mike grinned. "Yeah. Essentially, on this scale, if I put my sandwich in the conduit, it would appear at the keys instantly."

"Okay, I got it. So, that's what they're trying to do. What happened day before yesterday?"

Mike retrieved his keys and sat back down. "They had a breakthrough. Apparently, there was some kind of event a long time ago where this wormhole opened and dropped some stuff on our side. Nobody knows if it was a freak natural occurrence or someone on the other end caused it somehow, or what, but they've been trying to reproduce it ever since. Really smart men have worked on it, like Einstein. No dice. They came up with all kinds of ideas, but nothing ever came close to working.

"Two days ago, they tried something and it was a partial success. They created a conduit through space." He paused. Bobby figured it was obvious he couldn't understand a technical explanation, so Mike needed to think about how to explain it in plain English. "Okay. Right. So, they made the tunnel. They dropped in a penny just to see what would happen, and it disappeared. A second later, the tunnel collapsed."

"That sounds kinda like a failure."

"If all you care about is the tunnel working," Mike shrugged, "then, yeah, it is. They've never managed to get a stable tunnel for even a nanosecond before, though, and now they have tons of data to work with, so it's only a matter of time. Heh, so to speak."

Bobby sat there, not sure how knowing this helped him. It was interesting and sounded exciting. He doubted it would help him with his current problems. This tunnel thing wouldn't have Elena or anyone else he cared about at the other end. "Alright. That's...real helpful." What was he going to do? Say it was useless information?

Mike brightened. "Good. Is there anything more concrete I can do to help Sam?"

Standing up, Bobby scratched the back of his head. "I don't rightly know. She's in a sort of a jail thing in DeeCee right now. I don't suppose you can get me into Area 51 so I can do a thing I gotta do there?"

"Seriously?"

Bobby chuckled at the comical amount of shock on Mike's face. "Yeah, I'm serious, but I think I can handle getting in on my own. Tell you what, though. Let me give you a phone number for a guy, name of Liam. He's trying to help me out too. If'n a body can figure out how you can help, it'll be him. He's a pretty smart guy. I wouldn't call him from here, though."

Mike offered him a pen and Bobby scribbled the number down on a piece of paper. "I'll call him when I can. Is he like you?"

"Ayup, he's one of us." He offered his hand and Mike shook it. "You be careful. Folks been killed over this stuff."

"Really?" Mike gulped. "I'll, uh, not hop in my car and start driving, then."

"That's a good plan." Bobby couldn't think of anything else to say or do here, so he gave Mike an encouraging smile and broke apart into the swarm. As the dragons went for the ventilation system, he heard Mike gasp in wonder, a reaction he didn't mind at all. If he intended to be public like he kept saying he did, he'd need to get used to all sorts of reactions. But not now, not yet. It was too early. He still needed the element of surprise, and had no idea what Privek would do if he caught a video of dragons on TV. The agent had the others at his mercy right now, and he didn't dare take that kind of risk with their lives.

Outside, he reflected that coming here had almost been a waste of time. Closing the book on White Sands left him feeling accomplished, at least. It must have been a setup before, a way for Privek to get one of his people in with them so he could find their home. A home he could slip up to right now. The side trip would only take him about five hours. He'd likely hit Groom Lake in the middle of the day tomorrow, or he could wait until tomorrow night to hit the other base.

Except he did promise he'd be as fast as he could manage. Liam was counting on him to find her and free her. Though she didn't seem to be in much actual danger from Privek, the longer she stayed under his thumb, the longer everyone else did too. Sebastian, Lily, Stephen, Jasmine, Hannah, Lily...all of them. He had thirty-four brothers and sisters and one nephew, and they all needed to be set free, even Liam and Paul. How fast or slow he sprang Elena dictated how fast or slow he sprang the rest.

He paused in Albuquerque long enough to graze on restaurant dumpsters and let the dragons strip a junkyard of what they wanted, then headed for Groom Lake. The scenery along the way, mostly empty desert, reminded him of fleeing Afghanistan and Turkey. He didn't want to think about any of that. The dragons didn't want him to think about any of that either.

Chapter 4

Liam

The facility looked about how Liam expected it to look. His father's company did government contracting. They built things and had research divisions, and most of it looked a lot like this. The only notable difference was the soldier at the guard post taking Riker's ID and looking it over. Sitting beside him, Paul took deep breaths while concentrating, trying to manipulate the outcome of this brief encounter. For whatever reason, making a bunch of people ignore Bobby earlier had been easier than getting this one man to let them through.

"This isn't a scheduled visit," Riker told the guard. "Surprise inspection with civilian contractors."

Liam, busy dwelling on Kaitlin's words from two hours ago, perked up and realized he needed to play a part "Is there a problem?" He asked with an air of annoyance. He could do bored impatience, no problem.

"They usually put the names of anyone coming on my list, Sergeant." The guard's expression held a peculiar vagueness, and he kept twitching his head. "This is a secure facility."

If only they had a clipboard. Liam pulled his phone out, hoping it would be good enough for the purpose, and pretended to take notes. In reality, he scrolled through his contacts to see if anyone could be useful here. Laurie owed him for fixing things up with her professor last fall, and her father happened to be an Admiral. He tried to imagine how to word what he needed, and couldn't come up with a way that didn't sound awful or go far beyond her debt to him. Also, he'd have to explain it out loud. The guard would catch on.

"Well, the security is clearly good, but it's not supposed to keep out people who should be here, only those who shouldn't be."

"He's resisting me," Paul muttered out of the side of his mouth.

"I'll just call it in," the guard said. "What name should I give?"

Liam seized the moment and ran with it. He gave the guard a sharp glare. "How about if I make a call instead, Private—" His eyes flicked to the name patch on the guard's uniform as he held up his phone. "—Hillson? Would you like to talk to General Hanstadt yourself, maybe make this go quicker?" He flicked his finger to scroll through his contacts list. The key was confidence, and Liam projected plenty of it.

Hillson swallowed and looked to Riker. Whatever expression the Sergeant gave him along with a curt nod, it convinced the guard. "Um, no, that's not necessary, sir. Sorry, Sergeant."

"It's okay, Hillson. Just doing your job."

"And doing it well," Liam added as he pretended to tap a note out on his phone. "Carry on."

The arm barring the way went up and Riker drove through. "Nice name drop," he told Liam as soon as the window rolled up.

Paul sighed. "His mind was too strong and alert, sorry."

"It worked out, nothing to apologize for." Liam noticed his hand shaking and gripped his leg to make it stop. He'd talked a lot of people into and out of things, but never anything with these kinds of stakes before. He took a deep breaths to calm himself.

When the car stopped, he was as ready as possible for the rest of this. "I think our best bet is if Riker and his men use their uniforms to get us through, and when that's not enough, I do the talking. You two back me up as needed. Okay?" He didn't really want to order them around. Kaitlin especially struck him as the type to dislike authority. Someone, though, had to step up, and this was his show. They came for Elena. That made this all about him.

"Whatever." Kaitlin shrugged.

"Let's use channel four," Riker told his men. They all fiddled with something at their belts. "Hansen and Platt, you're our getaway drivers." He handed his car keys over to Platt. "We're not outfitted for a hostile entry. Hopefully we won't need to be. If this thing goes fubar, aim to hurt, not kill. We're walking on the wild side here, but that doesn't mean we have to go all dark side."

The other four men nodded and two got into the cars while the other two fell in behind Paul and Kaitlin. Liam knew how to lead a group of people through a facility as if he belonged there. Every other time he'd done it, he actually *did* belong there, because he'd been giving a tour of one of his father's company's buildings to Important People.

He still wished he had a clipboard. Especially when they greeted the first hurdle, the security right inside the front door. A soldier sat in a small booth on the other side of the door with glass between them and him. They could see the shiny, red button for opening the door, so close and yet so far away.

Riker knocked on the glass to get the guy's attention and stood there, staring at him like he ought to be expecting them and should just go ahead and let them in. "Surprise inspection," he barked, voice full of command.

The young soldier jumped and slapped the button. "Yes, Sergeant!"

Apparently, the guard held a lower rank than Riker. Liam didn't have much experience with such things and chose to be glad Riker obviously knew what he was doing. He grabbed the door as it buzzed and nodded his approval to the young man. Although tempted to praise the soldier's efficiency, he had a feeling that would cause problems and kept his mouth shut. Knowing when *not* to talk helped at least as much as knowing what to say.

"We're in," Riker muttered once they passed the guard post, presumably to let Hansen and Platt know.

"Take a left," Kaitlin murmured. They had no reason not to follow her directions, so Liam and Riker turned down the next hallway to the left. "Go in the next room on the right." This put them into a small office with minimalist furniture and no occupant. Kaitlin shut the door softly behind them all and stood there with her ear pressed to the door and a finger to her lips to shush them.

A glance at Paul confirmed for Liam that they did this for a reason—the telepath rubbed his temple and stood as far from Kaitlin as he could manage in such a small room. All Liam's own aches and pains had faded into the background, completely overwhelmed by the rush of infiltrating a military facility pursuing secret research projects combined with the anticipation of seeing Elena again—finally—after a month apart.

He'd only met her two weeks before she was taken away from him. They'd been the most intense, wonderful two weeks of his life. After spending years chasing and being chased by skirts he had no real interest in and expecting his mother to find him a wife he'd have to settle for if he wanted to continue to live the lifestyle he'd become accustomed to, he'd fallen hard, in two weeks, for a woman he'd bumped into by accident. The thought terrified him and liberated him at the same time. But she was gone, and he'd done things he never would have otherwise to get her back. Like using his awful ability for total strangers, and breaking into a high-security military facility.

Would she still want him? He'd never been dumped in his life. His relationships—such as they'd been—always ended well, except for a few he'd had to get stern and unpleasant with. In those cases, it he'd done the dumping. The idea of Elena doing that to him crushed a piece of his soul, and he delicately avoided it. That she might be mad at him because of whatever Privek and his lackeys told her was fine, and he could live with it. Getting past those kinds of lies wouldn't be too hard. Dealing with the truth was always harder.

Kaitlin opened the door and walked out, beckoning for them to follow her. Liam let her lead without argument. She could, apparently, get them through this place without incident. For Paul's benefit, he spruced up his expression of blithe confidence as he followed Riker out. The telepath looked nervous and a little green around the gills.

"It's continuous right now," Paul breathed at him, staying by Liam's side. "She's walking around in the future or something. It feels like her mind is some kind of dragon that's going to pounce and eat me as soon as we both stand still."

Liam nodded to project more confidence than he felt. "It didn't happen in that room, so you should be safe. Stop fidgeting, it makes you look suspicious."

"First rule of not being noticed is to fly casual," Hegi murmured from behind them. "Act like you belong and aren't doing anything worth looking into."

"Easy for you to say," Paul grumbled.

Putting a hand comfortingly on Paul's shoulder, Liam leaned down and said, "Try imagining it's looking at something behind you it wants to protect you from."

The telepath blinked stupidly and whipped his head around. Aside from nearly clocking Liam in the jaw, he found himself face to face with Carter, who managed to avoid walking into him. Liam rolled his eyes and shoved Paul to get him moving again.

Kaitlin ushered them all through a door with an admonition to be quiet again. This time, they crammed themselves into a janitor's closet. Unlike last time, they could all hear the muffled voices moving past the door.

"I can't believe they're doing another surprise inspection."

"Nobody can just trust us to do our jobs anymore, Jesus. It's like they *want* to find the stuff they don't want to know about."

"Where the hell *are* these people? We can't damned well keep them out of the black sections if we can't find them."

"Black sections" made Liam raise an eyebrow. Obviously, the government researched things they didn't want anyone to know about. He wondered if any of the experiments or programs related to them. It couldn't be a coincidence that Elena had been moved here. Well, okay, it could, but it would be exceptionally unfair if they couldn't kill two birds with one break-in. Besides, if he understood the very little Bobby had said, Privek's project managed this site, so it made sense to be related.

They'd been stuffed in so tightly that Liam half-tumbled out of the little room when Kaitlin opened the door. It almost felt like a madcap comedy, except he had no reason to laugh. Being in that tight space with five other people all worried about a hiccup or sneeze giving them away hadn't improved his already frayed nerves.

They kept going, down a flight of stairs, up a hallway, down more stairs, around and around in what seemed to be a giant circle, spiraling into the pit of Hell. The longer they walked, the more he wondered if this would turn out to be the biggest mistake of his life. Horrible things, the consequences of being caught down here without some kind of official authorization, danced through his head, getting progressively more unpleasant with every minute that passed.

Glancing at Paul, he noticed an obscene amount of tension in the other man's shoulders and a tight, pinched look on his face. Walking beside a frantic ball of worry probably made things worse for the telepath. He stopped himself from apologizing and instead groped for something else to focus on than how horrible this situation could become.

Elena, the reason for this whole disaster in the first place, came to mind. Instead of thinking about how much he missed her, or how much she panicked him overall, he thought about her face, her laugh, and her smile. With her wide hips and strong nose, she would never qualify as conventionally pretty. To him, she stuck out as the most beautiful woman he'd ever met.

She'd be the first person to tell him to stop being stupid, and to stop worrying so much about something he had no control over. Her finger would lay over his mouth and shut him up, and she'd dance for him. With that thought came the memory of their first night together, spent in a grotto he never would've found without her.

The two of them lay on a bed of moss together, a gap in the rock overhead showing him more stars than he'd ever seen before. They huddled for warmth when the temperature dropped unexpectedly. Dazed by the incredible whirlwind that had fallen asleep in his arms, his heart swelled with the strange knowledge that he felt more connected to her without sex than he'd ever felt with any of the girls he'd jumped into bed with.

Somehow, the Spaniard who'd stopped randomly to ask him for help that morning had turned out to be everything he wanted. He stroked her hair and sighed. For once, he had no audience or expectations, and it allowed him to relax. That forgotten feeling surging through his veins was so strange that it took him several minutes to identify uncomplicated happiness.

Kaitlin stopped abruptly at a set of thick metal fire doors, jarring Liam out of his reverie. "From here, there's no evading anymore. Riker, you guys will just have to punch people. I don't see any way around that. There are cameras. I know how to shut them off, but that will bring people down here, expecting something's going on. We need to go into the third door on the left. That's not where Elena is. She's through the second door on the right. We'll have to grab her after. I'm not sure what's through the other door, just that we have to go in there. Maybe there's someone in with Elena that we need to avoid."

Everyone looked at Liam. He could tell. Taking a deep breath, he nodded. "Okay. You haven't led us wrong yet. I trust you."

"Good." Kaitlin gave him a firm nod. He wondered if she knew how to smile without it being a smirk. Probably not. "Because I'm not trying to screw with you, I just want to get out of here in one piece."

"Seconded," Riker said. "No shooting if we can avoid it down here. No telling what or who you might hit." He, Carter, and Hegi all switched over to their pistols, safeties on, letting their rifles hang from the straps across their bodies where they wouldn't get in the way.

Paul swallowed nervously as he watched them. "Didn't you just say 'no shooting'?"

Riker got a half grin. "They make good substitute brass knuckles in a pinch." The statement made Paul go pale, and Kaitlin smirked. For his part, Liam just nodded, because if he said anything, it would probably be a whimper or squeak.

"We'll follow you three in," Kaitlin said confidently. How did she manage to stay so calm? Did she know this would work out okay, making panic seem foolish? Maybe she just knew she'd be alright. That struck Liam as a lot more likely, given what he'd seen so far. "The panel to disable the cameras is on the other side of these doors. I'll take care of that."

Carter moved up and grabbed the handle for the fire doors, waited for the go ahead from Riker, then heaved it open. Riker and Hegi slipped inside. Carter followed right behind them. Kaitlin stopped Liam and Paul from following immediately. She counted to ten, then opened the door and darted inside. Liam looked at Paul, who happened to also look at him, and wondered if his own face held as much panic as the telepath's did. Hopefully not.

For a long moment, they both stood there. Then Liam, bolstered by the notion he'd find Elena through there, grabbed the door handle and yanked it open to see the three soldiers dragging bodies through the first door on the right while Kaitlin clicked a panel on the wall shut. "None of them are dead," Kaitlin whispered. "Come on, no dawdling, this'll be noticed pretty soon."

Liam held the door open for Paul, who came through it reluctantly. They followed Riker past the second door on the right. No one else so much as looked at it. Liam couldn't stop himself from staring, wondering, and stopping. The rest of them kept going while he put his ear to the door.

He heard noises on the other side, too muffled to decipher. His heart beat so fast he thought he might explode. Right then, he knew that no matter what he'd said, he could *not* leave this door, not even with a gun to his head.

Glancing up and down the hallway, he noted he hadn't been missed yet. Paul was probably too scared to keep track of him, and the others focused on what lay ahead, not behind. He grabbed the knob and threw the door open. There she was, like Kaitlin said she would be, only he couldn't have prepared for the incredible amount of anger tearing through him at what he saw.

The room resembled a doctor's office, with cabinets and a chair, and a rolling bed instead of a fixed exam table. The walls had even been painted a soothing light minty green color with darker mint trim. Between himself and Elena, a man stood with his back to the door, wearing a lab coat that didn't hide the light bruising on the knuckles of his right hand. To complement them, an ugly purple splotch tainted Elena's dusky skin around her eye and blood stained her lower lip. She'd been knocked out cold, and her attacker held a needle. Once he profaned her hand with it, that needle would probably be attached to the IV bag at the head of the gurney.

The guy in the lab coat turned and looked, then frowned. "Who are you? You can't—" His eyes snapped to Liam's, then widened in surprise and horror. It might have had something to do with the pure rage unfurling in Liam's chest, because that had to be written across his face. Instead of backing away like a sane person should, the very average guy with glasses put up his hands and blocked Liam from coming in any further. "You shouldn't be here. Get out. She's not your concern."

How dare he. Liam had no need to assert his manhood and didn't feel he owned Elena. But he loved her, and seeing her like that, when this man obviously did it to her... And now he tried to shove Liam away, to get him to leave Elena behind. No damned chance.

Brawling didn't come naturally to Liam. He'd never had trouble defusing the sorts of situations he found himself in where such things might happen, and thus had never needed to learn to fight. Despite that, Liam threw his fist at the man's face. There would be no chitchat here.

So much adrenaline pumped through Liam's body he didn't feel the impact as anything more than a confirmation of a solid blow. He used his body to shoulder the man into the wall and hit him again, wanting to make him hurt a hundred times worse than what Elena felt from the blow she took. Idly, part of his brain noticed the sudden end to the dull throbbing he'd managed to push into the background during the car ride. The hundred little aches from the crash evaporated. He felt pretty good, actually, aside from wanting to kill this man.

The moment he realized he actually *could* kill this man, Liam stopped and let him fall to the floor, panting from the exertion. He was in good shape, but had never done anything like this before, ever. Elena's attacker crumpled to the floor in what seemed like slow motion, with cuts and bruises on his face that seemed oddly similar to the ones he himself had suffered in the crash. That little slice there was eerie. Liam reached up to touch his own face with smooth, perfect hands where his own slice should be, only to find more smooth, perfect skin.

He'd transferred his wounds to someone else. The thought made him go cold all over and stumble backward until he bumped into Elena's gurney. He could take the wounds of others and regenerate the injuries, or he could take his own wounds and give them to someone else. God, that was scary. Worse, almost, than just healing people. Could he take someone else's wounds on himself and pass them on before he healed them? Could he bring someone back to life by killing someone else?

He didn't want to think about it. Turning, he let all that wash away at the sight of his girlfriend, lying unconscious with a bruise on her cheek. His fingers brushed that bruise lightly, pulling it out of her, along with the concussion keeping her down. His head split with a blinding ache for a few seconds. He'd gladly take it for an hour in exchange for seeing her eyes flutter open and her lips smile at him.

"Liam, what did you do?" Paul stood in the doorway, staring at the downed man in horror.

Scooping Elena up into his arms and holding her tightly, Liam heard himself say dully, "He hit Elena."

"Oh." Paul gulped and gave a weak chuckle. "Remind me never to say anything rude to her. We need to move, though. Before someone comes along and—"

"What's going—" Too late. A guy in a lab coat peered inside and blinked, then turned to run.

"I'll handle it," Paul said, sounding glad to have something to distract him from the contents of the room. He turned away, leaving Liam and Elena alone again.

"They told me—" She barely spoke English and he barely spoke Spanish, so they used French. His mother had made him learn it, and he'd never been more appreciative of that than since he'd met Elena.

He put a finger on her lips. "It can be no worse than what they told me. They lied to us both." All his life, he'd chased blondes, women who looked like his mother. Sometimes he entertained a brunette or a redhead, but he couldn't ever get blondes out of his system. Now, he had the most lovely woman imaginable, and she had such dark hair, dusky skin, and brown eyes. For those two weeks, he'd taken her for granted, but after a month forcibly apart, he never would again.

"I worked for them." She held onto him as tightly as he held onto her.

"I know. We're going to make sure this never, ever happens again. We have to leave, though, and hurry." He had to force himself to let go of her, and only managed it because he could take her hand. They hurried out of the room together.

CHAPTER 5

BOBBY

Bobby skirted around the bright lights of Las Vegas until he found the installation he'd come looking for. They hadn't bothered trying to hide it from above. The airstrip even had its lights on tonight. As the swarm slipped up on the buildings, of which it had fewer than White Sands, he noticed a small plane-thing taxiing into position to take off. That explained the lights. The craft had a weird shape. They must've been doing a test flight of some fancy new aircraft. That explained the choice of night for the flight.

Nothing about this base that he could see from above explained how much fervent conspiracy theory surrounded it. The installation appeared to be nothing more than an experimental aircraft testing facility. It had some hangars, an air traffic control tower, emergency services, housing, and a few other buildings that probably served the other basic needs of the folks stationed here. Putting it out in the middle of nowhere meant less danger to regular folks if anything went really wrong, and their planes and stuff could stay out of normal commercial air traffic lanes.

Of course, he'd been created by a top secret cross-species breeding program, and had no idea what kind of facility the actual process had been carried out in. His mind supplied a darkened room full of men wearing glasses and surgical masks, playing with medical equipment and shipping the engineered embryos out for implantation in special orange coolers labeled "live organs" or "biohazard," or whatever else would keep anyone from opening them up for inspection. In this fantasy, the room existed inside a decrepit old warehouse, one easy to ignore as another example of urban blight. Atlanta had places like that.

The dragons wanted him to quit it. Letting his imagination run with the idea distracted and irritated them. Time to focus on searching for Elena. He sent the swarm in to infiltrate the place, looking for her and anything else interesting, though he had low expectations. It surprised him when one dragon vibrated with excitement.

He threw himself into that dragon to see what it found. It had buzzed into a site building. From the outside, it appeared to be an ordinary storage warehouse. Inside, as expected, it had rows of shelving full of boxes and crates. The dragon directed him to the back corner, where he found an elevator. Its housing had no room to go up, only down.

This certainly qualified as "something interesting." Why didn't any of the other dragons find any evidence of an underground facility? It should have ventilation, his favorite way to get into places.

If it had originally been set up as a nuclear fallout shelter, something he remembered seeing crappy videos about in school, it might be sealed and not vent to the surface. Though he had no idea how that might work, it seemed plausible.

He grumbled, not sure how to breach such a place without being noticed. The elevator doors had a keypad next to them, which meant a code, and he had no way to guess, hack, or otherwise get around that. The dragons flew all around the housing for the elevator, looking for ways inside it without finding so much as a tiny crack. There must be some way to service the thing, but he didn't see anything like an access panel.

So far as he could figure, he had two options. One, he could sit around and wait for someone to either come in or leave. The other involved a lot of trying to disguise himself and convince someone to escort him down there.

By the time he'd given up on the idea of faking his way in, the sun had crept up, making the waiting option seem perfectly reasonable. People working at a place like this probably got started pretty early in the morning. He remembered his Daddy—when he'd been stateside—having to be at work by six, so he got up much earlier than Momma did. Bobby sometimes got up early so he could spend five minutes with the man while he ate his breakfast and packed his lunch, then he'd watch him drive away and go back to bed.

Should he take the whole swarm though, or just bring the one dragon? With one dragon, getting caught seemed less likely. On the downside, he wouldn't be able to talk to anyone. Though that might work in his favor, he had a feeling he might want to chat with Elena when he found her. At the very least, she'd recognize him as...the guy with that vampire who knocked her unconscious by drinking her blood. Suddenly, he felt confident this would go sideways no matter what he chose. Might as well drag the whole swarm down there, so he had as many options as possible when he got an opportunity.

It only took a few minutes for the swarm to converge, and he tried not to think too hard about how much he would like to have his Army desert camouflage uniform right now. He could have gone to the farm first and picked it up. But if he had, he wouldn't be here now, he'd be here at lunchtime instead. These folks might not leave until late in the day—who knew how dedicated they were to their jobs or when they actually all went down there.

A few minutes later, he appreciated his choice more, as a group of three men walked in and headed for the elevator. Two wore regular Air Force uniforms. At least, he thought they were Air Force. His Daddy had been a Marine and he knew those uniforms. He sometimes got the other branches' uniforms mixed up.

As for the other guy, Bobby didn't consider himself a fashion expert, but he was pretty sure no one wore ties that wide anymore, and he thought slacks ought to reach all the way to your shoes. Light blue and blood red argyle socks clashed horribly with the brown of his suit. His graying dark hair hung long and loose and, combined with his somewhat scraggly beard and thick rimmed glasses, made him seem averse to the concept of a mirror and of personal grooming in general.

All three men had ID cards on lanyards around their necks. When they reached the elevator, chatting about the weather forecast for the weekend, the guy in the suit punched a six digit code in, which made a panel slide to the side. He held up his ID card to the new black panel and bent enough to let it examine his eye. A little light went green, a little "bing" noise announced the arrival of the elevator, and the doors slid open.

He saw no space between the doors and the shaft, and he'd never get more than one or two into that elevator without them being noticed. So much for sending in the whole swarm. He picked one dragon, jumped into it, and flew it into the elevator. The rest got instructions to stay nearby and out of sight.

One of the two uniform guys stuck his hand out to stop the elevator doors from closing. "Did you see that?"

Bobby's dragon froze, hoping the carpet and brushed silver walls provided enough camouflage.

"See what?" The other man in uniform put his hand on the gun belted at his waist and peered around.

The man in the suit looked serious as he asked, "Was it a UFO?" He barely managed to get the words out of his mouth before he cracked a grin.

First Uniform gave Ugly Suit a sour look. "I saw something flash in the light."

Second Uniform poked his head out through the doors and looked all around. "I didn't see anything, and I still don't."

Ugly Suit chuckled with a weird, snorting laugh. "Maybe it was nanobot aliens, trying desperately to communicate with us."

First Uniform let out an aggrieved sigh. "You know, Doctor, this is why no one likes you." He pulled his hand back and waved to Second Uniform, who shrugged and stepped back in, letting the doors shut. The elevator moved downward without them doing anything else. It had buttons, but none of them got pushed or lit up. Likewise, it had a display over the door that showed nothing.

"Ouch, that's not a nice thing to say." Ugly Suit didn't seem perturbed, just amused. "Seriously, though, what could you possibly have seen that the scanner won't pick up?"

Scanner? Bobby didn't like the sound of that. If they scanned the elevator for anything, they'd probably notice him in this one dragon. Without knowing what it would actually scan for, he couldn't say if climbing onto the nearest pant leg would do him any good.

The only way out might be sacrificing this one dragon. He wanted to avoid that. Aside from how the dragon wouldn't like it much, he'd be left with an aching hand and no way down. He got the dragon to slowly inch its way to where the doors would open in the hopes it would be able to zip out before anyone or anything noticed him.

First Uniform huffed, then shrugged and crossed his arms. Second Uniform rolled his eyes. Ugly Suit continued to smile cheerfully. The elevator trundled downward in silence for over a minute. From his distance to the rest of the swarm, Bobby guessed they'd gone ten or twelve floors underground when it finally stopped and the doors slid open. The dragon grabbed the bottom of the door and rode it open. It waited for the three people to walk past, then grabbed the pant leg of Second Uniform and held on for the ride.

He couldn't think of anything else he could do to defeat an unknown scanner, especially without being able to open the door at the other end of this brightly lit, blank white corridor. This strange, short, empty hallway actually reminded him of some movies he'd seen. In them, the hallway or room had hidden cameras all over the place, and that's where the scanning equipment was. Someone on the other end of those would check the people over and be able to kill or stun an unwanted intruder.

"Barnes, there's something on your left ankle." The voice came from nowhere in particular, with a bit of distortion, enough to make it clear the owner used some kind of device to get it into the hallway.

Bobby focused on not panicking while the dragon let go, darted up to the man's belt, and grabbed the edge. Barnes bent down and checked the hem of his pants.

"It's moved to your belt," the voice said, "in the back."

Before the dragon could decide where to go next, a hand smacked it. "I've got something," Barnes said as he managed to grab the dragon and pulled it around in front of himself.

Afraid the dragon would be crushed, Bobby took over and refused to allow it to struggle, bite, or burn. Appearing harmless seemed like the best way to avoid disaster here. He hoped Barnes had kids or found himself around kids frequently. Under his orders, the dragon stayed still as Barnes used both hands to keep it contained. An eye peered inside the dark space.

"It looks kind of like a toy." Barnes sounded confused. "I have no idea how it got there."

"You'll have to be detained, Barnes. Put it in the box."

"Seriously? I really have no idea what this thing is, or where—"

The voice cut him off again. "You know the rules."

Barnes sighed heavily and dumped Bobby into some kind of glass or clear plastic box. It slid into the wall and a cover blocked out the light and his sight of Barnes. The box kept moving in the darkness. Bobby had the dragon knock on the side and scratch at it, finding it to be solid and stronger than he could affect.

The last time he'd felt this completely trapped had happened years ago, when some kids beat him up for no reason other than being scrawny. That time, he'd crawled away with two cracked ribs, more bruises than a body could shake a barrel of hissing cats at, and a bunch of bleeding cuts all over the place. He had a rather strong feeling the likely outcome of failing to escape this situation would be at least as unpleasant.

The box slid out on the other side, into a less harshly lit room with computers and screens and people with earpiece headsets. Peering at him through the box, he saw a slightly overweight man with glasses in uniform, the chunky kind of guy Bobby would peg as a computer geek.

"Well, well, what do we have here? Hey, guys, take a look at this thing." At his gesture, two other men, also in uniform, rolled their chairs over and peered at the dragon. Bobby kept it still, figuring performing for them would only earn this dragon a dissection. It was a little surprising he could hear them through the box—even though their voices were muffled, they were still perfectly understandable.

"A dragon bug? Freaky. And awesome."

"Why bother making it all detailed like that?"

"It looks more like a mini than a bug. What's a douche like Barnes doing with a mini?"

"Maybe it's supposed to throw us off."

"Crack it open and let's see if it's a bug or not."

The original geek appeared to weigh the options and shrugged. "I'm gonna go scan the bejeezus out of it." Geek Guy picked up the box and carted it elsewhere.

Bobby had no worries about where he'd wind up. What Geek Guy did with him when he got there mattered a lot more. He needed the box to get opened in a situation that allowed him to escape unnoticed.

Geek Guy stuck the box into a machine. For an eternity, Bobby saw lights of every color and heard a wide variety of sounds. He figured something on the other end would use whatever it collected from all that to decide what kind of animal, vegetable, or mineral the dragon should be categorized as. Though he doubted he'd understand any of it, he kind of wanted to see the readouts and reports.

Eventually, Geek Guy took the box out and set it on a table. Bending down, he peered at Bobby, his nose less than an inch away. "What are you, little dragon?" He shook his head and tapped the side of the box with one corner of his mouth quirked up in a smile. "Not giving you back, little dragon, but I don't think I'll turn you in, either. If you can keep a secret, so can I, and we'll just say you were destroyed."

It sounded like Bobby would get an opening to make a break for it at some point. It could wind up being long enough for his stomach to hate him. With the rest of the swarm up in that warehouse, though, he could easily go take care of himself. He only needed to have the dragon put into a situation where he'd have no reason to worry about it.

Geek Guy opened up the box and grabbed the dragon, which Bobby let him do, and stuffed it into his pants pocket. "It was nothing," Geek Guy told his coworkers as he returned to his post and sat down. The pocket got tight enough the dragon had to go flat to avoid potentially losing a wing, and couldn't wriggle out without alerting Geek Guy to its movement.

"Are you keeping it?"

"That would be against regulations."

"Uh-huh." The other guy sounded unconvinced, but didn't press the subject. From there, the conversation turned to their job, which apparently consisted of monitoring cameras and other things, as well as playing some sort of computer game involving shooting and blowing things up. It sounded positively boring to Bobby, so he left the dragon behind with instructions to stay still until he got back.

Returning to the swarm, he took stock of his options. This military base had nothing around it for miles and miles. He could either chance the mess hall or take off and leave his one dragon behind for a couple of hours.

He thought he remembered Jayce being from Las Vegas, which wasn't far from here. If he could find it, maybe Jayce's stuff would all still be at his place. Finding people hadn't been too hard when he'd done it before, and "Jayce Westbrook" seemed like an uncommon enough name to make it doable.

Determined, he left the base behind, flying up high enough to not be noticed, and spent the next hour heading for Las Vegas. There, he walked around, grabbing food out of the garbage and fending off weariness as he looked for a way to find Jayce's address. Once upon a time, he spent a few bucks to use an internet cafe for stuff like this. He didn't have a few bucks right now. He even checked all his pockets to make sure Kaitlin hadn't stuffed some money in them, anticipating his needs. She didn't see everything coming.

After spending a half hour walking around, he found himself in front of the Monte Carlo hotel and wandered inside in search of a drinking fountain and some relief from the heat. While there, he decided to try the "aw shucks" approach with an employee. No need to pretend at being a hick, because he'd never seen a place as ritzy as this one before. He naturally gawked all around at everything, from the marble floors to the glass chandeliers to the heavy wood and plush velvet furniture.

The front desk, made of polished dark wood, had him sticking his hands in his pockets to keep from accidentally touching and sullying it. It took him off guard that the cute girl standing behind it in the crisp uniform with her brown hair tied up neatly in some kind of bun smiled pleasantly at him, like he must be an honored guest. He guessed her to be about his age, probably a college student working her way through school.

"Hello and welcome to the Monte Carlo. Do you have a reservation?"

"Uh, no, I don't. Um, actually, I'm kinda lost. My buddy says to stop by if'n I'm ever in town, but I done lost my phone someplace 'tween home and here, and I ain't got no idea where to go. Any way you could maybe look up an address here in town for me? I'd bug someone else, but I got let out nearby and ain't got no clue where nothing else is."

Her polite smile crinkled, becoming more genuine. "Sure, I can do that." Leaning toward him, she lowered her voice. "Just don't tell anyone." She winked.

"I sure won't," he nodded with his own answering smile and echoing her volume, "and thank ya kindly. His name's Jayce Westbrook."

Her eyebrows jumped up. "Oh, you know Jayce?"

"Um, yeah," he answered warily, not expecting such a reaction. "That a bad thing 'round these parts?"

"No, not at all. He works here. Or, he did, anyway, until he got arrested. I'm supposed to call the police if anyone comes asking for him. But, you know, I don't really believe what they said, and..." She bit her lip. "You don't look like a terrorist."

Five hundred hotels in this town, and he managed to pick the one where Jayce had worked. "Huh. Weird. No, I ain't no terrorist. My Momma says I'm kinda a pain in the ass, though."

She flashed him a grin. "Sorry I have to be the one to tell you that."

"Yeah, it's okay. Guess I'm in Vegas with purt near nothing and knowing nobody." Why in the heckbiscuits was he hitting on this girl? He could feel himself putting on a kind of pout, trying to get a pity date. Lily did make it clear she wasn't interested. He still hoped and wished and wanted, and couldn't make himself give up yet. "I don't suppose you could look up his address anyway? If he done got out and just ain't ready to see about getting his job back yet, I can maybe still get a place to crash for the night."

"Well," she said with a sigh. "I don't need to." She grabbed a piece of paper, scribbled something on it, and offered it to him. "Look, if he's there, would you tell him—" She sighed again. "I know it was just a casual thing to him, but we had a really good time, and I thought maybe— I just— Would you ask him to call me?" Tapping her name tag, which read "Beverly," she gave him a pleading look. "I'll listen, even if whatever happened while he was gone was really bad."

Bobby blinked and took the paper. What was it about the guys in this stupid secret project that made so many of them have such an easy time with women? Heck, even Greg managed better than him. Except Bobby, always except him. Everyone else got all the looks, everyone else smiled and got girls to shed clothes, everyone else didn't get into half as much trouble as he seemed to wander his damned fool head into. "Yeah, sure, I can tell him. Beverly at the Monte Carlo says to get offa your ass and stop feeling sorry for yourself and give her a call. That about right?"

He'd successfully amused her again. "Yes, that's about right. Thanks. I hope he's okay."

"Me too." He used the slip of paper to wave at her, biting back the urge to ask if he could count on her as a backup option for tonight. He'd become a tomcat out on the prowl for some reason he couldn't put his finger on, and needed to stop that, right now. Maybe it only happened because he had nothing but a fight to look back on and nothing but more fights to look forward to.

Hurrying out of the place, he checked the paper. On it, she'd put directions to get to address, which he appreciated. Next time he saw Jayce, he actually would tell him to give Beverly a call. She deserved that much, at least. Assuming he actually managed to find Elena so he actually could see Jayce again, which dawdling here didn't help in the slightest. He slipped behind a palm tree to cover himself breaking apart into the swarm, then swirled upward to follow the directions from above.

Jayce had an apartment on the top floor of a decent four-story building. Bobby got in without a problem to find it trashed. Someone went through it without much regard for Jayce's things, and Bobby got the distinct impression it had been the cops. His rent must have been paid up for a bit to keep the landlord from sweeping it all up into a dumpster.

Leaving the fridge alone seemed prudent—he couldn't imagine what might have survived this long in there, and had no desire to get a whiff of what didn't. In the cabinets, he found some cans and boxes of food. With a can of beans in one hand and fork in the other, he paced around the place, peering through the mess. He had nothing in particular to look for and only did it to not wonder later if he'd missed something by ignoring it.

The closet had Jayce-sized dark suits and Bobby found a motorcycle helmet under a crumpled sheet. Most of the debris came from magazines, mail, and the stuffing that had been ripped out of the couch and bed. His clothing drawers had been dumped out too, along with a small collection of kitchen utensils. It interested Bobby that Jayce kept no knickknacks or other mementos, not even pictures stuck to the fridge or mirror. Then again, the cops might have taken some of it as "evidence."

Until he headed into the bathroom to use it for its intended purpose, he thought he'd wasted his time coming here. That room had been taken apart like the rest of the place, but he found something unexpected along with the usual bathroom stuff. Sitting on the counter, someone had left a digital camera lying on its side, mostly covered by a towel. Had he found it in a different room, he would have dismissed it as unremarkable.

Leaving the can and fork behind in the sink, he picked up the camera and turned it on. The battery had plenty of charge left, and he fiddled with it until it showed him the contents of its memory card. The pictures went backward in time, starting with various things in the apartment when it was already mussed, then a handful of pictures from before they did any-thing, showing it all neat and tidy. After that, he found one in a very differ-ent location, of Jayce flanked by two suits in a room that reminded Bobby of the place he'd been interrogated when he'd first been picked up.

What struck Bobby about this picture was Jayce. He had a droopy and goofy look about him, one Bobby found weird and jarring on a man he'd never known to be a pushover or a heavy drinker. His posture entirely lack the solid, straight-backed professionalism the Native American man always had, even when he cracked jokes or batted his eyes at a pretty girl. Two suits flanked him, struggling under his weight without him resisting. One side of the frame had a sliver of another suit's arm.

As he stared at it, he noticed other details. The suit on the left had a familiar jawline, and had to be Privek. That guy showed up everywhere. How did he get from Vegas to Atlanta in time to pick them both up, and had he been there for Ai and Alice too? He thought the one on the right might be Hagen, who seemed to be his favorite lackey.

Bobby hit the button to get to the next picture, expecting to see a few more of the same. The difference between this next picture of Jayce and the previous one made him pause and examine it.

In the new picture, Jayce stood with his back straight, glowering at the suit with his back to the camera. That suit had to be the one from the previous frame, this time captured with one arm raised, a hand reaching for Jayce's face. It took staring at the picture for nearly a minute for Bobby to decide the pose of the hand had nothing to do with slapping. The owner of that hand wanted to touch Jayce.

He also noticed something wrong with the hand, something weird about the skin. Where the shirt under the suit jacket ended, the skin tone almost matched Jayce's. It had some weird distortion, though. The camera had too small a screen to get detail beyond that.

No one with a hand like that had been there when Bobby got arrested. Privek grabbed him from the police station, took him to some other jail, made him change, then loaded him into a van for the most unpleasant and boring ride in his life. As far as he could tell, he could account for every minute of that journey except for the time spent sleeping. After he'd been stationed in that weird cell, he had missing time, yeah, but not before. At least, he didn't think so. Thinking back over the experience, though, he had to admit it had been a blur in some parts.

Jayce hadn't ever said anything about missing time or gaps in his memory. Did that mean it might have happened to Bobby without him realizing it? He did remember getting punched in the face by Privek. After that, he'd tried to talk to those suits, then he gave up. Maybe Jayce did more than wriggle a bit and try to chat them up, so they used a bigger gun. Or, maybe they saw him as a bigger threat to begin with because of his security guard background.

Bobby flipped through the last two pictures of Jayce as his normal self. Neither showed the mystery hand or its owner. He knew that person had to be important, somehow. Unable to come up with any brilliant ideas, he slipped the camera into his jeans pocket.

He'd discovered something, for sure. The trip to Vegas had been worth it. Now, he only needed to stuff his face enough to last however long he needed to at Groom Lake. Yawning, he gave the shredded bed a longing look. Later, he'd sleep. For now, he broke apart into the swarm, grateful it would keep him from noticing how much he needed to rest.

CHAPTER 6

BOBBY

His solo dragon had stayed in Geek Guy's pocket, stuck there. Bobby had good timing. After only a few minutes of listening to him lose at whatever video game they played on company time, Geek Guy announced he needed a break. Sitting around on his ass goofing off was, apparently, hard work. As soon as he got up, the dragon climbed up the pocket to stick its head out and look around.

The other two guys grunted. As absorbed as they seemed to be in their game, he chose not to take the risk they'd notice something small moving in their peripheral vision. This room wouldn't be the best place to get out and find the ventilation system anyway, since he couldn't see a vent.

Geek Guy used a different door than last time. This one opened into a hallway with other closed doors. At the end of the hallway, he went into a kitchen sort of space with a coffee machine, a fridge, and a microwave. Bobby saw a vent near the ceiling and no other people, making it a perfect place to get out of the pocket and disappear.

The dragon flew behind Geek Guy's back and skimmed the ceiling to reach the vent, then wriggled through it. He flitted down the tunnels, checking every access point for anything worth seeing. The ductwork felt vast and cavernous, and the place had endless strings of offices and conference rooms.

Next, he found labs full of people in lab coats and face masks, all bent over glass tubes and big machines and microscopes. Nowhere did he find Elena. Until he checked the whole place, though, he wouldn't give up.

Which was why he found her. Not Elena—she definitely wasn't here. He found *her*. Slim and willowy, she sat in a floral print armchair, downcast and listless, folding a piece of colored paper carefully and delicately. Her skin looked almost translucent and her dull yellow hair hung limp and straight to her chin without bangs. They had her wearing a white t-shirt with an Air Force logo on the upper left, just above her minimal breast, and a pair of blue running pants.

He stopped and stared because of her icy blue eyes. The same as his own, as all of theirs, hers looked out from a face with high cheekbones and a more angular feel than any human he ever saw. Pointy ears just poked out of the curtain of hair. This woman had to be the one he'd been told about more than once, the one who started all of this.

His real mother.

Not only had he found her alive, he'd found her in the custody of the US military, as a prisoner. If he had to guess her age, he'd say somewhere in her twenties, though that made no sense. He'd been told they found her in Roswell, in the 1940s or 50s. Had she been stuck in a prison since then?

Did this mean she had no unusual abilities, or did they keep her dosed up to prevent her from using them? Either way, he had to find a way to get her out of here. Even if he had nothing more in common with her than half his DNA and the military being interested in them both, he still felt that he owed her something. Blood is thicker than most anything, so the saying went, and if not for her, he wouldn't be. Besides, no one deserved to be stuck in a box just for being different.

He had one dragon to get her out. She wouldn't fit into the ducts, and even if she could, they didn't go anywhere useful that he'd found yet. As he'd suspected, this underground facility used some kind of closed system without a vent to the surface. It meant no way to get the rest of the swarm inside, which meant no way to actually break her loose. Nothing that he could think of, anyway. Leaving her here bothered him a lot, though.

Was this really any different from leaving the others behind? In fairness, he felt horrible about that too, so it didn't really matter. If he could have, he would have grabbed them all and to heckbiscuits with Liam and his stupid girlfriend. But he wanted them all on the same team, he wanted not to have a rift between them all if he could help it. That led him to here, staring at his biological mother with no idea what to do about it.

He could get the swarm to bust into the place, but he couldn't carry a person that far, not up through that elevator shaft. No, he'd have to find a way to get someone to release her, or transfer her somewhere else, or something like that. Paul would be a big help. Or Sam—she could make fake electronically delivered orders. With the whole group, they could assault the place. Dammit, he needed backup.

No, he didn't. There had to be a way to get her out. Seeing her sitting there, like habit kept her going, like she'd forgotten the feel of the sun kissing her skin... It hurt him, someplace deep down. That kind of ache made no sense, yet he had it all the same.

Before he could eagerly drop in to go meet her, the dragon noticed a pair of cameras in the corners. The next room had a sink, making it a bathroom. Odds were good they didn't let her have even a moment of privacy to use the shower, so whatever he decided to do, he needed to come up with a distraction to keep those three security guys busy watching elsewhere.

He went back to the next closest vent and found a soldier outside her cell—no matter how cushy the chairs, he considered it a prison—sitting at a table, reading a book. If she walked out, he'd stop her, so this guy needed a distraction too. Checking the area over, he noticed a fire alarm on the wall and wondered how the base would react if he set it off. Would they evacuate her or focus on finding the nonexistent fire?

A real fire would cause more chaos, especially if he started several in different parts of the facility. He could do that. The dragon danced in place, excited by the idea of actually accomplishing something and getting to her. Why did it care? Might as well ask why *he* cared, and he had no answer for that either.

This place featured concrete, hard industrial floors, and fire retardant ceiling tiles. The furniture he saw everywhere but in the cell had been made of metal and hard plastic. This guard had a paperback book, which made him think of paper, leading him to recall seeing garbage cans. They had a bunch of kitchen-style break rooms scattered across the place too. He could probably find something flammable in those.

Now with a genuine plan, he zoomed around the base, randomly lighting up whatever would burn here and there and everywhere. Within thirty seconds of the first fire, alarms went off. Then sprinklers made it rain inside. Despite the fires being small and put out almost as fast as he could start them, people shouted and screamed, grabbing up laptops and papers and running around. Since he didn't really want to destroy the whole place or cause a genuine fire, this was perfect. The security guys would have their hands full dealing with the chaos and panic, leaving them unable to do their real jobs adequately.

By the time he returned to her cell, he'd started more than twenty fires. The guard stationed outside set down his radio as Bobby arrived and hit the button to open the cell door. Bobby took a chance and swooped in behind him. "Asyllis, we're going to the bunker." He said "bunker" like it should have a capital letter. More importantly, it sounded like her name was "Asyllis," which appealed to Bobby for no reason he could explain.

She took a spiritless breath deep enough to move her head. Her eyes blinked heavily. "No." The voice that made the one word was stale like cardboard, but he knew, somehow, that it could be musical and beautiful. It pissed him off that it wasn't.

The guard glared and made a fist. "It's kind of an emergency, and I'm not asking you. Get up, we're going. I'll use the stun stick if I have to." His other hand went to a baton on his belt with a button on the end of the handle.

Bobby refused to stand by and let the guard deliver on his threat, and he needed her to get up and leave the room. Only one solution came to mind: more fire. Dropping down fast enough to avoid notice, he blew fire at one of her chairs until it caught, and kept blowing at the chair until one of them noticed.

The guard made a wordless sound of unpleasant surprise, cuing Bobby to peer around the side. The dragon couldn't be hurt by fire, so he didn't care about the chair burning. Interestingly, it didn't seem that this room had any sort of fire suppression system. He watched the guard grab Asyllis by the arm and haul her out of the chair. She didn't resist. He wondered if she ever truly resisted anything at this point, aside from doing so to avoid moving.

Once on her feet, Asyllis stumbled after the guard while still watching the fire. A tiny flicker of fear crossed her face, so muted he thought she might be too dead inside to feel anything. Since the guard watched ahead, Bobby had the dragon fly out where she could see it. She stared at the tiny dragon, putting a hand out to let him land. Obliging her made the dragon happier than a biscuit in gravy. Recognition lit up in her face. Either she'd somehow seen one before, or guessed it would help her gain her freedom.

Nodding to the dragon, she closed her hand around it and moved more smoothly, like she decided to actually run with the guard instead of being dragged by him. "The Bunker is too far," she told him, "we should use the door and go to the surface. Who knows where the next fire will break out?"

The guard stopped running and Bobby heard them both panting. "You know you're not allowed up there."

"Please, Cander, I haven't seen the sun in so long, I've forgotten what it looks like. You did it for my safety, until the source of the mysterious fire could be determined. To protect the precious prize your superiors charged you with." The more she spoke, the more Bobby could hear her light accent. It was strange, foreign in a way he couldn't explain. Aside from the fact he figured she must be an alien, which completely explained it in every way. In light of that, she had a stellar command of English. Then again, she'd had a long time to learn it. With little else to do over several decades, he could probably master a language or five.

"I don't know, Asyllis. I could get into a lot of trouble. We should go to the Bunker." If he knew where it was, Bobby would take off and go set a fire in this Bunker to cross it off the list of Safe Places.

"I have no dignity left to shred for you, Cander. I beg you to just grant me this one small favor. Please." Bobby imagined her getting to the guy's personal space and trying her damnedest to appeal to his decency. He couldn't have resisted her even if he wanted to, and wished he could scream at Cander to give in already.

Cander didn't answer for one agonizing second that stretched into an eon. "Alright, but you have to stay close to me." They hurried on their way again.

"Thank you, Cander. Thank you."

"Don't thank me yet. For all I know, this'll make them think you're more trouble than you're worth."

No one accosted either of them as they moved swiftly through the halls. Bobby didn't feel like this might really work until they ran down that blank hallway and slid into the elevator. Apparently, Bobby had successfully managed to thoroughly distract the security guys, because they said nothing about Cander and Asyllis walking right out the front door with the strange dragon that had officially been destroyed and unofficially still sat in Geek Guy's pocket.

Bobby jumped back out of the dragon, certain it would stay there and be fine. No one else had evacuated to the surface, leaving Bobby free to re-form and walk right up to punch the soldier guarding Asyllis in the face. Too stunned to react, Cander stood there and let Bobby hit him again, then follow up with a third that knocked him down enough to keep him there for a short time.

"Asyllis, this here's a jailbreak."

She wasn't listening. She wasn't even standing there anymore when he turned to look. She'd walked out the door of the warehouse already, staring up at the sky. "It's so blue," she said softly.

He hurried to her side. "If'n you want to spend more'n a few minutes looking at it, we should grab a vehicle and get the heck outta Dodge. 'Less you can fly?"

"Fly?" She blinked and looked at him. "No, I can't fly." She stood at the same height as him, putting them eye to eye. Reaching for his face, she brushed her fingertips across his cheek. "Who are you?" To his joy, her voice gained more color and melody with every moment she spent in this patch of sunshine.

"This really ain't the time, but pretty sure I'm your son. If'n you got any special ways to get yourself away from here, you oughta pull it out, but if not, we gotta take care of that. Your other choice is going back inside." He jerked a thumb back toward the elevator.

She looked at Cander, lying unconscious on the floor. "They won't let me go so easily."

"Yeah, that's what I thought about myself, but I done escaped. Ain't giving up now, not ever." Unsure how this would actually work, he offered her his hand.

Turning again, she gazed out over the base. "We may both be killed."

Was she trying to talk him out of it, or just making sure he understood the stakes? If anyone understood the situation, it was him. They were extremely lucky not to have sirens wailing already, and that the base hadn't yet been locked down with guys carting machine guns hoofing it all around. "Wouldn't you rather go down in the sun than waste away in the dark?"

A fierce grin transformed her into a warrior angel, a woman come down to kick some ass and not bother taking any names. She let go of the dragon and grabbed his hand, watching with wonder as it darted to his thumb and stuck back on. "You? You're the *drathikê?*"

Instead of answering, he ran, pulling her willingly along behind him. He already knew the layout of the base and took them to the motor pool. It had only a few vehicles, and a handful of dragons would have no trouble grabbing a set of keys. When they stood with their backs against the wall, waiting for his dragon scouts, he looked at her and nodded. "I'm them and they're me." It made no more sense now than it had before, but she had a word for them, which made him want to talk about it.

"How? How is that possible?" She touched the smooth stump of his wrist, running her fingers over it.

Why did he expect her to have all the answers? The question disappointed him. "No idea. I kinda thought you could tell me."

"Me? Why? I've never seen anything like this before. It's strange, bizarre. What are you?" The edge of disgust to her voice hurt to hear.

"I'm your son," he reminded her with a mild glare. "They done took your stuff and crossed it with human and made kids. There's thirty-five of us. None of us is your responsibility, but we *are* your kin."

"Why would they do such a thing?" She let go of him and sighed, staring off into the distance. "I had no idea. Not that I could've done anything if I did. I haven't been allowed outside since I was moved here, and I was drugged for that trip."

Whatever he expected, she failed to live up to it. He had to admit to himself that, fair or not, he thought she'd be a lot like his Momma. That noble woman accepted him immediately when he told her what he'd become. She also carried him and raised him and knew him. Asyllis, on the other hand, had nothing more than DNA in common with him. They were strangers.

"It kinda seemed like you cooperate with it all."

Before she came up with a way to respond, the dragons returned with a ring of keys. She watched his hand re-form with rapt attention. "Are the others like you?"

"Not exactly. But we gotta move now. There's a Humvee, I'll point to it. Move quick, just get right in and hopefully we'll be able to drive away before anyone realizes we shouldn't oughta."

They slipped through the cracked open door, moving low and quiet to avoid attracting the attention of the two soldiers inside. Bobby pointed to the vehicle he wanted Asyllis to get into.

A soldier jogged to the Humvee with a clipboard in hand. Bobby grabbed Asyllis before the soldier could notice them and pulled her down behind some barrels. The soldier hopped into the vehicle Bobby intended to take and did a bunch of things to start it up, scribbled something on his clipboard, then got out, leaving it running. That whole process took a couple of minutes. He watched the soldier just walk away from the running Humvee and frowned down at the keys in his hand, confused. Never mind. They'd never get a better opportunity than this.

Hauling Asyllis up, he practically threw her at the passenger door and ran around to the other side. Her door shutting must have echoed, because as he planted his butt in the driver's seat, a voice called out, "Hey, who're you?" Good thing he let the other guy start the Humvee up, because he saw nowhere to jam a key in, and it had all kinds of lights and switches and buttons. At least the shifter had labels, and he yanked on it, only to realize he had to push the button and twist the handle to make it move.

Despite the differences between the two vehicles, sitting in this seat reminded him of driving Lily's car, taking his turn to get her and her boy to the farm. He had things he needed to say to her, most of it an apology for being such a dumbass. If she gave him five minutes, he knew he could make things right with her. Probably. Maybe. So long as he didn't say or do anything else stupid. Probably not, then.

He needed to stop thinking about her. One of the soldiers came around the front of the vehicle with a gun out. Bobby did his best not to hit the guy as he slammed the gas pedal to the floor. "Hold on," he said. Asyllis already had her seat belt clicked in and she gripped the seat and door so tightly her knuckles went an odd shade of purple.

The reason for her distress probably involved the sight of the door ahead, only open about halfway and possibly not quite enough to get this thing through it. With the added obstacle of the soldier in the way, Bobby missed, slamming his side of the vehicle into the door. Unlike in the movies, the door failed to fly off. It did buckle enough to get through. The sound of metal scraping on metal grated enough that he clenched his jaw since he couldn't cover his ears. Somewhere in there, he started making noise to urge the Humvee on, as if him growling would make it go faster.

Gunshots announced the fact that the soldiers weren't going to just let them get away. Asyllis ducked down and covered her head with her hands like it would make a difference. Bobby swerved some, not sure if it helped, but at least they didn't hit the tires yet. This "plan" probably wasn't going to get them very far. He needed to think of something else to follow up with. Driving like this wasn't going to make that easy.

Glancing back to check on the soldiers, he caught sight of something worse: a small helicopter. He'd heard about drones, and guessed this one had either a camera or a gun. Both options sucked for them. Dragons could take care of it, but he kind of needed both hands to keep control of the Humvee.

"I'm not sure this is better than being locked up down there."

Bobby cranked the wheel and refused to give up.

CHAPTER 7

LIAM

Another door down the hall stood open. Paul must have left it that way when he came looking for Liam. He pulled Elena through it, giving Paul space to muck around in that man's head. They slipped in behind the others, all staring through a pane of glass into a dim room.

"Hi, Elena," Kaitlin said offhandedly, only barely glancing back. "This is something, huh? Didn't see it coming, no idea what to make of it." She pointed at the glass, indicating the vast array of gurneys on the other side, most of them filled with people. There were at least two hundred of them, no more than ten or twelve empty. They held people of both genders and varying skin tones, though they seemed to all be in a particular age range: late teens to mid twenties. Each had a sheet for a covering and an IV bag going into a needle in their arm.

Elena blinked and waved uncertainly at Kaitlin's back. Liam squeezed her hand and tried not to be freaked out. "What are the chances this is actually of some interest to us?"

"I was sent here. There's got to be a reason." Kaitlin put a hand on the glass, her fingertips resting on it gently. She sighed and shook her head. "We have to free them."

Riker reached out to restrain her the second she started for the other door, the one that would let her into that room. "We don't know what's really going on here. If you go in there and just pull those IVs out, you could hurt them worse than leaving them there."

Kaitlin stared at him, then blinked. Paul whined behind Liam. "Dammit, does that have to keep happening, over and over?" He shivered and pressed a hand to his head.

"If we don't free them now, there will be blood shed over them. I'm not sure, but some of it might be theirs." Kaitlin put her hand back on the glass, only this time, she clearly did it to support herself. "This isn't exactly a goddamned picnic for me, either, Paul."

"Say we do free them." Liam tried not to look, because he knew that he shouldn't leave them behind while Elena got to walk free. He was selfish, and he knew it and had no intention of doing anything about it. When he'd insured her safety, then he'd look at the idea of freeing other people. "Then what? We're not prepared to get them out of here, and if any of them have medical conditions, we're not prepared to handle dealing with them. I don't want to leave them here any more than you do, but we aren't going to magically find a tour bus in the parking lot to evacuate them with, and even if we somehow did, we'd never be able to prevent some of them from getting hurt or killed in the escape."

"We could take one or two, Sergeant," Hegi offered. "But I don't know how you'd pick."

Riker grunted. "If they're out cold, we can stuff them in the trunk or something."

"That's my sister," Paul pushed his way to the glass, even though that put him next to Kaitlin. "She's been missing for weeks. We thought she ran away from home again, but she didn't come back. She always came back after a few days or a week, looking for a place to crash again and more money. Mom and Dad were ready to send her to a rehab place, then she disappeared again, but she didn't come back this time."

Only one thing about that made no sense to Liam. "And Privek didn't use her against you?"

"No." Paul still stared at the one girl, not shaking his head or otherwise moving. "I wouldn't have believed him anyway. When she didn't come back after two weeks, we figured she was dead. I mean, my parents didn't come out and say it, and neither did I, we just kind of all silently agreed."

Kaitlin crossed her arms and seemed to be having a contest of wills with Riker. "Is she one of us?"

"No, we were both adopted."

Riker rolled his eyes. "We can't afford to stand here and argue and chat. Hegi, you carry the sister. Carter, you go pick one out at random. We'll question them when they wake up, find out if there are any similarities in their stories. I'll take point with Kaitlin, Paul fall in behind us to handle whatever you need to. Liam, take the rear. You'll be able to maneuver better than these two."

While the others hurried into the room to grab two victims, Liam turned and explained what just happened to Elena as succinctly as he could. She didn't understand any of this, but thankfully, chose not to ask questions. They fell in behind Hegi. The soldier had a young, pale, brunette girl wrapped in a sheet tossed over his shoulder like a sack of potatoes. She had more piercings than he considered flattering, making Liam wonder what she got up to when she disappeared.

With Kaitlin guiding them and Paul there in case anything went wrong, their exit seemed assured. Liam's phone rang. He pulled it out and frowned at the caller ID. Why was Privek calling him? He hadn't shirked any duties in particular that he knew of. "Hello?"

"Moore, where are you?" That was Privek: all business.

To help him feel an excuse he hoped the agent would swallow, he shrugged. "I went out for some air. Did you need something?" In this moment, he realized he wouldn't be able to pull anything on Privek face-to-face anymore, not knowing what he knew now, not having rescued Elena like this.

"Some air. I see." He heard Privek take a deep breath. "Yes, you're wanted here. There's been a development and I'd like all hands on deck. How soon can you get back?"

"Well, I took a drive and kind of got lost. The GPS can't seem to connect to any satellites for some reason, so I really have no idea. At least an hour."

"Mmhmm." Liam had a sinking feeling that noise meant Privek didn't buy it. "Call me when you reach the city again." He hung up without giving Liam a chance to say anything else.

Liam stared at his phone, feeling like he'd missed something. That conversation went more or less fine, but it felt off, and he couldn't— They'd taken Paul's car. His own car sat in the parking lot. The bastard probably stood next to it when he called. Now Privek knew. As soon as he got reports about everything going wrong today, he'd blame Liam. For all of it, even whatever trouble Bobby managed to get himself into.

He cursed, then repeated it because he hadn't meant to say it out loud in the first place. Their breathing room with Privek had evaporated, and they'd lost any chance at a surprise assault. Their exit from this building might even have just gotten more complicated.

Paul's phone rang, giving Liam a sudden rush of panic. "Paul, it's

Privek. He's going to ask where you are."

Turning around with his phone already in hand, Paul paled. "What should I tell him?"

Liam's brain froze, imagining all the horrible things that could happen to Elena. As a Spanish citizen and not an American, she could be detained, or deported, or worse.

"Tell him you're busy," Riker said, "there's a girl."

Why did he say he'd gone out in his car? He could've said he'd gone for a walk. Though he couldn't have claimed to be lost, he could still have said it would take him an hour to get back. Liam bit back another curse for his incredible stupidity.

Paul nodded and answered his phone. He said what Riker suggested, mumbling nervously. He hung up the phone and shook his head with a frown. "I don't think he believed anything I just said."

"Worry about this when we get to the car. We're not out of the building yet." Riker reached over and patted Paul on the shoulder encouragingly. "Nobody's perfect, we just do what we can with what we've got."

"How come you never say anything nice like that to me, Sarge?" Carter joked.

Riker turned back with a grin. "Because you're a thick-skull dumbass and only shouting gets through to you."

"Oh, right. I forgot." Carter chuckled and Hegi snorted.

The banter faded into the background for Liam. He glanced at Elena, hoping that what he and Paul just got her into was really worth it. No, he didn't mean that. Obviously, being free made her instantly better off than locked up, especially if he'd prevented her from being stuck in one of those beds. Just as obviously, he benefited from having her by his side. He worried, though, that he'd jumped into a rabbit hole without knowing whether she'd get hurt by following him or not.

Between the efforts of Paul and Kaitlin, they walked out the front door to find their cars waiting, engines already running. Liam wondered how long it would take Privek to hear about this and whether he'd connect them to it. He imagined the guards getting a call any second now, asking about suspicious or unexpected guests. In his head, soldiers fired guns at them, tires squealed, someone got shot, and he had to watch Elena die because the bullet hit her between the eyes.

One thing kept him from falling apart: the precog. Paul wanted to stay as far away as possible from Kaitlin. Liam pushed Elena toward the car Kaitlin chose. They shared it with Riker, and Platt drove, with Kaitlin's random male damsel in distress draped across their laps in the back seat. As awkward as it felt, he suspected having Paul's teenage sister there instead would be worse.

"Where are we going?" Platt asked as he pulled the car away from the building. "I can figure out 'off the base' on my own. I mean after that."

Riker turned around to check with Kaitlin, who had the unknown man's head in her lap as she sat next to Elena. She leaned back against the seat with her eyes closed. "I don't know, stop looking at me. I'm kind of wiped from all that in there. It takes energy to do that, and I was doing it almost the whole time we were in there. I really need something to eat soon, and a nap."

Liam rubbed his eyes with one hand. The other refused to leave Elena's shoulders. "For now, head toward Chicago. Maybe something will come up before we get there and we can pick someplace else."

"That's what, ten, twelve hours away?"

"Something like that, yeah," Riker nodded. "We can't drive all the way there like this, though. Not with minimal cash and a body in the backseat."

Liam pulled his phone out of his pocket and stared at it. He didn't like paranoia. It always struck him as silly and stupid, the province of mentally unstable people. Yet, here he found himself pursuing the worst possible dark fantasies imaginable. "I'm concerned that Privek is tapping my phone or I could call my father and arrange to meet his plane at the airport."

Without missing a beat, Riker offered his phone. "Odds are pretty low he's tapping mine yet. That'll probably change when he's had a chance to look over the security footage. Might as well use it while we got it."

"Who is Privek, anyway?" Platt asked as Liam took the phone and dialed.

"He said he was NSA," Liam answered absently, "but I really don't know." The last time he spoke to his father had been before Afghanistan. His parents didn't even know he'd gone there. He hadn't told them about Elena yet, either. He'd intended to introduce her when he got home. Then Privek took her and he'd lost sight of everything except getting her back. The one time he spoke to them, he only said he'd miss his next semester at Harvard Business School. They expected so little of him that his father didn't even give him a hard time about it.

"Hello?" His father's voice, full of suspicion, jarred him out of his thoughts.

"It's Liam, I'm borrowing a friend's phone." He didn't need to explain. Robert would assume he'd let his phone's battery run dead, or he'd left it in some girl's purse. "Can you send the plane to DC for me?" As soon as the words left his mouth, it occurred to him that he should have made this request the way he usually did, by calling his father's secretary.

Robert left a pause. "Are you alright?"

The entirety of the last six weeks tried to push its way out of his mouth. From the joy of meeting Elena to being on the run right now, he burned to share it all. "Yeah," he heard himself say in a voice so easily controlled by years of practice in the fine art of keeping his parents happy that it happened with no effort. "I...I think I met someone."

"Ah. This is all about a girl." He sounded so relieved that he must have expected something devastating, something he'd dread explaining to his wife.

"Yeah, it kind of is. She's..." He turned and kissed Elena's temple. "Something special."

Robert chuckled. "Good to know. I'm glad you called. When you decided to blow off school, your mother got a little difficult, but I convinced her to give you your space. You're welcome for that."

"Yes, thank you, I appreciate it. Things have been, I don't know, crazy, I guess. I'll add Chicago to my list of places to take her soon."

"See that you do. I'm looking forward to meeting her."

Liam felt the urge to say goodbye and hang up. That's what the conversation demanded. How could he explain what he'd seen and done, what he'd become? How could he even ask about who he really was? He wanted to know and understand, yet he wanted to do it without causing a problem or driving a wedge into the middle of his family. "Dad, um." It must have sounded awful coming from him, something so inarticulate and needy it made Elena look up at him with concern.

"It sounds like you fell, hard, son," Robert chuckled again. "Don't let her use that against you too much. See you soon."

Liam pulled the phone away from his face and stared at it when his father hung up, caught between the shame of not being able to figure out how to ask a question, embarrassment at sounding like an idiot, and something tight in his chest he didn't have a name for. His father cut to the heart of things, guessing right while also guessing wrong. He did fall, and it was hard, and it was wonderful, and he loved her.

People tossed that word around in the circles he ran in, using it to mean "like" or "lust." He feared saying it out loud, worried it would cheapen what he felt. Worse, he had no idea what he'd do if she didn't feel the same things back. He had no fear of rejection, yet found the idea of *this* rejection terrifying. He could live if everyone else rejected him for the rest of his life, for everything, so long as Elena didn't.

Reaching back, Riker took his phone and pocketed it. "You think that hard for too long, you're gonna blow a gasket. We going to Reagan?"

"Yeah." Liam frowned. Elena had been taken from him there. He'd wanted to show her around the city for a couple of days before taking her home. With the still unconscious man laying across their laps and three other people in the car, he preferred not to make any grand displays of affection, yet he needed Elena's support now. He pulled her closer and leaned into her, brushing a finger down her cheek. "We'll probably beat the plane there."

"Gives us time to eat," Kaitlin said with a yawn. "We should go back to the farmhouse. It's kind of a mess, but no one will look for us there."

Liam thought about that. "Privek already knows where it is." Her logic, though, took no effort to follow. "But he'd never expect me to go there. Even if he thinks Bobby is with us, he wouldn't expect Bobby to go there, either, because that would be stupid. Going there makes no sense when the people we need to free are in DC."

"Sounds like a plan, then." Riker nodded his approval. "We go there, make an assault plan, meet up with Bobby, and prepare to hit them hard, where it counts."

They arrived at the airport with enough time to pick up food for everyone, then boarded the plane while the Moore family pilot took care of refueling. The middle-aged retired Navy aviator said nothing about the number of people or the two still unconscious ones carried inside still only wrapped in sheets. He was a professional and worked for wealthy people. Although Liam didn't think any of them had ever done anything this strange, his father paid well enough for the man not to comment.

Liam pulled out spare clothes his parents left in the drawers for the times when a business meeting in another city went from a few hours to a few days and left them next to the still sleeping bodies. Paul sat with his sister on the bed in the back of the plane, holding her hand. Kaitlin took a nap on the couch. Liam and Elena sat together at one of the windows. The five soldiers played cards at the table. The other victim lay on the floor.

About two hours into the flight, the guy on the floor curled up in distress and mewled. He appeared to have a seizure, or something similar.

From the back, Paul called out in a panicky voice, "Something's wrong. She's waking up, but something's wrong!"

Riker nodded toward the back. "Hegi, go check on the girl. Platt, this guy." The two men tossed their cards and followed orders.

Liam cringed, knowing he should do something and not wanting to. He much preferred to stay quietly by Elena's side and enjoy her presence. The piteous noises coming from the guy's mouth punched him in the guilt, and he left her to crouch beside the young man. The poor guy hurt so much that he twitched, and it sounded like Paul's sister had the same problem.

Hesitant to take on that level of pain, Liam rubbed his forehead nervously and took a deep breath. "I don't want to do this," he whined.

Platt gave him a sympathetic pat on the shoulder. "Nut up or shut up."

The abruptness and crudeness took him off guard; he expected some kind of short inspirational speech. Liam barked out a laugh and put his hand on the guy. Nothing happened. He could tell the man suffered. He could also tell his ability wouldn't fix it. All amusement disappeared and he frowned "I think...I don't know. It's like— His body is attacking itself, but that's not really the right way to explain. It's not like cancer, not a tumor. It's something different." Even he knew that made no sense.

Riker gathered up all the cards calmly. "Maybe they were being kept sedated so they didn't have to suffer through this, whatever it is."

"That makes sense," Liam agreed. "If I had to guess, I'd say he's mutating." That thought led to another, which made him want to know how Privek got all these people. "Okay. They've had blood from at least a few of us for months now. Assuming they have lots of money and access to lots of intelligent people they can keep under control one way or another, I'm going to guess that a facility connected to this whole thing was conducting research into our abilities."

"I'm with you," Riker nodded, "and I see where you're headed. They're trying to make more of you guys. They've got the resources to try it, and given secrecy level Ridiculous, they could pretty much do anything they wanted, including human testing."

Platt shrugged. "If we had some morphine or something, I could give it to him, but I don't see anything I can do or diagnose. What I don't get about that theory is where they got these people."

Riker shrugged and gave the guy a closer look. Liam did the same thing. He hadn't paid this one much attention before, thinking of him as nothing more than some guy in a sheet.

He was young, maybe twenty at most, with light brown hair and beard. He seemed decently fed but lean, without a lot of muscle mass. Something about him made Liam guess he'd had a hard life before he'd been grabbed, though he couldn't put his finger on what.

"Probably not military," Riker said with a shrug, "unless he's been in that facility for a while. Hair's too long. Beard only suggests a couple of weeks at most since he last paid attention to grooming. And the girl is obviously not military—too young and pierced."

In the back, Liam heard Paul quietly begging Hegi to do something. He couldn't blame the guy. If it was his own sister or Elena, he'd probably feel the same way. He got up and put a hand on Paul's shoulder, hoping to distract him. "Come on. There's nothing we can do here, you need to stop looking. She'll come out of it eventually and we need to talk."

"You don't know that. She could be stuck like this! It could kill her." Paul looked up at Liam, naked helplessness on his face, crinkles of pain tightening it. "I can hear her screaming in my head. She doesn't even pause to take a breath in there."

"Paul." Gripping his shoulder more forcefully, Liam pushed him back. "You have more control than that. You can block it out. I know you can. Listening to that won't help her, it only makes it harder for you to do anything useful. As soon as we land, we'll try to get some kind of painkiller or sedative, or something, but we can't do that right now. There's nothing we can do except try to figure things out. We need your help to do that."

Paul nodded and let go of his sister. He covered his head with both arms and cringed with agony. When he opened his eyes again, he averted them from the girl and stood up, following Liam away from her. "She's going to be fine," he said a few times, probably to himself.

They sat down in the two seats vacated by Platt and Hegi, who moved the unknown young man to lie on the bed beside Paul's sister and stayed with them both in case anything changed. "Paul," Liam said gently, knowing he was still upset, "you said your sister ran away from home. What's your best guess for what she would have been doing out there?"

The telepath rubbed his face with both hands. "I could find out, I'm sure it's there, under all the—" He finished the statement by waving his hand and slumping his shoulders.

"Just guess for now," Riker said in the same perfunctory tone he always used. "You know her, right? What do you *think* happened?"

Paul shrugged. "She was probably on the streets. Mom checked with all her friends and Dad looked for her. He's a cop. There are a lot of places a...someone like her can get lost."

It wouldn't help to suggest that Paul actually meant "a young pretty girl" instead of "someone like her," so Liam politely refrained. "Seattle is a long way for these guys to go just to pick up a test subject."

Paul snorted. It managed to be depressed and amused at the same time. "They could have picked her up at the same time they picked me up for all I know. I mean, they lied to us about everything else. Why not this too?" One hand gestured back at Elena, who sat looking out the window. "You remember how Maisie said she was picked up by guys in suits, then Privek and his guys rescued her? How can we think that was anything but a setup at this point? Camellia said something similar, so did some of the others."

"Yeah." Liam sat back and stared glumly at the table. They'd all been played, hard, and it annoyed him to discover he had such an obvious blind spot. All his life, he'd been able to finger the women who only wanted him for his money. Privek walked up and manipulated him effortlessly. Elena was his Achilles Heel and always would be. She'd been used against him so easily and effectively that he was ashamed of himself.

"I think maybe it's time for you guys to fill us in on the whole story, from front to back." Riker's voice startled him out of a brood. "We're here because we trust Bobby, for the most part, and I'm getting the basic picture, but if you could lay it all out, we can help more effectively."

"I don't think we know the whole picture," Liam admitted, sounding grumpy because he felt grumpy. "Not as much as Bobby does."

Sitting up and rubbing her eyes, Kaitlin yawned. "I know the whole picture, so listen up, kiddies. This is the bedtime story to end all bedtime stories. Roswell. There was really at least one alien. They got DNA from her, one way or another. In vitro fertilization comes along and some asshats say 'hey, what would happen if we crossed this alien DNA with human?' They try it through a program that looks like a social service organization, managing to actually impregnate thirty-five women across the country.

"The program loses funding, the kids all go on to grow up without knowing they were part of an experiment. Their parents don't know, either. One day, one of us gets a superpower, someone notices, government gets interested. Four of us get picked up by men in suits, of which Privek is one. Bobby was one of the ones they picked up. They fumble the whole thing and all four manage to escape after their superpowers become active. Led to believe they were part of some crazy experiment, they go across the country, with a list they conveniently happen to find while escaping, to try to convince the rest of the thirty-five to band together for the purpose of self-defense.

"We were going to try to work together to determine what to do, how to live in this human world without fucking it up for everyone and getting war declared on us for existing. Turns out, ten of us were actually taken by the other team," she gestured to indicate both Paul and Liam, "and convinced the rest of us are the bad guys and need to be stopped and locked up until we can be convinced not to cause trouble. You guys came in the middle of the night and ripped us out of our beds, shot us with tranquilizer darts like animals and bundled everyone off to freezer drawers.

"I only escaped because I just barely knew what was going to happen. Since then, we've learned there's another one of us we can't account for, Kanik Okpik, who must be the first one of us that got his power. He's got to be part of this whole thing, somehow, but whether Privek is using him or the other way around, we don't know yet. Looks now like they're experimenting, probably with the intent to create their own little army of supers. Who knows what their ultimate goal really is. Depends on how crazy they are."

Everyone stared at Kaitlin as she spoke. She met Liam's eyes the whole time. He wanted to look away, but felt that would be cowardly beyond even him. When she stopped, she smiled without even the tiniest trace of happiness. "We wanted to be left alone, and you fucks came and killed Tiana's cat. I buried it myself."

The moment she said that, Liam flushed with shame. Paul paled and covered his mouth with a hand. "We didn't know," Liam murmured. He regretted the words instantly.

"Yeah, no shit." Kaitlin snorted and shook her head. "I bet you all thought you were doing the right thing and deserved a fucking cookie and pat on the head for being such good boys and girls."

"Sounds like it's time to make amends," Carter said, too lightly for the situation. "Can't take back the past, but you can own the future. We need a plan to break the others out of the freezer drawers, show the rest how they were played, and then what to do from there."

Riker nodded. "If all those people in those beds are going to have superpowers like you guys, good chance we'll have a war on our hands until we can convince them they're being used. Even if we can, it's possible they'll have someone with mind control, right? Have to plan for that."

"Bobby is good for riding to the rescue." Kaitlin stopped glaring at Liam, which had no effect on how much he felt like an asshole right now. "When we meet back up with him, he'll have ideas."

"His mind can't be controlled," Paul offered, his voice subdued. "He's in too many parts. And Cant's mind is shielded. Roulet's blocked from me too."

Kaitlin shrugged. "I don't know anyone's last names."

"Um, Stephen and...Andrew?"

"Stephen is a vampire," Kaitlin said. "He drinks blood, is super strong and can fly. Can't handle sunlight. Andrew can block anyone's power and make it not work. He's going to be a big help if we're up against others like us."

Riker nodded thoughtfully. "We'll need both of them on our team. Here's hoping our bad guy doesn't figure that out and shoot them in the head rather than risk facing them."

When the conversation stalled, Liam got up to try to ignore the guilt he now felt on top of his shame. She was right. He did all that for a cookie and a pat on the head, and didn't really stop to consider how he might be wrong, how they might all be wrong. It had been all for Elena. That failed at making it okay. Losing her shouldn't have prevented him from using his brain.

Dropping himself down next to her, he took her hand and reveled in how she smiled at him. He kissed her palm gently and explained all of that in French, bracing for her to hate him because of it.

To his surprise, instead of showing any disappointment in him, she climbed onto his lap and hugged him tightly and told him, "I love you too." After a pause she added, "I will try not to do anything that stupid to show it."

He didn't deserve her.

Chapter 8

Bobby

"I need you to kinda take half the wheel, Asyllis. Can you do that? I gotta use dragons to get that tail offa our tail." Bobby aimed the Humvee at a place where the base had minimal fencing, probably only meant to separate military and public land. It'd keep the weirdo conspiracy guys out well enough, but wouldn't do much to keep a vehicle like this in.

"I don't see the connection between those two things."

"It's my hand and arm. I gotta let them off and I can't use it while they're gone."

"Why can't you just make your leg into dragons? You don't seem to be using that one."

Bobby blinked a few times. "Uh." The thought had never occurred to him before. Every time he needed some, they popped off his hand, then his arm. A few times, he'd re-formed without a toe because of a dragon being missing, but he'd never tried it on purpose. "I, uh, don't really got time for experimenting right now. Kinda need my attention for the road."

She sighed in resignation and offered her hand. "What do I do?"

Oh, heckbiscuits, she had no idea how to drive. Because she spent her whole lifetime on Earth in a box. Great, just great. "Hold on here," he grabbed her hand and stuck it on the wheel. "Don't resist when I crank it around, just help me keep it straight while I ain't turning, okay?"

"I'll do my best."

Bobby had a powerful urge to quote a movie he liked, mocking the notion of 'your best,' but curbed it back since she probably wouldn't get it. Her room hadn't had a TV, after all. Instead, he put his effort into pushing his whole right arm into dragons and sending them out to defend the Humvee. They were to try not to hurt anyone or let anyone get hurt, but do whatever it took to stop anything following them. He couldn't control them directly, not now, so they'd have to...do their best.

"We're gonna hit a fence, it might rock us around a bit, so hold on." He glanced at her, hoping this risk turned out to be worth it. Of course, the look on her face when she'd seen the sun bolstered him. Nobody deserved what she'd been through, nobody. With her in tow, he'd be able to convince Liam, even without Elena. They'd still find her somehow, because he'd promised.

His dragons swarmed the drone and chewed it up. The Humvee hit the fence and plowed over it without issue. None of the tires blew out on the razor wire at the top, and he could only hope none of them took on a slow leak. They had a long way to go yet. He had to somehow get Asyllis across the country to meet up with Liam, Paul, and Kaitlin without anyone noticing and with no money. Damn, he wished Stephen could be here to carry her.

His dragons returned, allowing Asyllis to take her hand back. All things being equal, he preferred having both his own hands on the wheel. She did nothing wrong, except give him one more thing to worry about while escaping from a covert military project.

Actually, he didn't think for one second they'd *really* escaped. Someplace like this probably had a satellite pointed at it all the time, or a giant radar installation staring at it. Heck, they might even have a tracking device in the Humvee. They needed to get lost in Vegas.

"So, I gotta ask you about what you're capable of and stuff. You seen me, how I turn into dragons and all. We gotta cover a lot of distance, can you do anything to make that go quick?"

Startled by his voice, Asyllis jumped, then curled her legs up and stopped looking out the window. "I'm not sure I understand the question. I have no special abilities. My mate and I, we were trackers and hunters, not magi. If I've ever been out of the ordinary, it was only in my skill with a bow. That you can do what you can do is fantastical to me."

Bobby frowned and tried not to let this distract him from driving. They hadn't reached a road yet, and he had to avoid the big bushes and things. "A bow? Like, you can control the arrows with your mind or something?"

"No, nothing of the sort. I am merely a good shot. Or, I *was* a good shot, anyway. The muscles have certainly withered from disuse by now. I could probably still hit a target—I still know how to do it—but not exceptionally well."

What did that mean? The Humvee bounced over a particularly rough bump, neatly distracting him from the quandary, and he spotted a road off to the left, which he turned to head for. They'd go much faster on it. "Okay, so, how's it that if you're normal, we're all not?"

"I have no idea. I knew nothing about what they were doing. Perhaps if we knew more, we could make educated guesses."

They'd done plenty of guessing so far, and seemed to have done a decent job getting close, if not right on. "Pretty sure all our daddies are different and human, else we wouldn't none of us look more human than you. Ain't a single one of us got pointy ears, we only got your eyes."

"Then it is reasonable to suspect the mixing of the two races is the cause of your strange abilities. Tell me, what of the others? You said there are thirty-five."

"Most of them're locked up in boxes right now, by a guy name of Privek. I can't figure why he's doing it, except maybe he wants control over us. The ones're out, aside from me and a couple others, they're working for him. But of the ones I know, there's a girl what can make fire, another can make ice. Hannah can make a force field, Jasmine can turn into a squirrel, Kaitlin sees the future, Violet can fly, all kinds of stuff like that. Some of them are harder to explain, but it's all stuff that don't make no sense, not really."

Asyllis nodded and went quiet for a few minutes, curled up in her seat.

Bobby had to pay attention to driving anyway. The way over to the road was bumpy as heckbiscuits and he had to keep a sharp watch to avoid putting them in a ditch or hitting something too big to give way. He let out a breath of relief when they reached the road and the drive smoothed out.

"I first arrived here in my sleep beside Tarilyr, my mate. You would use the word 'husband.' We slept in a hammock for the night, bound between two trees. Our son had just reached the age of adulthood, and we went off to spend time together, just the two of us, as we hadn't done for many years."

She sighed heavily. "I had a very strange dream. It happened so long ago, I barely remember it. Blue light, a feeling of being stretched. When we woke up, we were in a strange place, and there were men, human men, approaching. Everything happened so quickly. We tried to speak to them. We were frightened and confused, but their language was so thick and strange. More and more men came. They had guns. We didn't know what guns were until they demonstrated by shooting one.

"There was nothing to be done. Neither of us could resist them with such weapons, not with our two bows. They separated us, locked us in cages. Tarilyr went mad, he tried to escape and they cut him down. I saw it happen. I watched him die. I've been locked in a box ever since, though not long after that, they moved me to this place. I was drugged for the trip. I saw nothing. I learned English. They taught me so they could question me.

"They want to open a way between our two worlds. They've been trying to reproduce whatever brought us here ever since they realized what must have happened. I know this because of the questions they asked. There is no other possibility. After a while, they must have realized I'd told them everything I could, because they stopped asking questions and left me alone with guards. The soldiers grow older and get replaced. My people, we live much longer than humans do. I couldn't say how much longer, but quite a bit."

Bobby listened and kept quiet until she left a long silence. "I'm sorry about your mate, that musta been a real hard thing to see. And being all locked up like that...pretty amazing you didn't just lay down and let yourself die." He saw her turn away to look out the window. "That's what they're doing at White Sands. They want to open up that path and make contact with your world. It happened once, they must figure it can happen again."

What would they do when they managed it and went through? He could just imagine a tactical team with some kind of translator crossing over and deciding the only safe thing to do would be blowing the other place up. Or worse, they'd find it great and send settlers through after that. Like humans hadn't done that before. He'd seen some movies that made it pretty clear what had been done to the Native Americans. Only this time, the people on the receiving end wouldn't actually be human beings, they'd be people like Asyllis and her mate.

Not on his watch. Those people? They were his people too. He couldn't say if he really believed in God anymore, but he'd been raised Christian, and as far as he saw, that meant he ought to do whatever he could to keep it fair, at the very least. Now, more than ever, he knew they had to go public, and they had to do it as a group, not as one cowboy taking matters into his own hands and doing it his way. Granted, if he wasn't careful, he might not have a choice.

He glanced at Asyllis again, still watching out the window. The question of how to get her across the country without anyone seeing her still had no— Wait a minute. He wasn't alone, he wasn't the Head Cowboy. He had Liam's number and could find a phone. Maybe they could come here, or Kaitlin would have an idea, or Paul could do something. They could talk it out and figure something. Or Liam would tell him to stuff it because he couldn't find Elena. Still, at least then he'd know he had to stand on his own.

Part of him thought he should go back to the Monte Carlo and hit up Beverly again. She'd been nice, and he could lay it all out for her. If he meant to spill it all publicly anyway, what difference did it make if he told a person or two here or there along the way? He wouldn't be able to find a phone anywhere without letting people see Asyllis anyway.

Something else popped into his head, and the words spilled out before he could stop himself. "Hey, I wonder, do you know why they called your project 'Maze Beset'?"

Asyllis snorted. "Yes. One of the men—he was so pleased with himself for it, thought it was horribly clever. The two words are unrelated.

'Maze' is a wordplay. It sounds like 'maize,' Spanish for corn, which has yellow silk, like my hair. Also, it's a maze to get through the bureaucracy and red tape and whatever else to find out about me. And, as you saw, I was kept in a maze of a prison. As for 'beset,' it refers to how I am surrounded on all sides, and a bizarre notion that humanity is under threat of invasion or attack from my people. That threat is preposterous, of course. We have bows and swords, you have machine guns and nuclear bombs. Tarilyr and I were not advance scouts for an assault, either. They've never believed me that my people pose no threat."

Unexpected noise distracted Bobby from thinking about any of that right now, and he looked all around before spotting the helicopter heading straight for them. "We got a little problem," he said as he floored the gas, knowing they had no chance of outrunning it. The Humvee flew down the road.

"Can't your *drathikén* handle it?" She turned to face forward, full of grim determination, and braced herself again.

"That there is full of soldiers. I ain't keen on killing soldiers, so no, there ain't a whole lot I can do about it. If'n I knew how to disable it without sending it crashing to the ground, I'd do that, but I sure don't." The Humvee slowed and bucked, making sputtering noises. Bobby looked all around in a panic and noticed a needle that might be a gas gauge. The needle sat all the way to the empty side. "I take it back," he said grimly. "We got a big problem."

"Is that the city ahead?" Asyllis pointed down the road. They'd just crested a rise high enough to see the taller buildings of Las Vegas in the distance. More importantly and usefully, a residential subdivision perched not too far away. If the guys in the helicopter had orders to capture instead of kill, and they could run fast enough, they might make it to the houses.

Once there, they might be able to evade the soldiers.

That many ifs and mights gave him little confidence. The alternative, though, forced him to kill people, and Bobby wasn't ready to let his dragons do that again yet. Maybe he wouldn't be ready for that ever. Maybe that was a good thing. "Yeah, it is. We're gonna jump out and run like heck-biscuits for those houses nearby without stopping the vehicle. I'll help you, just jump for it."

Asyllis nodded her understanding and took off her seat belt. The helicopter came around in front of them, making this plan even better. He shifted the thing into neutral and took a deep breath. "Now." As the word left his mouth, gunfire sprayed across the windshield. He burst into the swarm and flew out with her, cushioning her fall as he'd done for Kaitlin in that car crash. The dragons found her light enough to carry a short distance, so he kept going, unable to pull her up higher than a few feet off the ground. Not that doing so would get the helicopter off their trail, but with luck, his speed would give them enough of a head start to get somewhere worth getting.

Some dragons noticed her breathing strangely, and a few caught sight of blood. Did she get hit by the gunfire or flying glass? Needing every last dragon to carry her, he couldn't check right now. Behind them, the helicopter let two soldiers out to scramble after the Humvee, then followed after the dragon swarm. That Bobby and Asyllis went into a residential area had to reduce their options. They couldn't just land a military helicopter on the street and send soldiers door to door. Right?

All the houses in the subdivision looked the same. In this particular part, the yards had rocks and low-growing creepers instead of grass with a few shrubs or trees mixed in to make the spaces actually worth looking at. Some had rock walls, most had no fencing of any kind.

When he reached the closest houses, Bobby had to stop and let the dragons rest. He set Asyllis on her feet as gently as he could and re-formed just in time to catch her as she collapsed. Now that he looked her over, he sucked in a breath and felt like someone kicked him in the gut. Three separate blood stains spread swiftly on her clothing. Bobby had no medical training at all, but he knew that digging the bullets out and burning the tissues could save her life. It had worked for Dan, anyway.

"I can fix this," he told her firmly. If he didn't, he'd spend the rest of his life wondering about her, wishing he'd had time to get to know her. Three of his dragons popped back off and dove at the three injuries.

She hissed with sudden pain. "It's alright," she said, voice breathy and strained. Her hand weakly gripped his arm. "You gave me back the sky. Like you said: go down in the sun, not waste away in the dark. You're a good man, Bobby. I'm proud to call you my son."

He'd found her an hour ago and had barely learned anything about her, yet the sight of her drifting away brought pain to his heart and tears to his eyes. The dragons yanked on bullets, pulling them out. One found itself flooded with blood for its efforts and he knew that he'd killed her instead of saving her. "I'm sorry," he said softly. "I'm so sorry."

"Save the rest. Stop them. Don't let them destroy my home." Her words slurred toward the end and her grip weakened.

Nodding, he held her close, his world shrunken down to the woman in his arms. "I promise. I'll put things right."

She smiled at him, then her eyes slipped lazily to the sky overhead. "I wish," she began. Her last breath left her before she could manage anything else.

"Put your hands up," he heard behind his back, the voice exasperated and tense, like he'd already repeated this a few times.

"Fuck off," Bobby said as he pushed Asyllis's eyelids down. Rage boiled inside him. They'd killed her. She didn't deserve to die. After everything she'd been through, she deserved to be free. Now that she was dead, they'd probably cut her up and pin her open like a frog in science class. They'd study every bit of her, trying to figure how she lived so long. He could see those damned scientists all relieved she could be treated like a thing now instead of a person. If that had even been what stopped them before.

"C'mon, buddy, let the lady go and show us your hands. Otherwise, we'll have to shoot you."

"She's dead." His voice came out flat and hard and cold.

"Damn, you killed her?"

Bobby turned his head, so angry he could barely think. "No. You did." They were soldiers, not much older than him. If he let this rage loose, he'd kill them. "Back off." He didn't want to kill them. The dragons did. They didn't care who these men were, they only cared about Asyllis being dead by their hands. Bobby cared, and he was in charge.

"Put your hands up." One of them kept a gun trained on him while the other took a tentative step toward him, attention flicking between Bobby and Asyllis.

"Turn around and walk away now, before I lose control and you both die." By the end of the demand, he found himself begging. "What you saw was real. Just walk away."

Both of them froze and stared at him. "Are you sure she's dead?"

"Yeah." Bobby closed his eyes and took a deep breath. "Was an accident, right? Guy busted her out and she got killed in a crossfire. He carted the body off, but you're sure she's dead." When he opened his eyes again, they had both taken a step forward and looked ready to try to take him down.

"Right. Sure. Look, just come with us." The one with the gun put it up to show he wouldn't shoot. "We can sort this all out back at the base. I'm sure you didn't mean any real harm, buddy."

Bobby didn't know what to do, just that he had to do something. "I don't think you got the slightest idea what you're dealing with. I don't want to hurt any of you, but if you make me, I will." He heard the helicopter settle overhead, the steady thp-thp-thp of the rotor loud enough he had to shout. At least the wind from it helped him cool down.

"I don't want to hurt you, either, buddy. Just come along quietly and we can all avoid lots of trouble."

He put his hands up and thought about what he could do and still get out of here with her body. Like waiting in that geek's pocket, he had to watch for the best opportunity and take it, not bolt at the first chance. The helicopter moved off enough to land as the soldier gave him reassuring words about doing the right thing and he'd make sure to tell someone about it, and other pointless nonsense.

His opportunity came sooner than he expected. The helicopter door opened. Soldiers jostled in an attempt to surround him and load him up where he couldn't cause any trouble. Getting shot didn't scare him, leaving him free to act as he pleased. His left hand fell to dragons while he threw a punch at his captor with his right. Above their heads, two dragons sacrificed themselves in the engine, now making hideous screeches and crunches. More dragons burned and clawed whatever looked important.

Someone shot him while he shoved one soldier aside and knocked the other over. Dragons took the bullet and kept it from hitting anyone else. Thank goodness for that. The swarm blew out and carried Asyllis away again. Bullets flew around him. He ignored them.

What, exactly, should do now? By himself, he could fly for it and get to a phone. With a dead body, he needed a car. He broke into a random house and looked around. With luck, he'd have five minutes to find something that might help. Backup would come. Privek would find out.

Standing in the living room with Asyllis in his arms, he caught sight of a cordless phone sitting on a table. He first thought to call Liam. However, since Privek would toss a magnifying glass over everything here, the call would be traced, which could lead him to Liam. His attention went back to Asyllis, peaceful and still.

Setting her on the couch, he picked up the phone and called for an ambulance. The operator told him to stay on the line, but he hung up. He called information and got himself connected to a local TV station. "I seen a guy go into a house," he told the young woman who answered. "He had a lady in his arms, I think she was hurt, or maybe dead. Thing is, she looked kinda weird. I know this'll sound crazy, since we're so close to Area 51 and all, but I think she had pointy ears, like one of them elves in a video game. I'm just calling you in case it's something and they try to cover it up." He hung up on her before she could ask him any questions, then did the same thing with the local newspaper.

Tears sliding down his cheeks, he brushed his fingertips across her pale face. For some reason, he thought of the camera in his pocket and pulled it out. No one would believe a picture like this on the internet or news, not these days. He'd do it for Liam and Paul and Alice and Hannah and the rest, so they could see her face and know where they came from. Not only that, they'd help him keep his promise. Head Cowboy needed help. He took a few pictures, feeling ghoulish for doing so.

He heard sirens coming and thought about leaving a dragon behind to make sure she didn't get swept under a rug. Would that actually accomplish anything? He could burn the house down instead. No, the folks who owned the house didn't deserve that. His eyes strayed to a patch of sunshine on the carpet, and he picked her up, knowing what to do. If any press folks showed up, they might be able to get a picture.

As he laid her out on the driveway, a small white flower caught his eye and he picked it. "I done barely knew you, Asyllis. That ain't fair. S'all I got to say about it." He curled her fingers around the flower and sniffled. At the sound of screeching tires, he burst out into the swarm and flew up, unwilling to be further involved in this. Not now.

Since he had nowhere else in particular to go, he broke into a room at the Monte Carlo and used the phone. Liam told him they'd gone to the farm and let him hang up without talking much. Bobby stared at the phone for several minutes, still dazed by the roller coaster he'd ridden out here. He thought about taking a nap on the bed in the room with him. If he went to the farm, though, he'd be able to sleep in his own bed.

Seven or so hours later, the farm looked a tiny bit better than it had the last time Bobby saw it. None of the cars had been towed away, which surprised him. He recognized the spots where Jayce had been put down, where Stephen got shot, where Sebastian had been carried through and where his own dragon had been smashed. Since the lost dragon remained lost, he wondered if they'd taken it someplace.

Glinting metal caught his eye, surprising him again. The swarm set down there and devoured his missing dragon while he re-formed. For once, his belly didn't rumble, having been filled an hour ago in Denver. He drooped, though, weary from going so long without sleep and from everything he'd done and seen in the past day.

Scuffing the dirt with a shoe, he thought about lying down right here and taking a nap in the mid-afternoon sunshine. Inside would be more comfortable. Comfortable felt wrong, like a betrayal of Asyllis. The familiar squeak of the front door opening interrupted his brooding.

"Hi, Bobby." Kaitlin gave him a sympathetic smile from the front stoop.

"Hey." It came out as more of a grunt than an actual word.

"Don't worry, we're safe here. For at least another twenty-four hours."

He grunted again, noting that, if he wanted to avoid talking about it, he could fly away and do something stupid or stand here like a dumbass. He had a peculiar talent for both. His feet moved. So did his hand. As he passed Kaitlin, he slapped the camera into her unexpectedly waiting palm. With that gesture, he'd passed on the responsibility. She would make sure it got taken care of somehow without him screwing it up.

Riker and Hegi worked in the common room, picking up debris and dumping it into a wheelbarrow. He grunted in greeting and kept going until he found some strange guy lying in his bed. Frowning, he stepped into the tiny space and looked the guy over.

"He was in the same place as Elena." Until she spoke, he hadn't noticed Kaitlin following him. "Adelphi."

So, they found Elena. He listened while she rattled the gist of what had happened there, staring at this new victim of Privek's plans. Or Kanik's. Maybe both. Another place to hit after they freed the others. "We gotta stop them."

"Who's this woman, Bobby?" She held up the camera, he turned to look.

"Our real momma." He found himself unwilling to wait for the others before telling the tale of what happened at Groom Lake. Words poured from him, like they could draw out the impossible ache inside. "They'll know it was me," he ended with. "Ain't no way they won't."

"I'll pass all that along for you, so you don't have to explain it again."

"Thanks. You know this is my room?"

Kaitlin made a face. "No, I didn't realize that. Sorry. I would've made them pick another one."

"S'alright." He bent to scoop the guy off the bed, and froze when he groaned. Part of him wanted to turn around and walk away, to flop down on Lily's bed and sleep and not worry about anything until tomorrow. The rest of him pointed out that he'd made promises, and ignoring them would be cowardly and rude.

Time to get a grip and deal. "Hey there." Setting the guy back down, he leaned in and kept his voice down in case the guy had a headache. "You're safe and all."

"What happened?" His voice started weak and slurred. He gained strength with each second that passed. "One minute I'm..." He blinked several times and reached up to rub his face. "Where am I?"

"Colorado." Kaitlin moved in closer and peered over Bobby's shoulder. "We found you tied up and knocked out."

"Huh?"

Bobby held up a hand to stop Kaitlin from saying anything else. "What's the last thing you remember?"

"I thought I was taking a job, sort of. I guess not."

"Right. Okay. I'm Bobby, this is Kaitlin. We're looking to know details and stuff."

"Um, Shane." He took a deep breath and looked away. "I, uh...was a little... It wasn't like I wanted to be, you know, it just happened."

Bobby had enough shame of his own to recognize it in someone else. From the roughness of Shane's hands, to how skinny he was, to the look in his eyes, the source seemed obvious. "Living on the street?" He waved off Shane's meek little nod. "I eat outta dumpsters on a regular basis. Ain't nothing to be worked up over with me. What kinda job was it supposed to be? Where'd you meet whoever done hired you?"

As he suspected, Shane raised his chin again. "I was in a shelter. It was morning, over breakfast. A guy in a suit with sunglasses came in and told everybody he was looking for volunteers for a sleep experiment. Anyone who went with him would have a safe place to sleep for a week, plus food and some cash at the end. Guy got more volunteers than he wanted. He picked out all of us that were kinda in the same age group. Got ten from there, I think. We all piled into a van. They drove us around some, but after that, it's all blank. I don't remember why I blacked out."

"It's 'cause they drugged you up." Bobby nodded, pleased that something made sense. Grabbing homeless people meant no families or paper trails to worry about. What for, though? Looking for ways to replicate their abilities with adults, maybe? That was a creepy idea, one that fit what they knew already too well. "Okay, you feeling weird or anything? Got any funny itches or urges or anything?"

"Funny...how?" Shane's eyes went wide as Bobby popped a dragon off his thumb and let him get a good look at it. "No, nothing like that." Halfway through the gesture, he stopped and frowned. "Well, actually, there is one thing that's kind of weird. Not like *that* kind of weird but, well, um, I think I can see an extra color. I don't know what color it is, but I've never seen it before. It's like black, but not. Really hard to explain."

"Yeah, that's kinda weird." But, like he said, that came nowhere near to the level of what Bobby and the rest of them could do. Seeing an extra color sounded downright tame. It did probably match up with something regular people couldn't see. Unlike being a swarm of dragons, though, the power to see black-plus gave him no special defensive benefit. "Welcome to the club."

Shame gave him a small smile. "Thanks. I don't know what to do now, but thanks."

"We'll figure something out soon as we can. There's a bunch of us with crazy stuff we can do, and we aim to stick together and help each other out. Even if all you got's a new color, you're one of us. Somebody'll bring something and help you eat, yeah? Rest until then, we'll get you up and about soon." He patted Shane on the arm as he stood up.

"Okay." He looked up at the ceiling. "Were other people there, where you found me?"

"Yeah," Kaitlin said from the doorway, "and we're going back for them as soon as we can."

Bobby rummaged through his closet, pulling out clean clothes. "That's a fact. You don't gotta do nothing 'bout that, though. Just get back on your feet and relax for now."

"Thanks."

Leaving him behind, Bobby pushed past Kaitlin to head for the bathroom. Under the hot water of a shower, he tried not to think about Asyllis. Her death was his fault. The guys in the helicopter probably only knew that someone stole the Humvee and had maybe been told the thief might be nuts. Shooting at the vehicle probably seemed to be the best option to stop him, especially when it had to look like he meant to ram the helicopter with it.

Why exactly her death hit him so hard, he had no idea. He remembered when they came to say his Daddy was dead. The man had been part of his life for as long as he could remember, and when he was gone, Bobby mostly felt relief. They didn't have to worry about him anymore. Momma didn't have to answer the door with dread anymore. Their lives could go on without wondering if they should make plans with him for his next trip home or not. No more writing letters they didn't know if he'd ever get.

Asyllis, though, was just some woman he shared blood with. The dragons liked her immediately, and she affected him so deeply. He'd caused her death and he had to shoulder the blame for it. If he hadn't broken her out, she'd still be alive. In a box. Underground.

At least he gave her the sun.

A knock on the door startled him out of his thoughts. "Bobby, are you okay in there?" Liam's muffled voice actually sounded concerned.

How long had he been in here? He knew as well as anyone else that no amount of water could wash away his sins or make him stop seeing anything. Shutting off the shower, he grunted. "Yeah, I'll be out in a minute."

"We'll be in the kitchen. Things to discuss."

"Alright." His stomach rumbled at the mention of something related to food, and he scowled at the fogged up mirror. His belly never let the stain of death get in the way of hunger. Maybe Privek was actually right about him being a dangerous monster. He'd still do everything he could to get the others free.

He shrugged into a fresh pair of jeans and t-shirt and went barefoot to the kitchen. Riker and his men sat around the picnic tables with Kaitlin, Liam, and Paul, and Elena. Liam's girlfriend looked the same as he remembered her, aside from not wearing a suit. She hung on Liam's arm the way he wished Lily would do to him. All of them had bowls of thick soup and biscuits. Without tasting it, he knew none of it measure up to what Momma made. The thought made him frown.

Kaitlin patted the empty space beside her on the bench and waved him over. "C'mon, Bobby. Stuff some food in there before your blood sugar drops so low you fall asleep standing up."

"It's okay," Platt said with a cheery grin. "We can carry him."

One side of Bobby's mouth tugged up into an answering grin. "I don't need nobody to carry me." Taking the seat, he looked from one person to the next, ending with Kaitlin. "Y'all got a plan already, or am I supposed to come up with it?"

"We're still on the objectives part." Riker set his spoon down and fiddled with a biscuit. "We talked it over, and we're in this thing, Bobby. What we saw, that's not the kind of thing you can unsee, and it's not what we pledged ourselves to defend. There's no doubt we're already on a list of enemies of the state, but sometimes you have to be the bad guys to be the good guys. Besides, you saved our bacon, and there's nothing we like better than bacon."

"Here, here." Hegi raised his glass of water in a toast. "Well said, Sarge."

Bobby managed a single little huff of amusement. "Objectives, then. One, we gotta get the others loose. Two, we gotta free everyone we can of Kanik's influence. Them pictures make it pretty clear he can do whatever he wants to."

"If you ask me," Riker said, "that Kanik guy should be a target. There's a saying about power and responsibility, and he's got one without taking the other."

Paul gulped. "We should at least try talking to him. He's one of us."

"Yeah, we'll try." Bobby dipped his biscuit into his soup and swished it around. "Look, there's something I need to say. We gotta go public. Ain't nothing else gonna work. So long as we stay quiet, they're gonna be able to keep doing this. It's gotta look to folks like we ain't a threat and can police ourselves, and what we want is to be citizens of our country and have all the same rights as everyone else. Now we know for sure we're products of military experimentation. We gotta focus on that angle, I think, on how this happened because there's folks running amok, doing without thinking and that sort of thing. Also, we been hounded and treated like animals, and that ain't okay."

"We can't just step up to a microphone and say 'I'm a superhero!'," Liam said with a frown. "I know you think this is the right way to go, but what about those of us who don't want to be public? I don't want to be mobbed by people, which I will be. Seriously, they could decide I'm some kind of second coming of Christ, it would be horrible. I just want to have a life, not kill myself healing the world."

Bobby nodded. "That's fair, and I understand. Kaitlin's gonna be in the same boat, and I'm pretty sure there'll be lots of folks who ain't so keen to know there's folks what can mess with their heads. That's why I ain't gonna ask nobody to come forward aside from myself. What I can do, it's good for people to not know about it, but somebody's gotta break the silence, and I'm okay with being that somebody. Nobody gets outed without their consent. I'm pretty sure that list of names'll get out at some point, one way or another, so my second plan is we set up the farmhouse here again, as a secure commune for all of us. Anybody what wants to live away from all that, come here and be safe."

At the surprised looks all around him, Bobby snorted. "I had some time to think about all this stuff here and there. Y'all don't think I just sit there brain-dead when I'm not talking, do ya?"

Liam cleared his throat delicately after a few awkward moments of silence. "We were kind of led to believe you aren't the brightest bulb in the box. But no matter. I see your point, and agree. All the money in the world won't stop someone from targeting us one way or another so long as we all stay hidden and secret. Silence is helping them more than us."

"Then there's the wormhole thing," Kaitlin said. "Maybe we should go after that first, shut down that research."

Bobby took a bite of soup-drenched biscuit and chewed while he happily considered something besides his own failings. "I don't think we can stop it. We can slow it all down, we can make it public so folks know what's going on, but once science figures something out, it's figured out. Attacking there would just be to stop whatever they done got cooked up right now. I expect they won't have no serious problem building another one."

Liam nodded and frowned. "Publicity is the most likely foil for that. Carefully crafted publicity."

"Maybe we could film all of it," Platt suggested. "The breakout, I mean. Post it on the internet."

"People will think it's a joke," Liam said with a roll of his shoulders, "that it has special effects."

"That's fine." Riker looked off at the wall. "It doesn't matter if they believe it or not right away. What matters is we start showing it to the world. Platt, Carter, your jobs are to film the breakout. We need gear and supplies and a little more of a plan. You guys know the layout of the place with the freezer drawers full of people?"

Bobby stared at Liam without really seeing the healer. "I know it well enough. Actually, I can wake them all up myself. Where I'm gonna need help is the getting them out part. Everybody's gonna be groggy at the least, maybe not be able to do their thing. In some cases, that's maybe for the best. I'm sure Lizzie'd blow up the whole building if'n she could. It's worth saying here that we ain't harmless, we ain't all puppies and kittens, and everyone's gonna be pissed about the whole being taken prisoner thing."

"In which case, you setting them free is for the best," Riker agreed. "We'll still need a layout for an exit plan."

"Do we?" Kaitlin asked. "Don't we really just need to know who's going with who and has what job and where to meet up?"

"Aw, you can't make the Sarge go without a plan," Hegi grinned, "that's just mean."

"Paul?" A girl, maybe sixteen, stood in the doorway. She had pale skin and more piercings than Bobby considered attractive. Panting, she leaned against the door frame and clutched a sheet to her chest. "What's going on?"

Paul jumped up. "Sherrie, you're awake. Are you alright?" He rushed over and wrapped his arms around the girl.

"Where are we? Why are you here? What's going on?" She let him help her to the table to sit and leaned against him.

Paul pointed to everyone, offering their names for her. "You're safe here. I just need you to tell us what happened to you. Please. It's important."

Everyone stared at her. She looked down at the table. One hand snaked out and snatched two biscuits in a way that made Bobby take notice. Kaitlin said earlier that they had Paul's sister, and this must be her. He paid attention to the way she shifted her eyes around and wouldn't look at anybody.

"S'alright. She ran away from home, I'm guessing, and got picked up like Shane did. Some kinda promise of money or shelter or whatever, and once she was in the car or van, they shot her up with drugs that knocked her out."

"Yeah." She flashed guarded gratitude at him. "That's pretty much what happened."

In an effort to get her to trust him, he popped a dragon off his thumb and sent it to her. "Ain't nothing to fear here. Ain't nobody gonna take you again." Part of him knew he shouldn't promise that. This very place had been raided, and everything they'd just planned to do would make some folks eager to try it again. "Not 'less they kill me first."

The dragon landed next to her bowl and nudged the spoon toward her hand. She stared at it with awe and wonder. "I didn't actually wake up yet. This is a really weird dream."

Bobby shrugged. "You got any weird urges or itches or anything what feels or looks different than before?"

Sherrie gulped and looked around, finally actually seeing all the people in the large room watching her. "I...um...I knew where Paul was before I saw or heard him."

When she failed to follow that up with more explanation, Liam took a break from translating for Elena out of the side of his mouth to ask, "Can you be more specific? How did you know?"

She still hesitated. Bobby dipped his biscuit again and swished it around. "Look, my whole body can fall apart into hundreds of those little critters. I guarantee it ain't weirder than that. Nobody here's gonna judge you for whatever it is, so just tell us."

"Seriously?" Her jaw dropped open.

While taking a bite of the biscuit, he held up his hand and let dragons off until he had nothing past the middle of his forearm. The four dozen or so dragons landed all around her and on her shoulders. They trilled at her in unison. Five picked up her spoon and stuck it into her hand. One peered into her glass of water from the rim, then leaned too far and fell in with a plop. It sank to the bottom and looked all around.

He heard stifled chuckles and giggles and laughter from everyone in the room.

"Ah, come on," Bobby said with a roll of his eyes. "Get your little metal hide outta there. You ain't no ice cube."

"They don't need to breathe," Sherrie said with wonder, watching the dragon swim with all four little legs to the surface. It beat its wings, spraying water all around the cup, and managed to get into the air again. When it cleared the rim, another dragon joined it and breathed fire to dry it off.

Bobby could tell it felt sheepish and he called all the dragons back. He knew so much more about what they were capable of than he did when he first discovered them. "Yeah. That's handy sometimes. What's important right now ain't what I can do, it's what you can do. I showed mine, let's have yours."

"Uh, I don't think I can demonstrate." Sherrie gulped and watched with fascination as his hand re-formed. "I can...see minds? Not like read them or anything, I just know they're there. Sort of. All your dragons have separate little minds, but when you're you, you're kind of a weird jumble."

"That's exactly what I see," Paul nodded his approval. "Don't tell our parents, but I'm a telepath. I see them as little sparks and other people as bright lights. Except Kaitlin, but never mind that. You?"

"Um, it's not that...defined? I don't know."

"Makes sense." Bobby nodded. "It's like you're seeing heat, maybe, or feeling it or something, I bet. A little more useful than black-plus, but still a lot less than the rest of us. Folks, they're trying to cut corners to make more, and either they don't got it all sorted or you pulled these two out before the dose was all complete. Either way, every single one of those people you saw in Adelphi is one of us now."

Riker, sitting on Kaitlin's other side, nodded in agreement. "That makes Adelphi a high priority target. Once we have more hands on deck, we'll be able to split up and tackle both Adelphi and White Sands at the same time. A basic plan is taking shape, we'll just need to work up the details. Kaitlin and I can handle most of that."

Was it his imagination, or did Riker look at Kaitlin like he imagined her naked? Not that Bobby cared, she wasn't his sis—er, actually, she was. That didn't change how little he cared about who she did or didn't shack up with. It only struck him as interesting.

Liam frowned. "I don't understand why they don't just use military personnel. Isn't experimentation something you sign on for when you go in?"

Riker shrugged. "Not exactly. We can refuse, and there would be a paper trail, and we have families. Families ask questions and file lawsuits."

Nodding, Bobby looked off at nothing in particular He wound up staring at Liam's eyes. Family. He had his Momma already, and now he had a bunch of brothers and sisters, plus Riker and his men from the sounds of it. "What about you guys? You got families what ask questions and file lawsuits too."

"We all do, Bobby," Kaitlin said with an arched eyebrow.

"Yeah, but—"

Riker laughed without letting Bobby finish. "My family thinks I'm still in Afghanistan. We were told not to say a damned word, so none of us said a damned word. Fortunately, none of us has a wife to lie to."

"Alright, glad to hear it." Bobby grinned. "Is that gonna be a problem when we get on with the part where we go public?"

"Yes, but we'll live. Contacting them now would be detrimental to mission success."

"Ayup, that's how I feel about it." He really did want to call Momma and talk to her about the things he'd done. Most especially, he wanted to hear her tell him it would be okay, and he wasn't a bad person. Whether it was true or not, he'd like to hear her say it.

CHAPTER 9

BOBBY

After the meal, Bobby stood in the doorway of Lily's room, leaning against the frame. Everyone else batted around ideas for a detailed plan, or caught the last few rays of sunshine, or cleaned up. He'd told them through drooping eyes that he needed some sleep and no one gave him a hard time about it. Shane still lay in his bed, recovering from the drugs. Bobby had a thought to use Stephen's room, but couldn't stop himself from taking the detour to Lily's.

Sebastian had been grabbed right out of that little toddler bed, and his wailing screams for his mother still echoed in Bobby's head. They merged with the face of that little girl, making him want to hit himself with a baseball bat. Then he saw piles of shredded meat that had once been human. Asyllis, dead. The parade of images marched around him, over and over.

"I ain't a bad person," he told the room as he sat heavily on her bed. If he could make himself believe it, then it might be true. Stephen would agree and call him a dumbass with power he hadn't yet figured out how to control. That had to end now. People kept dying because of it.

"I'm in charge. Nobody dies 'less I say so. It's gotta be that way.

More damage we do, more likely they lock us up in a box for good. All they really gotta do is stick us in a box with no vents while I'm dosed on that drug and eventually, we all starve to death. So listen up. We gotta have rules to protect us as much as them."

They didn't answer; they never did. But he felt something. The only other times he ever felt anything from them while in full human shape had been when their rage threatened to rip them right off his body. This time, he got acceptance from them. Understanding. Almost drowning with Stephen maybe showed them how it could really all go to heckbiscuits.

"Okay. Good. Best to try not to injure anyone too seriously, neither. What I say goes, and you follow my lead. I know how people think, so you gotta trust me to know what I'm doing."

They got that too, even if saying those words out loud made him want to laugh at himself. Yeah, he knew what he was doing. Completely. Not. Regardless, he could trust the dragons now.

Still barefoot, he rolled onto the bed and shut his eyes, breathing in Lily's scent. It felt like no time had passed before a rapping knock on the door woke him. Somehow, he'd had no nightmares. Maybe Lily chased them away.

"Rise and shine, Sleeping Beauty!" Hegi's too cheerful voice echoed in the hallway as he walked away. "Thirty minutes 'til we leave."

Bobby groaned and rubbed the sleep out of his eyes. He got up and got dressed, choosing his desert camouflage pants and combat boots with a regular white t-shirt. He downed a breakfast on the go without tasting it, let alone looking at it long enough to figure out what it might be. In a few hours, they'd be freeing everyone else, and that thought rammed everything else aside. All along, this had been his goal. Finally, he got to do it. Granted, he'd thought he'd be liberating only eleven people.

One tense, quiet car ride later, Bobby dropped down into a seat on Liam's family plane and stared out the window. Half an hour into the flight, Liam, more cool and collected than he'd been in Virginia, cleared his throat and asked politely for everyone's attention. It had to come from having Elena's safety assured. Bobby wanted that too.

He swiveled his chair to see Kaitlin rubbing shoulders with Riker. Liam sat across the small table from the pair, next to Paul. They'd left Elena behind to watch over Shane and Paul's sister. Hegi, Platt, Hansen, and Carter sat in the rest of the chairs, all close enough to hear so long as no one whispered.

"We got a plan now?" Bobby asked.

Kaitlin nodded. "Yes, but first, I wanted to share something that I ran across while searching for stuff last night. Hannah must have seen it if she spent even two minutes looking, though she might have ignored it because of the date. It's a forum post about an article in the Juneau Empire, the paper there. Most of it's an environmentalist rant. There was a chemical spill in the city five years ago, caused by a train accident. It affected a mostly Inuit area the worst. A few people were killed and a bunch were hospitalized. This poster mentions Kanik Okpik as if he's some kind of martyr. He was injured and got acid burns on part of his body, but survived, at least up until this posting was made."

Something about that tugged at Bobby's memory. "You got them pictures I gave you?"

Nodding again, Kaitlin tapped and clicked on her laptop, then spun it around so everyone could get a good look at the pictures of Jayce. "Where did you get these, anyway?"

"I found the camera in Jayce's apartment." Bobby shrugged and peered at the much larger version of the image on the screen.

"What were you doing in Jayce's apartment?"

"I was in Vegas anyway," Bobby shrugged, "figured I'd have a look. Cops went through it something fierce. Kinda like they done did at the farm, only nobody was there to resist." He pointed at the screen. "Look at that hand."

Riker flipped between the before and after pictures for everyone. "That's freakish. I saw these before, but it's still just plain...freakish."

"It's the result of mind control," Kaitlin corrected. "But yeah, the hand. That could be acid burns."

Bobby noticed Riker putting his arm on the back of Kaitlin's chair, and his body shifting to lay claim to her. He thought Kaitlin noticed. Yep, those two definitely had something going on. "You know, I kinda wonder if there's something about the human-alien cross we are that makes us all more...frisky than usual folks."

Liam coughed, hiding a half a grin behind his hand. Paul blushed. Riker looked up at him with an arched eyebrow and said nothing. Kaitlin grinned. "I wouldn't be surprised, but we are all in the same age group, you know. Confined area. Shared doom and freakishness. So, you decide to get all up on Lily and—"

"Hey now," Bobby pointed at the screen with a chuckle. This foreign feeling, of being amused and wanting to laugh, made him hope they could all keep things light for now. They'd all have plenty of time for brooding later. "Plan time."

"Yeah, yeah." Kaitlin took control of the laptop back. Between her and Riker, they had good ideas, complete with maps. "The important part is we're up against someone who can do that kind of mind altering to probably anyone."

Paul cleared his throat uncomfortably. "Technically, I can do things like that too. I used it to get us out of the facility the other day. I can proba-bly defend against it, I've just never tried."

Hegi leaned in and fixed Paul with a suspicious glare. "How do we know you didn't put a mind whammy on Sarge to get us all to go along with this?"

Paul shrank from him. "I, uh," he gulped, "just because I *can* doesn't mean I *would*. I haven't really let loose and seen what my limits are because I'm afraid to. I don't want to be a monster with a horde of zombie drones to do my bidding. That's just...wrong."

If only Bobby had ever felt that way for more than a few minutes, a lot of people might still be alive right now. He crossed his arms and tried not to scowl too much at Mr. Goody-Two-Shoes. "This whole shebang may be up you and Stephen and Andrew and me, then. All of us can resist Kanik. We gotta change the plan on account of that?"

Riker thought about it and glanced at Liam, who shrugged. "Yes, I think we do."

"Let's get on that, then. We got, what, three more hours? There any food on this here plane?" Bobby spent the rest of the flight eating and try-ing to memorize what he needed to do. They had a plan, a backup plan and a retreat location. Here was hoping Stephen got his stuff back as quick as possible, because out of all of them, the vampire would probably be the biggest help.

They touched down in DC at 12:11pm, and found Riker and Platt's two cars waiting for them at the airport with sizable parking fees. Liam cov-ered them.

"You know, in all this," Bobby said, "I don't figure why that pig-tailed girl was so important."

Kaitlin shrugged. "Maybe it was just so you could feel justified killing that agent."

"I s'pose."

"Is that really the only detail that's bothering you?"

He rolled his eyes. "A'course not. Everything else seems bigger, though, like it matters. That one little girl, she weren't much. Just a kid."

"Are you talking about the little girl at Hill Air Force Base?" Liam, also in the back seat, leaned forward to fix him with a stern glare. "The one you tried to abduct?"

Bobby opened his mouth to agree with the first question. Before he could, the second one made him glare at Liam. "After what you seen, you still buy that line?"

Liam frowned. "Yes, and I guess I shouldn't. Her name is Elizabeth, she's the granddaughter of the Chairman of the Joint Chiefs, General Hanstadt. Her father is a Major in the Air Force. Elizabeth was there that day because her mother was recovering from surgery."

"Privek tell you that?"

Still frowning, Liam nodded. "Yes, actually. He was very forthcoming with certain kinds of details."

Riker and Hegi glanced at each other. Since Hegi happened to be driving, Riker turned around to face Bobby. "That little girl saw you turn into dragons?"

"Yeah." Bobby scratched his chin idly, watching the scene replay in his head. "That agent thought she was my kid, or Stephen or Dan's. He shot at her, not me. I took that bullet for her and killed him." His now jaded self marveled at how shiny and naïve he'd been only a few weeks ago.

"That might be the one thing that winds up keeping all our asses out of a sling here." Riker glanced at Hegi again, then back out the rear window at the car with the others. "We should take the party to his doorstep once we've gotten all your people out."

"What about the people at Adelphi?"

"He's the Chairman of the Joint Chiefs," Riker shrugged. "If he can't get that sorted out, no one can."

"I agree." Liam pulled out his phone and futzed with it. "There's no way we can just waltz back into that facility now. They'll be on alert and have pictures of us handy. I'm sure there was security footage of every one of us that went in, and it's been examined by now. Privek's suspicions about Paul and me have been confirmed, and he knows Riker and his men are on the other side, as well as knowing Kaitlin is with us. By now, he's checked and knows you're out too, and that you freed Asyllis."

Bobby looked out the window and tried to think of what Privek and Kanik might do, if they'd change things a lot based on what had happened over the past few days. The problem was, he didn't understand them, not really. What did they want? He had no real clue. Probably, if no one explained it all to him, he'd never understand. "I think the question we gotta find the answer to is why he took everybody from the farm. The real reason, I mean. Once we know that, seems to me we'll kinda have a handle on the why for everything else."

"I'm going to see what I can do to get us a meeting with the good General." Liam tapped his phone and held it up to his ear.

Bobby gaped at him. "Just like that?" Apparently, the company he currently kept was more rarefied than he knew.

Liam snorted. "We'll see."

Bobby went back to staring out the window, watching the scenery go by. If not for the need to be able to coordinate, he'd be out there flying instead of in here squished between Kaitlin and the door. Actually, he'd be there by now. In the background, he heard Liam on phone.

"Hi, uncle Glen, it's Liam. I was wondering if you could do me a favor." He chuckled at whatever Uncle Glen said. "No, nothing like that. I have a *friend* in the Army who's gotten into a little bit of trouble, and I was wondering if there's any way you could set us up with a meeting of some sort with General Hanstadt to discuss it as soon as possible. ... Yes, I understand that, but this is a fairly unusual situation. ... Tell him it's about Elizabeth's Hill dragons." From Liam's face, Bobby got exactly nothing. The guy must clean up if he ever played poker. "Yes, those words exactly, ... No, I can't explain right now. ... Sure, lunch next week would be great. I'll see you then."

"Next week?"

Liam kept his phone in hand, scrolling through his contacts again. "I'll meet my uncle for lunch next week. He'll text me back if he can get us in to see Hanstadt."

Reassured about the time frame, Bobby nodded. "Is that the price you gotta pay for a favor like that?"

"Depends. My Uncle is a Senator on the Armed Services Committee. If he has to call in a favor, then I'll have to make it up to him somehow. More than likely, though, when Hanstadt hears the message, that'll be enough."

The idea of meeting the top dog for all the military made Bobby squirm. Maybe if his Daddy hadn't been a Marine, it wouldn't be a big deal. He rubbed his face, wishing it could be a secretary or something instead. Liam's phone chirped a few minutes later. Bobby turned at the sound and watched the other guy read the message, then nod with satisfaction.

"Hanstadt will meet with us tonight at eight. Do we want to change the plan?"

For whatever reason, everyone looked at Bobby for an answer. Even Hegi flicked his eyes up to the rearview mirror to check on his reaction. Head Cowboy liked that. Bobby wasn't so sure. The boots seemed to fit, though, so he pulled them on and took a deep breath. "Nope. Us being quiet's got to not even seem like a thing he's got the ability to ask for. I ain't going quiet-like nowhere never again if'n I don't want to. Plus, if'n we're gonna face down Kanik, I want Stephen at my back."

Liam pursed his lips, like even though he'd expected that answer, he'd hoped for a different one. "What if Privek or Kanik are there?"

"I got a few things I'd like to say to Privek," Bobby growled. "Most of it's about him eating dragons."

"Bobby." Riker's tone reminded him of his Daddy. He looked up to find the sergeant staring at him intensely. "Don't walk in there looking to kill him. The job is to save lives, not take them."

Bobby turned away and tried to stop thinking about kids with their chests blown out. He wanted, so badly, for all of that to be Privek's fault. Privek set the whole thing in motion by grabbing him in the first place, by framing him for Mr. Patterson's murder, by sticking them all into those cells and the rest of it.

Actually, what he wanted more than anything right now was to go home and have Momma tell him all this had been nothing more than a crazy nightmare. Then he could wake up tomorrow and go back to work with no dragons or vampires or precogs.

Except he couldn't. Right now, he needed to get his head on straight. When they reached the building, the nine of them would break in and free as many of the others as they could. God, he missed Lily. Having her smack him upside the head or glare at him, or even throw his gifts back in his face was so much better than not having her around at all. He'd give a lot right now to have her look at him the awful way she did when he showed up in uniform.

He rubbed his face with both hands, trying to make the images go away. It didn't help. Pulling his hands away, they broke apart into dozens of dragons, all of which sat on his legs and looked up at him. They didn't understand right and wrong, not like he did. Each of them was too tiny to get the whole picture, that's why. They were fragments of him, little pieces of his soul.

No, he didn't really believe in the idea of a soul, not anymore. His stains weren't there to be judged by anyone or anything else. They were there for him to judge himself. Could he find a way to bleach them out? Maybe not, but he'd for damned sure try. For however long he had left in this world, he'd do whatever it took to atone for those people. Like Riker said, he had to walk with the goal of helping, not hurting. For Sebastian, for the world to be a place where a little boy could grow up not worrying about some asshole made of dragons swooping down out of nowhere and killing him and everybody he ever knew for no reason.

It was his fault and it would always be his fault. No one else deserved the blame for what happened. Privek bore some responsibility too, just not for any of the things Bobby did. Same for Kanik. Without them, he never would have been in those situations. He still might have done horrible things on his own.

"We gotta step light, hear?" He said it quietly, talking to the dragons and knowing the whole car could hear him anyway. He'd already said these things. This time, he did it for himself more than them. "Too many died already, let's not make more bodies if'n we can help it." The dragons nodded and re-formed back into his hands.

"It'll turn out okay," Kaitlin said with firm conviction.

He glanced at her. "You saying that 'cause it's true or 'cause you think I gotta hear it?"

Her mouth curled into a smirk. "I'm going to live through this."

"I think that means 'yes,' " Riker said with a half-grin.

Bobby snorted. "Reckon so." To keep his sanity, he focused on his best memories of Lily while the scenery went by. There would be new memories at some point, good ones. Hopefully.

Chapter 10

Bobby

The building showed no sign of heightened alert or extra security. Bobby broke into the swarm as soon as Hegi parked the car, eager to get inside and do his part. His dragons flew around, looking for a vent. As they poured into the first one he found, one noticed something strange: a squirrel sitting on a branch of the nearest tree, watching the swarm with more interest than a critter ought to have. He dove into one dragon and sent it that way, trusting the rest to find the drawers and open them up.

One paw waved at him excitedly, confirming he'd found Jasmine. She put out her paws and the dragon, still quite small compared to her squirrel shape, landed in them. He had no real way to explain the plan, and she presented an unexpected wrinkle. Did that mean Will was loose? Did they miss noticing Will at Adelphi? Kaitlin might not have recognized him, especially with so many bodies there.

He needed to get her to the others, because he needed them to be able to talk to her. Not just for Will. She could screw up the whole operation by trying to help. The dragon gestured to try to get her to stay put, but she ran down the branch to the trunk of the tree. Once there, she changed into Jasmine and held out her hand.

"Hi, Bobby," she whispered, not as cheerfully as he remembered her being. "They have Will. They said they were rescuing him, but they tried to shoot me and now he's inside. I followed them here, but I don't know what to do. Are you a dangerous terrorist? They said you were a dangerous terrorist, but they lied to me about Will. Did they lie to me about everything else too?"

Bobby nodded, grateful for finding her so focused and able to get to the heart of things. He wished he could give her all the details.

"Are you getting everyone else out?" Nod. "Is there a plan?" Nod. "Can I help?" Shrug. "Okay. I'll wait here, then. If I see a way to help, then I will."

He never expected something that useful and coherent to come out of her mouth. She'd always struck him as flighty. An intelligent, capable woman lurked inside, and he'd never bothered to look. Will probably knew already.

The dragon patted her hand as it nodded, then pointed off in the direction where she could find the others. That done, he took off to go keep the people that ought to be waking up soon from freaking out. Jasmine turned back into a squirrel behind him and ran down the tree trunk.

Jumping out of the one dragon, he re-formed most of his body in the freezer drawer room, where he found the doors already open. As he pulled the slabs out, he found the collection of people stashed here interesting: Stephen, Jayce, Owen, Anita, Dan, Lizzie, Matthew, and Andrew. Considering he'd been in this bunch, Privek might have chosen all the ones he considered the most dangerous to put here. Or, he thought with a smirk, the most difficult.

Stephen groaned first. Bobby grinned and thumped his arm. "Who's the dumbass now?" he chuckled at the vampire.

"Jesus, Bobby," Stephen breathed as he cracked an eye open. "I will never, ever doubt you again." His voice came out as a hoarse rumble.

"Where are we?" Jayce rolled and fell off his top rack drawer, crashing into Lizzie, Anita, and Matthew. The four of them landed in a heap on the floor. The girls and Dan wore nothing. The rest had some sort of pajamas on, except for Stephen, who still had everything he'd been taken with.

"In the guts of a Federal building," Bobby told them, trying not to laugh, "working on escaping. Less crashing and noise would be a good idea, since you're all drugged and can't do nothing but stumble around like idiots."

"You want to give pointers, then?" Anita flopped and glared at Stephen when he dropped a sheet on top of her.

"Sure," Bobby shrugged, still smiling. "Relax and let it work its way outta your system. I got a plan, and we got others on the outside. Kaitlin's free and I got two guys what were on the other side to help. Plus Jasmine is out there. Plan allows for none of you being able to use your stuff, so just take a minute to be able to walk on your own."

Dan sat up slowly, careful to avoid hitting his head on the bunk above him. "I don't suppose you thought to bring clothes for us?"

"Thought of it, sure. Couldn't manage it." Bobby gave Stephen a hand getting down. The vampire felt unusually heavy. "There's some waiting outside, in the car."

"Ung. I'm *starving*," Stephen rasped out. "Any volunteers before I go on a rampage?"

"They done knew you drink blood and they didn't give you none in the drip? That's kinda messed up." Bobby shook his head and waved him off. "Y'all been under for near on a week now. I done got ya out soon as I could. I got no idea where the rest are, there's only just this one bank of drawers, but everyone done got took, so they're someplace. Hopefully here. We gotta find 'em and get out, at any rate.

"There's still a few of us on the other team what might be around to try and stop us from leaving, and the guards here got them dart guns what they used to take us down at the farm in the first place. Out of the eleven they got, I got three, and I think the one named Kanik is actually Privek's master, or maybe his slave. So, we got seven folks to convince they're being used and one what probably ain't gonna be convinceable."

While he explained, Stephen scanned the room, his eyes flitting from one person to the next. He took a step toward Lizzie, but Bobby stepped in the way. "You need fresh blood, ya idjit. Without this stupid drug in their system."

Anita, now wrapped up in the sheet, held her arm out. "Here. You need enough to be sane, right? Take that much."

Looking her over with suspicion, Stephen asked, "Are you volunteering to take one for the team?"

She pursed her lips and looked away. It had to be hard to find something to rest her eyes on that didn't include Dan and Lizzie checking each other over more carefully than might be considered tasteful, a shirtless Owen on his hands and knees and breathing deeply, an equally shirtless Jayce sitting and rubbing his face, or Andrew sitting in a tight white shirt and briefs and staring up at the fluorescent lights. The scene reminded Bobby one of those weird underwear or cologne ads.

The long pause meant everyone watched her, even Lizzie and Dan. Bobby pitied for her, realizing that must have been a weird thing for her to offer.

Her hands all over Dan, Lizzie smiled. "It's okay, Anita, we can still all think of you as a raging bitch if you want."

Jayce snorted out a laugh. Matthew and Stephen both chuckled. Dan kissed Lizzie's neck with a dirty little smile and pulled a sheet down for her. Andrew and Owen both grinned, and so did Bobby.

"Fuck all of you," Anita snapped, She left her arm out, though, still offered to Stephen. The vampire took it and bit her. She gasped and collapsed into him while he drank. Still weak himself, he had to sit down to hold them both up.

"Do we know what Kanik can do?" Jayce stood up and stretched. Bobby could relate to the impulse. More importantly, it took attention off Stephen and Anita.

"He can mess around with your head. In fact, I got pictures proving he done it to you before, in particular. No idea why you and not me, but if you don't remember it, maybe he did do it to me and Alice and Ai, and we don't remember it neither. Then again, Paul—he's one of the two of them I got convinced—couldn't do nothing with my head, and he's a telepath, so maybe he didn't hit me with a head whammy."

Jayce nodded and held up a hand curled into a fist while he braced himself against the steel of a drawer. Nothing happened. "Nope, I can't do my thing yet. How long did it take you to get this crap out of your system?"

"I dunno." Bobby shrugged. "Ten minutes, maybe."

"It'll probably take us all twice as long, then." Stephen set Anita down on the floor and straightened. "I feel so damned heavy. I forgot what it's like to not be able to fly." He poked himself in the gut for no apparent reason, then swore. "I can probably be killed like this. All of us can."

Bobby shrugged. "So long as we stay in here, ain't nothing to worry about, not really. Least, I don't think so. I done planned on it taking a while to get out like this, expecting to have to explain everything and folks needing help. This room ain't got cameras so far as I could tell, and it don't get checked by the guards. There's a guard post right outside it."

The door behind him opened, and a guard stood there. Liam had said— But then, Liam also had said he thought maybe Privek knew to expect something. They must have changed the routine because of it. Fortunately, not having their powers failed to make these people useless. Bobby broke into the swarm to prevent the guy from leaving, Jayce stepped up and grabbed him, Stephen decked him, and Owen yanked the radio and dart gun off his belt. Once they had him under control, Bobby re-formed to shut the door again. The poor guy hadn't stood a chance.

"So much for your intel, Bobby," Jayce grunted. He shoved the guard up against the wall.

"Great." Bobby grabbed the guard's other gun, the nine millimeter one. "You know who we are?" he asked the guard.

The guard held his hands up in surrender. "N-not really, no. I was just told to check the room."

"He's lying," Stephen snarled. "Break his damned neck."

"Wait, no! I'm just a guard, I'm not worth it." The guard's voice went high pitched and panicked, his eyes wide and darting from man to man. "They said the people in the drawers were dangerous. I'm supposed to check to make sure all the dosing packs are the same and the drawers are locked. That's really it, I swear!"

Bobby nudged Stephen to get him to back off, hoping the guard would see it as him being in control. He wanted the guy to believe he'd be fine so long as he played straight with them so no one had to think too much about how far they wanted to go to get information. "How long before you get missed?"

"Um, a few minutes. There's another guard outside. I check in with him on the way out and go on the rest of my rounds."

Owen passed the radio to Dan, keeping the dart gun for himself. "What's on the rest of your rounds?"

The guard blinked and bit his lip. Jayce tightened his grip on the guy's shirt. He gulped. "Um, there's a pair of separate rooms. Just down the hall. One has a woman and a kid, the other has just a woman."

Bobby's jaw clenched, because he knew exactly who the woman and kid had to be, and could have found them when Liam broke him out. He wanted to kick himself for not doing it, but then, what would that have accomplished? It would have pissed him off even more. At the time, it probably would have made things worse. "Which way? Be specific. And what guards are between here and there?"

"Down the hall to the left, first door on the right. One guard outside this room, one more outside theirs. No others on the way. Two down by the elevators."

Glancing around, Bobby could tell no one else had any brilliant ideas. The guard needed to be handled, and every option—letting him go, taking him hostage, killing him, sticking him in a drawer—seemed stupid and counterproductive. "Jayce, let him go, he's got the point. Unload this and give it back to him. Owen, unload that dart gun too, and give that back. Dan, give the man his radio back. He's gonna walk right outta here like he's s'posed to, and he's gonna finish his rounds, then he's gonna take a break outside."

"Head Cowboy," Lizzie said, like she found it both annoying and delightful.

"This ain't no time for that. None of you got your stuff back yet. I do. He ain't going alone." Bobby popped a dragon off his thumb and held it up for the guard to get a good look at it. "You see this little guy? He's kinda cute, looks real harmless." It danced and flapped its wings, pretending to be a kiddie toy. Then it stopped and fixed the guard with a hard stare, one that matched Bobby's own. "He ain't even close to being harmless. You even think about tipping the other guards off, he's gonna blast his way into your mouth as hard as he gotta." The dragon let off a puff of fire and flashed its fangs. "Then he's gonna crawl down your throat until he reaches about where your heart is, and he's gonna rip his way outta your chest. We got an understanding?"

Standing there, the guard stared at Bobby, his mouth hanging open. "Jesus Christ."

"He ain't gonna help you," Bobby growled. "You do what I done told you to, and you get to walk away. We ain't got no real beef with you, it's with your bosses. Just on account I ain't sure I can trust you, I'm sending a few others with you, and they'll be happy to just burn and claw you wherever they can reach." He let off the rest of his hand, and they dove into his clothes. Bobby made sure at least one went into a pants pocket to threaten the guy's manhood, figuring that would be plenty motivating.

"O-okay, yeah, sure. I got it." The guard squirmed uncomfortably. "Finish my rounds and take a break outside."

Bobby shooed him off. "Get going."

The door closed behind him and Bobby turned around to see everyone but Stephen staring at him in shock. Actually, Lizzie seemed aroused more than disturbed.

"Stop it," the vampire said with a roll of his eyes. "Just because he's learned how to kill people efficiently doesn't mean he's suddenly a psychopath."

Giving them all his back again, Bobby rested his hand on the doorknob. Of course they thought he'd jumped off the sanity cliff. Right about now, some of them had to be wondering what exactly he did while they were out, maybe even back in Afghanistan. Jayce and Matthew could probably find all the right conclusions. "C'mon, we ain't got time for this. We're gonna knock the guards out without killing them, and get as many outta here as we can find."

"Are we going to blow the building up?" Lizzie asked hopefully. When he looked back, she licked her lips.

"Not unless we gotta. We're in the city here, DeeCee to be precise. Blowing it up'll get folks hurt. This ain't a base with a fence round it, nor a house in the middle of nowhere. It'd be best if we don't actually hurt nobody."

"Aww." She pouted as she held her sheet close. "When you threatened the guard, I thought you were—"

He cut her off, not interested in hearing it. "I ain't. You thought wrong. I want us to be safe and free. They ain't never gonna leave us alone if we go around killing and destroying and all that."

"They won't leave us alone regardless." Jayce put a hand on his shoulder and gripped it firmly. "The idea they will is a fantasy."

Bobby stopped and rubbed his forehead. "Look, yeah, I know. I got a plan. Most important thing right this minute is to get outta here. After that, we get into the rest. Ain't keeping ya in the dark, just trying to keep from explaining over and over so much."

His attention went to his dragons with the patrolling guard, because they saw Lily. "I'll be right back," he told Jayce, then he threw himself into the dragon doing its best to hide behind the guard's ear. Lily sat with Sebastian in a living room, reading a picture book with him. They looked normal and happy, and had no signs of any sort of mistreatment. He didn't know what to make of that. Lily noticed the guard and smiled, then ignored him. Sebastian completely ignored him. He jumped his dragon off the guard's ear as the man left, sending it to land on the book.

"Look, Mama, Bobby!" Sebastian scooped the dragon up and presented it proudly to Lily.

"Yes, that's one of his dragons. We should call Mr. Privek to let him know." Lily scooted Sebastian off her lap and, to Bobby's horror, went for what must be some kind of intercom.

Bobby wriggled out of Sebastian's grip. He darted to Lily, trying to get between her and the button on the wall. "Mama, Bobby wants you. "

"Yes, well, Bobby is—" She sighed and put her hand on the button. "I know, Sebastian. Mr. Privek said he might act strangely if he came here." Despite Bobby landing on her hand, she pushed the button. "Please inform Mr. Privek that Bobby is here. One of his dragons just showed up."

A male voice responded, "Yes, Ma'am. Thank you, Ma'am."

Why did she do that? Bobby had no idea why Lily would do that. She was mad at him, yes, and he knew it. He'd been a dumbass. It boggled his mind that she could be so angry. His stupidity didn't rate siccing Privek on him.

He told the dragon to get out of there and threw himself back into his body. "We got a problem. Lily just done told Privek I'm here. Any of you getting your stuff back yet?" He watched Jayce put a hand on the bank of drawers. A silver sheen slowly crept up his hand.

"Mine is coming back, but it's sluggish. Doesn't feel solid, either." He swatted Lizzie's hand away as she reached over, probably to squeeze his butt. "Take my word for it," he told her with a smirk. "It's just a thin coating on the outside.

She gave a husky chuckle and turned her palm up. It threw some tiny, harmless sparks. Her amusement died and she pouted. "It's so pathetic."

"It's okay, baby. It'll come back, we just need more time." Dan put his arm around her waist and kissed her neck.

"We don't got no more time." The rest of the dragons with the guard let him know Lisa was the woman in the other room, currently taking a nap. He had no idea why they'd singled her out. Nor did he understand why both women stayed with the door unlocked. Had Lily poured out her anger to Lisa? How would he ever get either of them to forgive him?

"I can still punch people," Jayce pointed out. "I just can't deflect bullets or break walls."

"Same here." Stephen stood on his toes, still unable to leave the floor.

"Don't look at me," Andrew grunted as he got to his feet. "I can scrap a little, but not nearly well enough to deal with trained guards. And if I help anyone walk, we'll never know when their powers come back. Why am I even in here with you guys?"

Bobby had no answer. Wait. Yes, he did. "Kanik. He does some kinda mind control. You turn powers off. Stephen's immune too." Now that he got rolling, he understood why every last one of them had been stashed here. "Jayce, you were really hard for them to put down. Dan, you were on camera making people shoot themselves. Lizzie done blew up Hill good, and Matthew got seen there as a werewolf. Anita, they knew you wrecked up that house. Owen, you woke everyone up at the farm. All of us're the ones they see as threats. Nobody else caused 'em no trouble, just us. We're the ones they used to motivate the others.

"Lily's gotta be under his thumb, that explains why she just called Privek on me. We gotta expect the rest are too. That means we're gonna be up against our own. Worst of 'em is gonna be...I dunno. Maybe Alice,

Andrea. Sam, depending on what they got set up here. Hannah's smart, Greg maybe built them something. 'Course, we got no idea about the ones we never met. My gut says they got some of 'em here, expecting this jail-break. Lizzie, you're gonna have to deal with Alice's ice. Don't blow nothing up you don't gotta, since there's ordinary office folk here.

"Jayce, Stephen, you gotta protect Andrew. He's the one what's gonna get everybody outta Kanik's grips." He hoped so, anyway. "We're going for Lily and Lisa first, on account we know where they are. Owen, I don't know what to suggest for you, just do whatever seems right." His eyes went from face to face as he spoke, ideas coming to him in the moment. "Anita, Dan, keep folks from shooting any of us soon as you can."

Matthew, who Bobby found himself staring at, used the rolled-out slabs to haul himself to his feet. "I know, I'm just a wrecking ball. I'll do my best to keep a lid on it. What're you going to do?"

Glad he didn't have to be the one to say it out loud, Bobby nodded. "Folks on the outside're gonna set up a diversion soon as they get the word from me. I'mma leave a couple dragons behind with y'all. When they squawk, get moving. I'll be spread over the building, getting you some warnings when I can." He dearly wished they had Sam. "If'n you hear a voice in your heads, it's just Paul and don't freak or nothing."

With that, he blew out into dragons and left through the ventilation system. Four stayed behind—one for Stephen, one for Jayce, one for Matthew, and one in case someone else had to split off. Most of the dragons broke off to search the building from top to bottom while a handful went out to where Riker and the others waited. Along the way, he found Jasmine again and beckoned to her, getting her to follow him. She'd be able to tell them at least a few things.

"Liam!" Jasmine stood into her human shape and threw herself into a hug that took Liam by surprise. He'd been squatting behind a shrub and she knocked him onto his butt. "Are you helping Bobby now?"

"Yes." He hugged her back as he got his feet under himself again. "Is Will inside?"

Bobby wanted to give her a real hug when he saw the fierce, unhappy determination on her face. More, he wanted to give her Will back. "That's where they took him after the helicopter ride. I haven't seen him come out yet. I saw them put a gun to his head. Do you think he's okay?"

Liam patted her shoulder. "I think he's alive." In one of the dragons, Bobby chirped and danced on Liam's shoulder. Another dragon sat on Riker's shoulder, and another on Paul's. He figured Kaitlin would be fine without. "Paul, can you reach the dragons individually?"

"Bobby, or dragon, or whatever, can you hear me?"

"Yeah, I hear ya." Relieved to hear Paul's voice in his head, Bobby passed along the important points quickly, and heard Paul repeat it all out loud for the rest.

Riker stared at the building hard enough to peel paint. "Are Privek or Kanik here? Can you tell, Paul?"

"There are too many people here for me to tell if anyone in particular is around, so I can't say who's here and who's not." Paul sighed heavily. "I want to help more than that, but I just can't."

"Do what you can," Riker said.

In unison, his four men finished for him. "Don't waste time worrying about what you can't." They all grinned.

"It's a Sarge-ism," Carter said with a chuckle. "How long should we wait?"

Distracted by goings-on back in the freezer room, Bobby paused and thought about it. Jayce smacked one of the cabinets again, checking his power and finding it still sluggish. Stephen rolled his head, neck cracking, and lifted half an inch off the floor. Seeing that, Lizzie cupped her hands and a little ball of fire boiled in the center. *"I don't know. It's gonna be a —"*The door to the freezer drawer room slammed open.

The guy with the icy blue eyes standing in the doorframe had short brown hair and skin tanned from time spent outdoors. He wore a pair of jeans and a plain t-shirt. "No one is going anywhere." His body melted into water and expanded to fill the doorway.

Inside the room, a strange metallic whump noise came from the back wall. When his dragon turned to find the source of the sound, Bobby caught sight of a person-sized blue-edged disc on the wall, outlining a view to someplace else. That other place had a dozen men in body armor with dart guns pointed into the room. Behind them, Alice stood in front of a wall of ice, probably intended to cut off anyone who tried to escape that way.

They'd set a damned good trap. Bobby let out an expletive for Paul's benefit, then threw himself into the dragon on Stephen's shoulder as it trilled in alarm. He sent an urgent call for the dragons to converge in the room again. A barrage of darts streaked into the room. Everyone dove for the sides to avoid them. Anita, too slow, took two darts and groaned. One hit Dan in the shoulder, another tagged Matthew in the leg.

Jayce ducked out from behind the open door and punched the nearly transparent barrier blocking their escape, only to recoil in pain from the impact. The swarm poured into the room through the ducts and settled over the blue disc opening to catch any more darts they might shoot.

Venomous rage settled over Lizzie's usually smirking face. She glared through the swarm, ready to run in and murder their attackers with her bare hands.

Owen opened his mouth and shouted, "Let us go!" He only managed to be a tiny bit louder than a normal voice.

Everyone seemed so stymied by this. Add a little stress to a situation and everyone panicked. Stephen, at least, had his back plastered to the wall beside the blue disc, and seemed to be trying to think.

For some reason, none of these people could come up with the answer that seemed so obvious to Bobby. He needed to be able to...to give orders. Damn, Head Cowboy had climbed up on his high horse. A handful of dragons flew to Andrew, trilling at him where he cowered in the corner, urging him to his feet. They pointed frantically at the water-guy in the doorway.

Andrew took forever to get the idea, then he lunged out and slapped his hand on it. Him. Whatever. Bobby had his own problems. Alice shot shards of ice at the swarm, ripping through the tiny bodies. Most of it, they dodged. She managed to hit twelve head-on, and encased twice that many in ice.

Stuck there to defend against the darts, Bobby had to let the dragons take it. While the guy in the doorway oozed back to his body, Alice kept shooting the dragons with globs of ice. Lizzie stood in the middle of the room now, staring so hard through the swarm he thought laser beams might shoot out of her eyes to hit Alice in the chest any second. She took deep breaths, her hands held out with tiny flames dancing in her palms. Slowly, they crept up her arms, but she needed more time to be able to fully counter Alice.

Stephen lunged at the water-guy and bit him in the arm. Water-guy moaned and dropped to the floor, revealing the girl standing behind him with a dart gun in her shaking hands. Bobby recognized her as the one who'd shot him at the farm, and she seemed as terrified now as she'd been then.

She squeezed the trigger while Jayce hopped over Stephen gulping down water-guy's blood. The gun clicked—she'd forgotten to switch the safety off. In one smooth motion, Jayce took the gun away from her, flipped it around, thumbed the safety, and shot her before she managed to do more than stumble back.

The blue disc and the view of the other room disappeared. As Lizzie screamed out a rage-filled cry of challenge, Bobby re-formed in agony, one arm missing because of all the ice encrusted dragons littering the floor. "Little help, Lizzie," he grunted. So many of his dragons had been smashed that he felt like a walking bruise.

"Baby," Dan said, still on the floor, "Calm down and help Bobby. C'mon, heat up the ice. You'll get your chance later when you've got more fire to burn."

"Nobody shoots you but me!" Flames flashed out, engulfing Lizzie's body and making everyone flinch away from her.

Bobby held an arm up to shield himself from the fire. "Lizzie, get a —" He bit back a few choice swearwords, instead making a wordless noise of exasperation. "—grip. We still gotta get outta here." Since she kept doing what looked to him like throwing a temper tantrum, he scooped up and chucked his frozen dragons at her. The ice sizzled and popped, and it seemed to soothe her.

Stephen sighed in contentment and sat up. "That's more like it. No drugs in that blood. I think it's chasing the rest of it away for me."

"We should take these two with us. How long will he—" Jayce used his chin to indicate Water-guy. "—be out?"

"A while." Stephen floated to his feet and picked Water-guy up easily. "Oh, yeah." Rolling his neck around made it crack loudly. "I'm good to go."

"Jayce, how you doing?" Bobby lobbed a large chunk of ice at Lizzie, and melting it both released five dragons and got Lizzie back under control.

"Not solid yet, but getting there." He picked the girl up and hefted her over his shoulder. "I should be able to repel the darts, but maybe not bullets yet."

"Good enough for now," Bobby nodded. "You, me, and Andrew are going to get Lily and Lisa. The rest of you go clear a path to the elevators and get a car for us. Do what you gotta, but remember not to hurt no one too much."

"We're the good guys, Baby," Dan said as he got gingerly to his feet and grinned. "At least for now."

Jayce handed the girl off to Matthew. The werewolf had a fresh dose of the drug, making him unsteady. He shouldered the girl well enough anyway. Bobby and Andrew followed Jayce down the hallway. A small group of guards clustered to defend the door they needed to go through. Jayce kept walking, letting their darts bounce off his metal flesh. Bobby burst back into the swarm and surrounded the poor guards, biting their hands and ripping guns away.

The pair of them knocked all the guards down in less than half a minute. "Good work," Bobby said as he re-formed, proud of his dragons for not killing anyone. They listened to him. That mattered. He pushed the door open, beckoning Andrew to follow, and took the first door in the new hallway to get to Lily.

CHAPTER 11

LIAM

Paul spat out a curse. "Go, go, go! They're under attack, I think."

Riker nodded and led his men through the parking lot at a jog. Liam didn't like this part of the plan very much, mostly because it involved a high probability he would have to heal people. A shame that just asking Privek nicely to let everyone go would never work. He stuffed Jasmine the squirrel into his pocket and led Paul and Kaitlin to the front doors, only to find them locked.

Liam frowned as he rattled the door again, refusing to accept their condition. "Why are they locked? These doors are never locked. Not even in the middle of the night."

"There must be an alarm going." Kaitlin made a face. "I didn't see that coming."

The wind kicked up, tossing small debris into the air. All three of them looked up to see two women dropping down out of the sky. Chelsea's feathery wings caused most of the breeze, and Dianna's ability to control the wind made it worse. They landed together, one on each side of the trio.

"What's going on, Liam?" Dianna put a hand on one hip and regarded her fingernails casually. The attractive black woman had taken to wearing spandex bodysuits now. Liam supposed that being able to fly would make skirts particularly unattractive, and loose clothing would get in the way. It made her look like she'd dropped off a comic book page. This particular outfit was dark red with a yellow sash across her waist and subtle black stripes up and down her body that brought a tornado to mind.

Chelsea, a pretty blonde with sparkling green eyes, turned her head in sharp, abrupt movements that reminded Liam of a bird studying a worm. "Where've you been for the past few days?"

Privek had arranged a welcoming committee, apparently. Liam shrugged, knowing he could fool these two at least well enough to keep them from doing anything regrettable. "Just enjoying the fact I'm not in Afghanistan."

"Uh huh. Who's this?" Dianna stared at Kaitlin.

"Kaitlin Tremont, here to meet Privek and hopefully join the home team."

Kaitlin gave them a good impression of a chipper person smiling and waving. "That's me, just looking to be on the winning side and all."

Dianna and Chelsea shared a look. Chelsea wrapped her arms around Kaitlin and snapped her wings out. "Let me help you with that."

Dianna put her hands out and the winds kicked up again. "The building is on lockdown until Mitchell is taken down, so we'll get you all in to see him."

Behind him, Paul made a little *eep* noise. Liam stifled down a sigh. "That's really not necessary, ladies. We don't mind climbing stairs."

Kaitlin screamed out, "Riker!"

Idly, as his feet lifted off the ground, Liam reflected that when the precog screamed, it was really more of a frantic yell without the shrieking high pitch some women are capable of. Nothing he could do would stop

Dianna, or anyone else, so he tried to keep his feet under him and not provoke her to drop him. Gunfire took him by surprise, though it shouldn't have. Riker was a soldier and he had a gun. Obviously, when a girl he liked made noises like Kaitlin did, there would be shooting.

Liam curled up to avoid getting shot and saw nothing. He went downward abruptly and slapped to the ground, letting out a grunt as something crunched under him and a sharp pain stabbed into his leg. Something small and furry tapped his face. In agony, he opened his eyes to find himself lying on the concrete with a squirrel trying desperately to wake him. Beyond Jasmine, he saw Paul lying on the ground, unconscious. The gunfire had stopped, so he looked around and caught sight of Chelsea crumpled on the ground, bleeding and gasping for breath. Next to her, Kaitlin rose unsteadily to her hands and knees, shaking her head.

He saw Dianna at least thirty feet up in the air. Someone else up there flailed one arm while the other clutched at his neck. Taking in the assault rifle dangling from its strap and military fatigues, he guessed it to be the man who'd been shooting: Riker.

More gunfire made Liam flinch down again, giving him a fresh rush of adrenaline. When nothing hit him, he rolled to see Riker's men shooting up at Dianna. Propping himself up on one elbow, he saw that his leg stuck out at a funny angle. Seeing it made it hurt, and he groaned, wishing he could heal himself.

Jasmine became human again beside him and pulled on his arm. "You have to help Paul!" She dragged him to the telepath and slapped his hand on the closest part, his knee.

The telepath could have prevented all of this if he'd only been prepared to handle this kind of stress. Now, he lay on concrete, bleeding to death on the inside with a dozen or more cracked bones, including his skull. Liam braced for the pain and still let out a tortured cry when his bones ruptured and repaired themselves.

Someone screamed, masculine and shocked, and then it stopped abruptly. Shouting followed while Paul groaned and Liam lay there in agony from his leg that stubbornly refused to heal. How high up did they get before Dianna threw them back down? It must have been at least twenty feet.

"Bring him here, quick," Paul called out.

Liam took deep breaths to keep from hyperventilating, knowing what to expect next. Even prepared for it, the intense torture of Riker's injuries overwhelmed him. Dianna had tried very hard to kill the soldier.

"What about Dianna?"

"The wind chick? She's toast," said Carter, or maybe Platt. They sounded too similar to tell through the pain. "Body's over there. This winged girl won't last much longer, either."

"Chelsea," Paul said, voice full of anguish.

Jasmine sniffled. "She seemed so nice."

Liam shut the rest of the chatter out to focus on not letting himself go mad. Sure, he'd healed men in bad shape before. No amount of experience would ever make it pleasant, fun, or easy the next time. "I'll heal Chelsea," he grunted as Riker's injuries faded from his body.

Someone dropped her hand into his. He found three bullet wounds, one serious enough to kill her. Liam gritted his teeth and healed all of it. With the others, the injuries had been all internal. Hers made holes in him and put blood stains on his shirt. She coughed and sucked in air while Liam gasped and wheezed. He heard the soldiers threatening her, Paul and Jasmine trying to ward them off, and Kaitlin fussing over Riker. No one, it seemed, felt he needed any attention.

The pain of everyone else's wounds faded, leaving only his own leg tormenting him. He needed someone to give it to. No one here qualified, until he listened to the tone of Chelsea's voice as she protested her treatment. It grated on his nerves, and he knew there would be no talking sense to her. Having a broken bone would keep her out of trouble. He opened his eyes and grabbed her arm. Her squeal of surprise bothered him as he pushed the bone break onto her. It scared him that he could do this.

"Liam, what are you doing?" Paul gasped.

He let out a sigh of relief. "Experimenting." To see what would happen and assuage his guilt, he tried to heal her. Nothing happened. "Sorry, Chelsea. You shouldn't have tried to take Kaitlin." Thankfully, she wasn't up to retorting right now. "Tie her up to be on the safe side, and let's get inside. They're bound to need help by now."

Getting to his feet, he averted his eyes from Chelsea, now curled up in a ball and crying over her own broken leg. That left him noticing the heavy stares of his team. He wondered if Bobby felt the same way when people gave him these looks. He'd done something horrible and he knew it, and everyone else knew it, and he knew they knew and judged him for it. Maybe, the next time he saw Bobby, he could cut the guy a break.

Riker sprang into action, pulling a rope out of who knows where and tying Chelsea up. Hegi hurried to the door and pointed his gun at it. A few short, sharp reports announced his method of lock picking. Carter grabbed what remained of the handle and yanked it open. The five soldiers assaulted the entrance, taking gunfire and returning it.

"You shouldn't have done that," Paul's mind voice accused him.

"I thought I could take it back and heal it, but I guess I can't." He winced at how defensive and petulant that must have sounded. *"Can you contact Bobby? We need to know what's going on."*

CHAPTER 12

BOBBY

Bobby opened the next door to find Lily and Sebastian as he'd last seen them, sitting with the book again. Sebastian lit up with a broad smile at the sight of Bobby and Jayce. Lily's face twisted with fear and she grabbed the boy up. Sebastian chirped with surprise and waved cheerfully.

"Bobby!" Sebastian tried and failed to wriggle free of his mother's grasp. "Mama, it's Bobby. Want a hug."

"Lily, what're you doing?" The expression on her face hurt. She hated him, enough to see Privek as better. "I ain't gonna hurt you or nothing. We gotta get outta here. No time for this kinda thing."

"We're not going anywhere with *you.*" She said it like he was the lowest of the low, something she scraped off her shoe. It hit him in the gut, worse than her slapping him and still being mad, worse than trying to accept there couldn't be anything between them, worse than just being avoided by her.

"Lily," he said helplessly, "please. Privek's gonna do things to Sebastian, you know that."

"Mama, let go." Sebastian squirmed in her arms, struggling against her desperate grip. He broke free and ran to Bobby, who bent down and picked him up. He settled the boy on his hip and small arms wrapped around his neck while he snuggled close.

Lily jumped up and screamed at Bobby. "Don't you dare take him away from me!" A white brick formed in her hand, and she threw it at him.

"What in—" Bobby curled away from it to protect himself and Sebastian from the brick. It hit him in the back, and it hurt. "Lily, what're you *doing*?"

She raised her hand and another brick formed. "You can't take him, he's not your son!"

He ducked away as she swung for his head. Thank goodness she'd never learned to fight. Setting Sebastian down, he turned to face her. She slammed the brick into his head hard enough to blow it into dragons. They snapped back into place and he grabbed her wrist to make her stop. Shoving his body at her, he pinned her against the wall, brick-holding hand over her head and the other bouncing around and smacking him ineffectually.

"What's going on, why in heckbiscuits are you hitting me with... bricks..." She had her power and wasn't sedated. Why did she have her power without being sedated? That made no sense. Privek wouldn't leave her like that unless he trusted her. He stared stupidly at her face as she screamed and raged. Things clicked into place. Kanik. He messed with heads. He must have made her think they'd protect her from that evil Bobby who wanted to take her boy away.

How was he supposed to break that? Could it be broken? Was she stuck like this forever? No, there had to be a way. "I'm sorry for this, Lily." He forcefully covered her mouth. "You gotta pipe down, just hear me out."

She bit him and his hand dispersed into dragons. "Get off me, you perverted freak," she snarled. "If you take Sebastian, I'll kill you."

In a storybook, kissing her would work. Bobby had a feeling she'd bite him again if he tried that, which wouldn't solve anything. "Lily, knock it off. I ain't taking your boy. I just come to see you, right? I know he ain't my son." She'd called him a "perverted freak," so maybe it would help if he explained and apologized. "I also know you're pissed at me on account I done some stupid crap. I didn't mean to spy on you, I just didn't think first. And I shoulda left you a note. I never seem to do nothing right, not for you, and I'm sorry."

While he kept talking, Bobby noticed Jayce slip in and, with a finger to his lips, snatch Sebastian up and out of the room. "I ain't never tried to take Sebastian before, why d'you think I would now?" He did everything he could think of to get Jayce to understand he wanted Andrew to come in and stop Lily from making any more bricks.

She must have caught Andrew running toward her out of the corner of her eye, because she turned with another shriek and a white glob formed in her hand. Andrew barreled into them both, knocking all three of them to floor in a tangle. Bobby opened his eyes to find himself face to face with Lily.

"What...happened?" She blinked and squinted, then her eyes went wide in horror. "Oh my gosh. I walked right in here, I let them lock us up. And I called Privek on you. Why did I do that?" Squeezing her eyes shut, she pressed her face into Bobby's neck.

Bobby slumped in relief and held her close. "Andrew, go get Lisa. Next room."

The Creole nodded and scrambled to his feet. They knew now that he could cut off whatever control Kanik had over a person without having to get at Kanik himself. That didn't really make sense, but Bobby's own dragons didn't really make sense, so he had no room to cast that kind of stone.

"It's okay, Lily. Your head got messed with. Ain't your fault, ain't nothing to feel guilty for." He reveled in the fact that she didn't pull away or punch him, or hit him with a brick again.

When she did finally pull back from him, he brushed tears from her cheek and tried to guess how this would work out. He never could quite figure out women, not really, especially this particular one. For all he knew, she'd wriggle away and focus on her son. To his surprise, she broke into a smile and kissed him.

Jayce cleared his throat. "Much as it pains me to stop you, we do still need to escape with as many of our people as we can."

"Yeah." Bobby lay there on the floor with her, marveling at how something so simple could wipe away everything else. All the doubt and guilt still huddled inside his head, of course. Somehow, the feel of her soft, warm body against his made it matter a lot less. He had a job to do and he'd get it done.

"We'll talk later," Lily said. She wriggled away from him.

The way she moved put all kinds of ideas into Bobby's head, enough so he had to adjust his jeans as he hauled himself to his feet. "Right. Yeah. Okay. Right."

Jayce grinned. "Do you need a minute?"

"Shut up," Bobby grumbled. "There's still a lot to do here, and we got places to go and all. Dragons outside're telling me they had some trouble, and one of ours is dead. They're coming in."

That wiped the smirk off Jayce's face. He turned without another word, leading them all back to the elevators. Everyone else waited while recovering from the drugs, some more patiently than others. Bobby saw no guards and figured they'd been stuffed behind doors.

Lizzie showed off a ball of fire in her hand, lighting up her pleased grin. Stephen punched the button for the elevator. "Everyone is doing alright now, except Dan and Anita." Those two both drooped, in need of a nap or a shot of caffeine. Behind him, the elevator dinged and the doors slid open.

Kaitlin stood there, in front of Jasmine, Liam and Paul. "Howdy, campers. We're holding the lobby. I see we have a bunch, but not everyone. These two are on our team. No molesting them."

"You have Maisie and Brian," Liam said, "Chelsea is out of commission and Dianna is dead. That leaves Kevin, Camellia, and Ray, plus the rest of your people. Kevin can turn invisible, Camellia does a chameleon thing, and Ray can make a protective shield. He's also good at punching."

Bobby nodded and thought about the situation. "Everyone get to the lobby and get out. Stephen, Andrew, Jayce, and me are gonna go through this building and get whoever else we can find." He ignored Lizzie's pout in favor of glancing back at Lily with Sebastian on her hip. "Don't bother being quiet. See what you can do to get us all outta here."

Lily smiled and kissed Bobby on the cheek on her way to the elevator. It warmed him to his toes to know she still wanted to be on his team. Somewhere inside, he'd been half worried she'd slap him once she had a minute to think about it. She'd put a dumb grin on his face, and he didn't care that everyone could see it.

Stephen grabbed the door to the stairwell and hauled it open. Bobby gave Andrew an encouraging pat on the arm and led the way up. The room they'd seen through the portal had to be here someplace, and the upper basement seemed the most likely, making it their first stop.

"I'm gonna—" Bobby stopped on the landing for the next floor when he saw Lizzie step up next to Andrew. She had a hand on her hip and her expression dared him to challenge her. "What're you doing?"

She rolled her eyes. "I'm coming with you, duh. What are you going to do when you find Alice? Run really fast so she doesn't ice you up?"

"What're *you* gonna do when Kanik tries to take over your mind? Burn him up first?"

"That's an idea." She grinned and held up her hand, now engulfed in flames. "Jayce can't defend against it, either."

Jayce shrugged. "If he gets me, he can't blow up the building."

Pushing the door open with a roll of his eyes, Bobby burst into the swarm as an unexpected volley of darts flew at him. Ice filled the space along with his dragons, catching and encasing more than half of them. Fire roared into life behind him, then Jayce's metal fist slammed through the rapidly melting sheet of ice, followed by his body.

"I really don't want to hurt anyone," Jayce said as he barreled into the group of men in tactical gear. In the time it took the dragons to get through the space now hosting a duel between fire and ice, Jayce knocked two of the shooters down and out. The swarm streaked in and shoved guns around, forcing several to clatter to the floor. Stephen stayed back for the moment, ready to knock Lizzie aside if he needed to. Andrew kept his back to the wall and out of sight.

Jayce clocked a third man with his steel fist, then a fourth with his elbow. "Why can't we just all be civilized?"

Bobby spotted Alice and went for her. She stood behind the men, peering around a corner to throw ice. They needed to get Alice and Andrew together. Hoping to circle around behind her, the swarm streaked up the hall, away from the fray. By the time he found her from the other side, Alice screamed with wordless frustration. He slipped up behind her and re-formed in the act of grabbing her arms and pinning them behind her back.

"Come on, Alice, why're you fighting us? Andrew's cooking ain't that bad, is it?"

"Dammit, Bobby!" She squirmed and struggled, kicking out and flinging her head back. His head blew into dragons that re-formed again immediately. "Let me go!"

"Lizzie, cover Andrew over to here!" One slow, difficult step at a time, he hauled Alice in that direction. Her body chilled in his arms, and his breath came out in little white puffs. If she kept that up, he'd wind up in the swarm again.

A curtain of fire sprang up, forming a curve around Jayce and the last few men still resisting him. Andrew sprinted around it and crashed into Bobby and Alice, not bothering to try to stop on the now slippery, icy floor. Without Alice affecting it, and with Lizzie's fire roaring, the temperature shot back up.

"What the..." Alice shook her head to clear it and Bobby let go of her.

"Welcome back," Bobby said as he relaxed onto the floor. "We're gonna need your help getting folks outta here. You up for that?"

Panting, Andrew wriggled out of the small heap of bodies and sat up on his knees. "I hope the rest are easier."

Alice sat up and stared stupidly at Lizzie, now by their side and offering her a hand up. "All I wanted to do was freeze everyone except those guys."

"Yeah, we know." Lizzie grabbed Alice's hand and yanked her to her feet. The fire dropped and disappeared, revealing Jayce standing in the midst of ten bodies in black tactical gear. Her eyes flicked from body to body and she licked her lips. "Isn't it great to watch? All those bulging silver muscles. It's all over, you know. *Everything* is metal. Can you just imagine?"

Jayce ignored her and, with Stephen's help, pulled weapons off the unconscious men. "I hate these darts," Stephen said with a scowl. He dropped a handful of them on the floor and stomped hard, smashing them. "Like we're rabid dogs that need to be controlled."

"Using them against our own may make things easier," Jayce said with a nod, "but I'm feeling like we shouldn't actually do it. I know I shot that one girl downstairs with her own dart gun. I just don't like it." He unloaded the one in his hands with a smooth motion, popping the loaded dart out and letting it fall to the floor. "Lizzie, can you burn them all up without hurting these guys?"

Instead of answering, small pops announced her doing it.

"Good deal." Bobby got to his feet. "Alice, there anyone else on this floor?"

"No, it was cleared out two days ago. Ever since they realized you were loose, they've been prepping the building for when you come back. Security was tightened and all nonessential employees were told to stay home. Some of us are here, some went to another facility. Sam's got the building wired, I'm not sure what all for. They're using Greg for something too."

Aside — Privek

Everything was not precisely going according to plan, but it came close enough. Privek glanced over at Kanik, hoping the lunatic would stick to it. Right now, the kid paced back and forth frantically across the thick shag carpet, ignoring the monitors and muttering to himself. He did that a lot. Privek had learned to ignore it a while ago.

Those monitors, with the camera feeds provided by Sam, showed a large group of them converging on the lobby, along with those five soldiers helping them. He should have known better than to post those men anywhere near someplace Mitchell might show up if he ever got loose, but their involvement wasn't any more of a disaster than anything else.

His eyes zeroed in on the actual problem: Moore and Pearson. He hadn't expected either of them to want to wake Mitchell up, and definitely didn't expect Moore to find Elena. The telepath shouldn't have been persuaded away from their goals, either. He should have seen through Mitchell just like Kanik's implanted suggestions told him to. Kanik's ability, apparently, wasn't as foolproof as he thought. At least it had kept Pearson from successfully reading his own mind.

Actually, in some ways, the worst part had to be Kanik losing his control over Westbrook early. After making the effort to set those first four up to flee those ridiculous experiments, and planting those lists so they'd do half the work for him, he'd lost his ace in the hole. At least everything had gone well prior to losing him. If the suggestions had only lasted a little longer, he wouldn't have had to send Camellia to find them. Things would be much better if he had Westbrook now too.

Privek pulled his phone out and sent Sam a short text, trusting the improvements she and that Greg kid made to the structure to be enough to handle the escapees. In a minute, several would be dead, and the rest would blindly flail around, blundering into the rest of his trap. Good thing Mitchell decided to take all the ones who could actually survive this sort of thing on his side trip.

He imagined himself slapping glossy photographs down in a line on the President's desk, each showing Mitchell's handiwork, or that of one of his band of freaks. The fireballs wouldn't be terribly compelling, but the corpses with their chests ripped out would make a statement. Agent Kaffer's body too; all those tiny bites and scorchmarks hinted at a slow, painful death of a thousand cuts.

The President and all his advisors—the Vice President, the Chief of Staff, the Chairman of the Joint Chiefs, the National Security Advisor, and more—gaped at the pictures, sucking in breaths and riveted by the grotesque images.

"These things represent a clear and present danger to the security of the Unites States, Mister President."

The President kept his hands to himself, as if refusing to touch the photos could make them less real. He was a weak man, a politician. A few long, stunned seconds passed before he reached for the one showing Mitchell and a handful of the others. Picking it up, he stared at the faces, imagining his own teenage children in their place. "They're just kids," he protested.

Privek slammed a hand on the desk, making all of them jump. "Don't let them deceive you, Mr. President. They may look like ordinary humans, but I assure you, they are not. They're dangerous halfbreeds, too alien to handle the power they've developed without letting it consume and corrupt them. We need to hunt them down before they kill like this again. I have the tools to do the job, I just need resources to deploy them."

The President nodded and sighed in resignation. "Give him whatever he needs to deal with this. I'd give you a Cabinet position, Mr. Privek, but then you'd be subject to Congressional approval. This should be kept quiet, and your vigilance and patriotism will be rewarded. Handsomely."

Kanik's voice broke into his fantasy, dispelling it for now. "I don't understand what we're doing anymore." He seemed to have regained some measure of lucidity. When Privek had first found the kid, he'd been paranoid and ranting and obsessed with revenge against the executives of that rail freight company. Privek had seen the potential immediately. Kanik was his golden ticket. So sad he'd probably need to kill the kid to seal this deal. Someone would have to take the blame for everything. Privek would miss having such a useful tool at his disposal, though.

"We're getting back at the men who hurt you."

Bringing up his old pain never failed to distract Kanik. The kid went off on a spittle-flecked, incoherent rant about injustice and the marginalization of the Inuit people, and all the rest. Funny how out of all these freaks, the one who could plant suggestions in others' minds turned out to be the easiest to manipulate.

"The test subjects," Privek said loudly enough to interrupt, "will be waking up soon. You should go and make sure all of them are under your control. We'll need them to keep you safe."

Kanik paused in his pacing and nodded fervently. "Yes, yes, the railroad men are coming. They won't get me. No one will get me. We'll stop them and their pawns." He hurried out of the room, rubbing the old burn scars on his hand.

Privek smirked and turned his attention to the monitors just in time to watch the real show begin. With proper motivation, Sam and Greg did good work. Maybe he'd keep them around. Just because they were freaks didn't mean they couldn't be controlled for the long term. It depended on how this whole thing went down.

Chapter 13

Liam

Packed with people, the elevator dinged and the doors slid open. Liam stood away from the back wall, ready to pile out with everyone else, when he noticed Paul roll his shoulders uncomfortably. Liam checked Kaitlin. Her eyes slid closed and her lips parted.

Paul shrugged it off and stepped out of the elevator with the others. Owen carried Maisie in his arms and Matthew had Brian slung over his shoulder. Lisa helped Anita. Lily let Dan lean on her while Sebastian walked beside her, holding her hand. Jasmine sat in Liam's pocket again, trying not to take up space.

"Wait," Kaitlin said.

Fearing the worst, Liam reached out and missed Anita's arm.

"Come back." Kaitlin grabbed Lily's shirt.

Outside the doors, Liam heard a mechanical whirring. It sounded very different from Bobby's swarm. His foot moved back and he had a sinking feeling he knew what Kaitlin had seen.

The lobby erupted with gunfire.

"Get down!" The voice came from the lobby, and Liam thought it might be Riker. "We need cover!"

Liam grabbed Dan and hauled him back in, healing the fresh injury to his leg without thinking. How many bullet wounds would he heal today? At once, he hoped it would be a lot and only a few—the lobby had few places to hide and that sounded like a lot of weapons firing. Apparently, Privek had expected something like this.

The deafening roar of guns trampled over voices shouting in the lobby. Jasmine crawled out of Liam's pocket and raced out of the elevator as the doors slid shut, cutting off the clamor.

"What are we supposed to do?" Liam looked to Kaitlin, begging her to have an answer.

Her eyes darted around wildly. "I don't know. It's like with the assault on the farm. I only know what to do for me, not anyone else, and only at the last minute."

"What about Riker and his men?"

Kaitlin went pale. "I...I don't know," she whispered. "They were in the lobby last we knew."

Sebastian reached a little hand up to the buttons. "Mama, don't run away." He pushed the number one and watched the doors open again. The fire sprinklers hissed, soaking everything and putting a metallic tang in the air. They heard a gun sputter and stop. Lily grabbed her son, pulling him away from the doors and shielding him with her own body.

"I got it," Anita's voice called out, strained with pain. "One left."

The last gun clicked, still shooting without bullets. "Clear," Jasmine shouted from near the ceiling. "Is everybody okay?" A lot of silence answered her.

Liam pulled himself to his feet and poked his head cautiously out of the elevator. "Hold the doors open." Dan stuck a hand in the way and peered out with him. A haze of dust and smoke hung in the air. Bullet holes riddled the walls. Chunks of concrete or plaster, or whatever the walls and floor were made of, littered the floor. Everything was drenched. Brackish water formed small puddles bounded by debris.

Flinching away from the rain, Liam held up a hand to shield his eyes. He caught sight of Anita, huddled on herself and shivering behind a pillar, her power holding up a broken piece of bullet-ridden plexiglass from the security station as a shield.

Jasmine clung to something on the ceiling, dangling next to the empty machine gun still chattering away. She must have disconnected the ammunition somehow. As he watched, she shrank down to her squirrel shape again and raced across the wall to get down.

The front wall remained intact with only the glass door damaged. He saw Riker standing there, doing the same thing as him: checking the situation for safety and survivors. A wide smear of blood on the floor suggested all his men didn't get out in one piece. So long as they all lived, he could take care of them.

Thanks to the sprinklers, the air cleared quickly, and Liam made out a limp hand in the debris. "Can someone shut off the water?" He hopped and hurried to that hand, hoping he'd find it attached to an arm.

"I can only affect people," Dan grunted from close behind him. "Anita, did you get hurt?"

From what he'd seen of the Hill footage, he never would have guessed Dan would show concern for anyone else. But he offered Anita a hand up and looked her over. The Hispanic girl took his help, letting out a squeak as she tried to put weight on her foot. Distracted from his other goal, Liam leaned over and took her other hand. Another bullet wound added insult to all the injury his pants had suffered already. The pain made him grit his teeth as it flashed in his leg and rapidly slipped away.

Riker, Hegi, and Platt reached the other people first and shifted the debris off them. "Liam," Riker called out, his tone sharp enough to cut through shock, "what can you do about dead?"

"Nothing." Liam took a deep breath and forced himself to go find out who Riker had found, knowing he only asked because he found a body. What he wouldn't give for an umbrella right now.

"Day-umn." Dan's comment covered the situation. Paul was dead, his body riddled with bloody holes. Alongside him, four more: Lisa, Maisie, Brian, Owen. It looked like they'd been used a thousand times as targets in a shooting gallery. The guns broadsided them, because Brian should have been able to shield them, and Maisie should have been able to get them out of there.

"Wait, where's Matt?" Dan looked around, then he pointed at a hole in the wall, big enough for a person to get through. "Never mind. We don't want to find him right now. He's got no control as a wolf."

"Liam, quick," Platt said, holding two fingers to Maisie's neck, "this one is alive." Riker gave up on Owen and crab hopped to grab Maisie's hand to shove it at Liam. Debris drunkenly flopped off of her, probably Anita's doing.

In a daze, Liam took it, then he collapsed to the floor, overwhelmed by all the damage done to her body. Bullet wounds and cracked ribs and internal bleeding all warred for his attention, and he let out a gurgling scream as it washed over him. Something else kept her unconscious, but she'd be fine.

"What do we do now, Sarge? Guns popping out of the ceiling wasn't anything we expected." Platt picked Maisie up.

Riker pushed Paul's glassy, staring eyes shut and scowled. "Outside. Liam, take care of Hansen. He'll live, but we could use him at one hundred percent."

"Lisa's pregnant." Kaitlin shook, hugging herself. "I didn't see this coming. Why didn't I see this coming?"

"You're not per—" Riker cut himself off, and he, Platt, and Hegi all cocked their heads to the side and listened to something. "Change of plan."

The front door swung open. Carter helped Hansen, cradling his arm and limping, hurry inside. "There's four of them."

"Elevator, now!" Riker barked.

Everyone else hurried that way. Liam stood there, staring stupidly at Paul's corpse. The telepath had risked everything because Liam asked him to. Consumed by his need to find Elena, he begged and cajoled until Paul relented and helped him wake up Bobby. His death was Liam's fault. Elena was safe and Paul was dead.

Someone shouted his name, maybe more than once. It made him look up. Three women he'd only previously seen pictures of filed in through the door, accompanied by Raymond. He thought the thin, waifish Asian wearing blue leggings with white polka dots and a matching blue top might be Ai. The second, a blonde with curves in black pants and a red blouse and boots could either be Hannah or Violet.

As for the third, they only had two black women among them that he knew of, and Dianna's dead body still lay outside. That made this one, with her hair swept up in an elegant bun that clashed with her plain shirt and jeans, Tiana. Ray looked like he usually did: a burly black man in military camouflage pants and a dingy white tank top, holding a large silvery shield.

It took him a long second to register the strange, futuristic guns they each carried. By then, the foursome had those weapons raised. Each showed him cold indifference, a willingness to cut him down where he stood and be unmoved by it.

Something took control of his body and made him run, ducking down and hopping around to be harder to target.

The guns threw pulses of sickly greenish light across the lobby to slam into the already broken surfaces. He heard sizzling where they hit, the light either cooking or eating the surfaces it struck. Liam's mouth went dry as he considered what that would do to flesh. Where did they get guns like that? His body ducked into the elevator and the doors slid shut behind him.

"Jesus Fucking Christ with a biscuit," Dan spat. "Run next time, ya idjit."

Riker grabbed Liam's arm and smacked it onto Hegi's, causing his healing gift to activate and take the soldier's pain as the elevator trundled upward. "They might have been there to herd us, I'm not sure. Rundown of superpowers present?"

Sebastian, the cute little boy holding Lily's hand, pointed at each person and recited all their abilities as if he had the list memorized somehow. "Healing, precog, telekinesis, body control, weapon creation, portal-based teleportation, squirrel shapeshifter. Uncle Matty is a werewolf."

Everyone stared at him except Jasmine, who sat in Kaitlin's hand as a squirrel. Liam didn't blame her for not wanting to be in his pocket anymore.

"Right." Riker recovered from the surprise well before Liam did. "Thanks. What kind of weapons?"

Lily she sighed as she pulled her son into a bewildered hug. "So far, I haven't tried a lot. I can make functioning bullets of any kind you show me, bricks, blades, hand tools, and inflexible sheets. None of it lasts more than an hour."

Riker nodded and pulled the clip out of his rifle. Popping one bullet off, he handed it to her. "We may need more of these before we get out of here. Anybody get an empty spare clip, give it to her so she can fill it up. What's wrong with the teleporting girl here?" He slammed the clip home and checked his pistol. His men followed suit, checking their weapons too.

Dan shrugged. "Jayce shot her with that drug stuff. She was on the wrong team. She'll be out for hours."

"She's not a threat to them, then, so she's low priority if we need to bug out. What button did you push?"

Platt shrugged. "I didn't."

Sebastian beamed up at him. "I pushed the six!"

CHAPTER 14

BOBBY

"The elevator just went past. I heard it."

Bobby nodded. He shouldn't have called back all his dragons. The situation go out of control so much and so fast that he thought he needed all hands...er, *claws* on deck. Now he had no idea what else might be going on with Riker and Kaitlin and the rest. That needed to change. "I'm gonna scout ahead and go see who's in the elevator and what's up. Stick together and don't do nothing stupid."

"That's your job." Stephen finally sounded like himself again.

"Yeah." He blew into the swarm and left a few behind. Most of the dragons poured down the hallways of the second floor, searching through the place. A handful went to find a way to wriggle into the elevator. Another handful went down to check the lobby. Since they hadn't gone past the second floor yet, the dragons heading for the lobby reached their destination first.

They streaked out into a war zone.

Bobby threw himself into one of those dragons, stunned by what he found. Tiana, Ai, Violet, and a man he didn't know picked their way through, holding weird looking guns. Violet stooped to check the bodies.

"These are dead. Leave them."

Tiana peered into the giant hole in the wall. "Should we check this way?"

"Nah," the black man said with a shake of his head, "our job was just to get them to take the elevator. Mission accomplished."

"I'm going up the stairs to make sure they get a proper greeting." Ai blurred as she ran to the stairs.

"Andrew!" Bobby had enough dragons near the Creole to at least form a kind of mouth. It was weird and freakish. He chose not to think about it in favor of grabbing a chance to get Ai. "Stairs!"

Fortunately, Andrew hadn't gone anywhere yet and decided not to be disturbed by what he saw of Bobby. He tossed the door open and flung himself through it, just in time to collide with Ai as she sped up the stairs at a hundred miles an hour. They tumbled together in a squawking heap, her gun clattering to the floor and shooting off a pulse that singed Andrew's arm. He groaned. He also slapped a hand on Ai's arm and squeezed so she couldn't get away.

"Oh, my head." Ai groaned. "What did I just hit?"

"Me. And the floor. What're you in such a hurry for, anyway?" Andrew let her go and they each leaned against the other and the wall to get to their feet.

"I was..." She frowned and shook her head. "Why did I even care about that?" Her eyes went wide and her mouth fell open. "Oh, Andrew, Lisa is dead! And Owen. Down in the lobby, with some of the others I don't know. I tried to shoot one of us too! Oh my gosh, why did I do that?"

"Easy, easy." Andrew hugged her. "They're using some kind of mind control. I'm the antidote."

Bobby wanted to hear everything she had to say, just not right now. He sent his dragons back to their search and threw himself into one racing to the top floor. They streaked out into a hallway near the elevators, where he saw Andrea pacing impatiently. The dragons crawled across the ceiling, trying to go unnoticed. Though she couldn't disintegrate people, that wouldn't stop her from targeting the elevator.

He watched in horror as panels in the ceiling slid down to reveal guns. The elevator dinged to announce its arrival before he could come up with a plan. Bobby dove inside it the moment the doors opened with the rest of this small group. Five dragons pushed on the second floor button frantically as bullets flew through the air. Fortunately, everyone had already ducked down—probably Kaitlin's doing.

The doors slid shut, cutting off the gunfire. The first two hits made small dimples in the metal doors. The next two thumped in farther, somehow meeting less resistance. Bobby could see how this was going to go and threw himself back downstairs, calling his dragons together and re-forming most of himself near Jayce. "Elevator! It's about to fall."

Jayce opened his mouth, then shut it and sprinted for the elevator, with Bobby right behind and calling out for Stephen. The three men cranked the doors open and looked up.

"I'll slow it down." Stephen jumped into the shaft and flew up while Bobby helped Jayce brace himself so he could stop the falling car and hold it.

How were they going to get Andrea to Andrew? It sure wouldn't happen with them all standing around waiting for disasters. "Keep everyone together," he told Andrew, pointing at him to make sure he knew that was his job. Before he could respond, Bobby burst back into the swarm and streamed up to the top floor.

The swarm poured out through the same vent as before and streaked toward Andrea, now standing at the gaping hole where the elevator doors should be, peering down the shaft. He would never get a better chance. The swarm shoved her, hard, and watched her fall. Someone down there would catch her. They had to. She screamed up enough of a storm that they wouldn't be able to ignore her.

In that moment, watching her swallowed up by the darkness, hearing her terror, he knew what they had to do. The swarm dove after her and noticed she stopped screaming with a sound of confusion. Anita caught her. Dragons flew around her and out through the gap as Riker and his men climbed down and helped everyone else.

"Andrew, take care of Andrea soon as you can." Bobby re-formed again, feeling like he kept going in circles. He'd had about enough of that. "Lizzie, you remember how I said not to blow up the building?"

"Yes." Lizzie pouted at him with a sullen nod.

"Forget it. Set the whole damned thing on fire." He watched her face light up with glee.

"Bobby," Andrew said as he hurried to the elevator, "we're kind of *in* the building right now."

"Yeah. Not for long. Blow out a window, and we're getting outta here." Pointing down a hallway, he stayed put while she ran off. "Time to get outta here. Jayce, Stephen, and Anita're gonna ferry whoever they gotta. You see anybody what needs to be helped out, you help 'em out, but get 'em straight to Andrew. We ain't playing this maze of death crap, and we're getting our people back."

He picked Sebastian up, who hugged him around his neck. "You wanna take a ride with the dragons?"

"Is Mama coming?"

"I'll be right behind you," Lily said, smiling at them both.

Lizzie shouted, "Fire in the hole!" She sounded positively rapturous. An explosion rocked the building.

"That's my girl," Dan smirked, the last one out of the elevator. The second he got clear, Stephen and Jayce let the car go. Everyone hurried to find Lizzie. She hadn't gone far, and the size of the gaping hole in the side of the building surprised Bobby. The pile of rubble strewn across the ground below it attested to how much force she put into the fireball that caused it. He could see chunks of masonry at least fifty feet away.

As soon as she saw Dan round the corner, Lizzie ran and jumped into his arms, planting a kiss on his lips as he spun her around. Bobby ignored them in favor of peering out through the hole. He saw a small horde of animals converging right where they'd land if they jumped out from here. Tiana must be nearby, which meant— Something green and painful tagged him in the shoulder. Sebastian, protected by the wall, was fine.

Whatever that gun shot, it made his entire shoulder burn. Dragons all around the injury popped off, some of them dissolving. "Stay back! Andrea, can you get that thing? It's Violet, so look up."

Andrea, still near Andrew, was about to move closer when Violet swooped right up and started spraying the area with that weird green stuff. Bobby's arm came back together and he threw a punch at her face. It probably hurt him more than her, but it distracted her long enough for Andrea to make her gun disintegrate into a fine layer of dust. Violet squealed and flew away.

"I'll get her," Stephen growled, a burning streak on his face healing over. He ran for the opening and jumped into the air behind her, chasing after her. Stephen and Jayce seemed to have taken the brunt of the burst she fired in, and Liam healed Jayce.

Bobby peered out again and spotted Tiana. "I ain't keen to get chomped to death by rats and cats. Anybody got any ideas?"

A squirrel zoomed up and changed into Jasmine lying on the floor, peering out. "I can help!" She screwed her eyes shut and pressed her lips together.

Liam blinked and stared at her. "Do we want to know what she's doing?"

"Probably not," Jayce said with a smirk.

Kaitlin cleared her throat. "Bobby, if we set the building on fire, there are some people who'll die in here."

Of course there were. Nothing about this could be easy. No, that just wouldn't be right. Bobby sighed and set Sebastian down. "You know where they are and what's guarding them?"

"Fourth floor, four of our people, no guards. Just locked doors."

"Alright. I got that. Stay with your Momma," he told Sebastian.

The boy nodded gravely. "Come back."

He ruffled the kid's hair affectionately and gave Lily a sheepish grin. "That's the one thing I seem to be pretty good at." The sight of her grinning at him warmed him to his toes as he blew into the swarm again and streamed up to get to the fourth floor. Somehow, he knew it wouldn't be as simple as Kaitlin said, so he took the time to fly through the fourth floor, looking all around for anything that might be amiss.

There were no hidden guns or trapdoors, no people, nothing. He did find cameras scattered around, and smashed all of them. That done, he set to the task of breaking the four doors open to find Greg's boyfriend Albert, Lisa's husband Clive, Jasmine's fiancee Will, and, strangely, Christopher the empath. Chris had been either drugged or controlled, he figured.

Once he'd opened all the doors, Bobby re-formed in the middle of them. "Time to go, guys. They're trying to—" Chris and Albert flung their arms around him and hugged him tightly. Clive and Will gave him strained, anxious smiles.

"I don't care how uncomfortable this makes you, Bobby," Christopher said with a teary warble in his voice. "I'm really happy to see you."

"Um, yeah, look," Bobby squirmed, "I'm glad you're free and stuff, but we gotta get outta here."

"Where's Greg?" Albert let go first. "Is he okay?"

"I don't know. Stairs are this way." He avoided looking at Clive while herding them. "Jasmine's okay, she's helping us. Ain't seen Greg yet."

"What about Lisa?"

Bobby scratched his cheek and wished he had better news. More, he wished he knew Clive better so he could break it to him in the easiest way possible. So many people lived at the farm and he'd spent so little time there that he hadn't really met everyone yet. He opened his mouth to say something, not sure what it would turn out to be.

"You're not getting out." Although well timed, Bobby curled his lip at this distraction. Sam and Greg stood side-by-side, blocking the hallway. Sam had her arms crossed over her chest, showing a completely uncharacteristic amount of confidence. Though she had no weapons Bobby could see, he figured she meant to use his dragons. Greg, on the other hand, had adopted a genuine mad scientist look with red tinted goggles, a lab coat, work gloves, and a really big futuristic gun held in both hands.

Bobby put up his hands in surrender. "These guys was just bait for the rest of us. I know it and so do you. Let them go."

"Greg? What are you doing?" Albert pushed past Bobby to stand in front of him. "Did you make...a gun?"

Greg's face contorted in confusion. "Two different kinds," he said.

"But...you refused when those guys from the Pentagon came. Remember? Last year, two men came and tried to recruit you, to work on the next generation of weapons. You said no, that you'd never make a weapon. That was a perversion of science, that's what you told them."

"This is all very nice," Sam said, "but you're still not going anywhere. Get into that room, all of you in the one." She shooed all of them with both lanky arms. No one moved.

"Greg, this isn't you, it's not who you are! Why are you doing this?" Albert stood there defiantly, his hands held out in invitation.

Sam's eyes narrowed and Bobby had some suspicions about what she might try. He took a swift step around Albert and punched her in the face, hating himself for hitting a girl. Again. She stumbled back to hit the wall and Bobby followed her, vaguely registering that Albert grabbed at the gun, and Clive and Will helped him overwhelm the super-geek. Chris stepped aside with his hands held up, useless and panicky. Sam pulled something out of her pocket, and Bobby didn't realize he needed to dodge it until she jammed it into his gut and jolted him with electricity.

He broke apart into the swarm, losing a few more dragons to everything Privek set up in this stupid building. That must have been what Sam wanted, because he immediately found himself fighting for control of his dragons. He wanted them to get Sam to drop the taser and keep her busy so she couldn't interfere with the others. They all wanted to fly off into that room and stay there. Neither happened. Instead, they buzzed around in the air, doing nothing but taking up space.

"Don't hit him," Albert wailed as Clive slugged Greg across the chin. Greg fell to the floor, stunned by the blow, and Albert followed him down, protecting his head.

Clive grunted and shook his hand out. "Do something, Chris!"

"Like what?" Chris wrung his hands together and kept his eyes screwed shut against all the violence.

Bobby wanted to grab him and slap him. Sam wouldn't let him re-form. At least they refused to do what she told them to. That was something.

"You do emotions, don't you?" Will grabbed Chris's chin and turned his face to look at Sam through the swarm. "Open your eyes and make her...I don't know! Scared or something. Distract her. She's obviously doing something to Bobby."

Chris breathed fast and shallow, opening one eye tentatively and wincing away from the whole episode. "I've never done that before!"

Clive picked up Greg's gun. "Try, dammit! She wants to kill us all."

Will squeezed Chris's shoulder. "Come on, Chris, you can do this. We need you to do this."

Gulping audibly, Chris nodded and stared at Sam so hard Bobby thought his head might explode. She shrieked and scuttled away. Bobby regained control of his swarm and they re-formed fast enough for him to chase her down and grab her. At least he didn't have to hit her anymore. "Good job and keep it up Chris. We gotta get 'em both down to Andrew, he'll fix it so they're themselves again. Don't leave that weapon here."

Clive stopped fiddling with the gun, keeping a firm grip on it. "She's dead, isn't she? That's why you won't answer."

Unable to look at him and say it, Bobby hauled Sam toward a window on the side of the building where the others should be. "I'm sorry, man. It happened in the lobby." Considering what the dragons saw down there, he figured Sam and Greg might be responsible. He had no intention of saying so. Not when it wasn't really their fault. "Privek and Kanik done it." How he wished he could blame those two for everything.

Clive pressed his lips thin and nodded, then pushed Chris to get him moving. Will helped Albert pick up the still-stunned Greg and carry him. At the window Bobby found, he grabbed a lamp and smashed it into the glass, shattering both. He stuck his head out to see a massive pile of squirrels converged at the base of the building with almost everyone else in the center of it. Jayce stood under Andrew, ready to catch him if he fell while climbing a rope to get down to the ground.

"I got six more up here," he shouted down.

Stephen shot upward and gave Bobby a smirk. "It's possible you may never realize how much I appreciate you picking the shady side of the building for our escape path."

Bobby chuckled as he wrangled Sam through the window and into Stephen's hands. "Hey, man, Head Cowboy takes care of the herd. Make sure to get Andrew on Sam and Greg. They done tried to kill us. Have him hit everyone else too, just to be on the safe side."

"Aye, Cap'n. I can carry two at once." They pushed Greg through and Stephen carried both down, then returned for the rest. Bobby's swarm flew down with him the last time, and he got to see Jasmine jump up and send squirrels flying as she ran for Will and flung herself at him. Thanks to Liam, Greg and Albert got to be reunited, and Sam collapsed into a heap of sobbing as soon as Andrew touched her. Matthew lay in the grass, off to the side with no squirrels near him.

All of that mattered, just not right now. Bobby had a feeling he'd come to hate the word "prioritize." It made him feel like a dick to interrupt everyone while they reunited and took stock and watched Lizzie gleefully blow up the building. He had to do it anyway.

Lily, he noticed, glanced at him, gave him a tight-lipped smile, then put her arm around Clive's shoulders. He hoped she'd done that because she could tell he had something to say and needed to get it out sooner rather than later. Striding to the center of the group, he cleared his throat and found almost everyone staring at him as a result.

"Folks, we can all hear the sirens a'coming. Some of us're still missing, and we still gotta get to Adelphi and free all them people, but there's another thing we gotta do first. Today, we gotta let folks know we're here and we ain't gonna let ourselves be locked up, nor experimented on, nor treated like we ain't worth the same as humans. If'n you don't want to be public, get scarce. I got lots to say, and it's gonna be heard, and that's that, but ain't nobody else gotta be seen or known about if'n you ain't comfortable with it. No shame neither way."

Stephen stepped forward first. "I'm in, for all of it." He flashed his fangs in a grin. "I can hardly wait to have teenage girls climbing all over each other to let me suck their blood."

Jayce nodded and so did a few others. As expected, Liam wasn't interested, and he didn't hold it against the healer. When they were sorted out, Riker and his men stayed, along with Jayce, Stephen, Lizzie, Dan, Ray, and Matthew. None of the rest wanted to be seen right now. Several said they needed time to think about it rather than outright refusing.

Lily waved to him as she carted Sebastian off, pointing to the boy as the reason she wouldn't stay, and Bobby nodded. He understood. He also sent a dragon with them so they'd be able to find each other later. By the time the fire department showed up, all of them managed to get at least a few blocks away and the building had become an inferno.

Ignored by the firefighters, the twelve of them stood there, watching it from the curb. "Riker, you guys sure you want to have your faces flashed on TV?"

Riker shrugged. "If we're going to be court-martialed and charged with treason anyway, we might as well try to control the media coverage a little."

"My mom is going to kill me for this," Hegi said with a sigh.

Bobby snorted. "You always got a place with us, even if I gotta smack heads together to make sure of it." He turned, because the first news van screeched to a halt mere yards away from them. "Man, they musta been in the neighborhood already."

Stephen sneered. "Vultures."

"Says the vampire." Jayce chuckled.

"Excuse me!" An attractive woman in a skirt suit jumped out of the van and looked right at them. "Did you see what happened? Would you be willing to talk about it on camera, live?"

Bobby smiled warmly. "Sure thing, ma'am. I done saw the whole thing, and I'd be right happy to tell the whole world all about it."

The reporter's eyes lit up with a jackpot smile and she beckoned frantically for her cameraman to get set up.

CHAPTER 15

LIAM

Liam clicked the radio on in his car. Since he had his keys and the car still sat in the parking lot, he figured he might as well get it while he could. The Roadster had only one passenger seat, and he brought Clive with the rather large gun he refused to let go of. A few others took their own cars too, he noticed, and everyone who wanted to got away from the site without a problem. Chelsea, as it turned out, regenerated slowly. Once Liam explained things to her, she flew away.

He glanced at Clive, wondering if he'd been stupid to take the only other person suffering an acute loss. They had something in common right now, so he figured they ought to stick together. Granted, Elena hadn't been the one he lost there, so he had no idea how to relate to Clive on that level. Paul, though, had been his friend, a *real* friend. All his life, people had valued him for his parents' money, or his ability to get them out of trouble or do them favors, or his looks. Paul had asked for nothing and gave everything.

"...According to eyewitnesses," the radio voice told them, "part of the building exploded out a minute or two before the entire structure was engulfed in flames. People were seen jumping out from the second floor, and the area is now swarmed with first responders. Several unconfirmed reports— Hold on, I'm just being handed additional information about this, which is kind of a surprise. Usually with something like this, it's just a standard...sort...oh my God." The radio personality left two seconds of dead air, then a commercial started.

Clive reached over and snapped the radio off. "Bobby's really spilling it all."

"He said he would. If there's one thing I've learned about Bobby over the past few days, it's that he keeps his word." Liam let the car go quiet again. The electric engine made no noise, leaving them floating down the road in a tense, heavy bubble of silence. After a long pause, he asked, "Can I take you anywhere in particular?"

Clive stared down at the weapon on his lap, one hand idly patting it. "Adelphi."

Liam regretted asking the question. "I was thinking more of a bar or something."

"Why? Do you think getting drunk will bring her back?"

"No. It's just what I could use after all of that. I've never healed so many people at once and been so utterly useless at the same time. I couldn't save your wife, and for that, I'm sorry."

Clive turned to stare out the window. "I want Privek to...to hurt."

"I can relate to that." It was a bad idea, but he got onto the highway that would take them on as much of a roundabout route to Adelphi as he thought he could manage without Clive getting suspicious. Privek probably had that place set up with even more defenses. They'd need backup. Of course, Bobby planned to assault it. They just needed to wait until he got there. A handful of them would probably be able to trash the place in minutes. He remembered the footage from Hill. That's what happened when a small group of them worked together. This would be a bigger group.

The scenery flashed by. Liam expected Clive to break down and cry at some point. He didn't. The man struck him as the mild-mannered type, with a boring job he did to pay the bills rather than out of love for it. The way he kept patting the weird gun seemed out of place and disturbing.

Liam's phone rang as he rolled to a stop for a traffic light at the end of the off-ramp in Adelphi. Glancing at it, he didn't recognize the number. Once, he would have assumed it unimportant and ignored it. Now, he sighed and answered it, expecting it to shatter his expectations or world yet again. "Hello?"

"Hi, you don't know me. My name is Mike." He spoke in a hushed voice. "I work at White Sands Missile Range, on the Maze Beset Space-Time Anomaly project. I know Sam, and Bobby Mitchell gave me your phone number. He asked me to call you if I wanted to help all of you. This has been my first real chance to do that, and I don't have long. They just successfully sent a penny through the wormhole and it didn't collapse. When they shut it down and opened it back up, they got the penny back, along with some other stuff. A little scoop of dirt and plants, maybe some small animals or insects."

Liam's heart sped into overdrive. They'd done it. They'd created a wormhole to another world. An insistent horn from the car behind him startled him back into awareness of his surroundings. He flipped off the guy behind him and got the car moving. "Um, okay. Thanks for letting me know. Do you think they're going to keep trying today, or be sidetracked by studying the dirt?"

"Best guess, they're going to poke at it for a few hours, then go back to tweaking the machine and try it again as soon as possible."

"Good to know. I don't suppose there's anything you can do to maybe slow them down a little? Like, a day or two, I mean. Not grand sabotage or anything."

"Oh. I don't know. I'm already taking a pretty big risk by calling you. Can you tell me something? How's Sam? Bobby said she was in some kind of jail."

"She's okay." Liam hated lying to strangers. He assuaged his guilt with the knowledge that he'd only lied in one sense—physically, she was okay. Kanik's gift was all the more horrific for letting his victims remember everything they'd done under his influence. She'd done quite a bit. "We got her out. She's free. You might want to give her a little time to recover from what happened."

"Sure, yeah. That's cool. I'll just email her and let her know I'm here if she wants to talk or anything. Thanks. Oh, crap, I gotta go. I'll do whatever I can here." Mike hung up.

They reached the facility. Liam stopped the car on the street about ten yards from the driveway, acutely aware he had no real way in on his own. "We can wait here for the others. With them—" He stopped because Clive tossed the door open and hopped out. Liam hit the button to shut the car off and stepped out too.

Clive pointed the gun at the guard shack and fired. Liam expected a laser beam or some sort of projectile. Instead, the ground trembled and some force churned up and tossed a wide cone of asphalt, dirt, concrete, grass sod, and everything else in front of Clive. The gun pitched upward in his hands from the recoil. Some kind of shockwave flung the debris at the guard post, crashing into it and ripping it apart.

Liam cringed away and screwed his eyes shut, not wanting to see what happened to the soldier inside. That guy had been doing his job a few days ago, and Liam had blustered their way past him. Now, he probably had been battered to death by one man's grief.

Looking down at the gun, Clive fiddled with the levers and fired it again. This time, he held it steady. He'd made the cone more precise: narrow, focused, and longer.

"Clive! Stop, you're going to kill people." Liam hurried around his car to find the gun pointed at him. "What are you doing? I'm on your side."

Now, when Clive had found the perfect tool to vent his rage, tears streamed down his face. "Leave me alone. You sit in your fancy car and wait for the others. I'm going to take care of this, once and for all."

Liam raised his hands in surrender and tried to imagine how the other man felt, tried to stand in his shoes. "This isn't the way, Clive. If you go in there by yourself, you're going to get killed." The moment he said the words, he realized that was the plan. "At least try not to hurt anyone else, Clive. They're just doing their job. Most of them don't even know what's going on here. It's a research facility, not an evil mastermind lair." How long would it be before the others showed up? He had no idea how long he could keep Clive from rampaging by talking to him.

"Ignorance is no excuse!" Clive shot the gun at the ground between himself and Liam, then turned and ran for the gate.

Pure force flung Liam to the ground. He rolled to his hands and knees, coughing and spitting and blinking. Something plastic scraping on the asphalt reminded him that he'd managed to keep his phone in his hand. There had to be someone he could call that would actually be helpful somehow. Paul was dead. Dianna and Brian were dead. Ray had a phone. Andrew had freed him and those three women, so he'd be safe. He'd stayed with Bobby, so he'd also be useful.

"Answer, Ray, pick up. Pick up, c'mon, pick up." When he really needed them, where were they? Ray picked up on the third ring. "Ray, listen to me. I need help at the Adelphi facility. Whoever can get here fast. No time to explain, just grab whoever can fly and get them here, now." He hung up without giving the other man a chance to ask questions and hurried over to the guard post.

As he checked the guard, who'd barely survived the assault, he surveyed the area and caught sight of dust clouds leading deeper into the base. Clive had a plan, apparently, and it included causing a lot of damage. Liam had no way to stop him.

Someone bigger, faster, or stronger would have to stop this. Meanwhile, he'd slog along in Clive's wake and heal anyone left alive.

His superpower sucked.

Chapter 16

Bobby

"You can stand there and try to deny it, but we ain't special effects, and we ain't going away." After only ten minutes of media circus attention, Bobby wanted to smash a camera or shove a microphone someplace unpleasant. A sea of both devices had been shoved at him, their owners jostling and shouting at him to be recognized and have their special question answered. Past them, a fleet of vans with TV station logos blocked them all in.

They'd put on a show already, and kept it up. His left arm being dragons meant every single cameraman had a chance to get a close-up of one. Lizzie let fire dance across her hand and arm and body over and over again. Jayce changed from steel to cloth to concrete and back again and again. Ray held up his shield and changed its size, color, and shape. Stephen lounged in the air, not touching the ground.

With all of that, every reporter asked the same stupid questions.

Someone's phone buzzed behind him, and he turned to see Ray holding his out, looking to Bobby in question. Bobby nodded. For all he knew, it could be important.

"Are you the leader of all of these 'superheroes'?"

Someone had already asked that question. He answered it again anyway. "I'm the group spokesdragon." The loose dragons trilled in glee.
While an amused chuckle ran through the small crowd, Ray touched his
shoulder.

"Everyone who can fly needs to get to—" Ray looked up at the cameras and microphones. "The other A site. One's there already, and there's a
problem."

Not sure what to make of that, Bobby nodded and turned back to
the cameras. "Sorry, folks, we got more work to do. Like I said, some of
us're still prisoners, and we gotta do what we gotta do to be free. We'll be
available for questions again soon." Turning away from the reporters, he
smirked and waggled his eyebrows at Lizzie and Dan. "Keep 'em off our
back for a minute. Don't hurt nobody." The rest, he waved to follow him.

Lizzie squealed with delight and Dan wrapped an arm around her
waist. The pair of them would be enough to tie up those reporters for a few
minutes. "It's Adelphi, everybody get there fast as you can. Stephen, take
Jayce and get there already. Riker, you guys drive the rest. Ray, if'n you got
phone numbers, use 'em. I'll round folks up and be there soon as I can."

Head Cowboy watched in satisfaction as everyone leaped into action
without arguing. They'd decided to accept that he had a level head and
wouldn't knowingly lead them into disaster. Even better, no one questioned his suggestions—he delicately avoided admitting to himself that the
word "orders" fit better—for how to get things done.

He let his dragons peel off for pure showmanship and scattered the
swarm. It was a real shame he couldn't spare the time to ride over with Lily.
They had things to talk about.

Chapter 17

Liam

Liam coughed on the thick haze of dust and dirt covering the base as he knelt beside a downed soldier and checked his pulse. This one had a concussion that Liam healed for him. The next one had no life-threatening injuries and already had rolled to his hands and knees. They'd both be fine. He left them without a word as soon as his splitting headache faded.

Clive still ran rampant, smashing and chewing up walls and vehicles with that weird gun. At odd moments, Liam caught his voice screaming Privek's name in challenge. Then he'd destroy something else and fill the air with more dust, more dirt, and more noise. Eventually, he'd have to stop on his own, too torn up and frustrated to do anything but collapse and weep for his wife. They could all hope so, anyway.

"Liam, what's going on?"

Looking up to find the source, Liam had to blink several times to understand what he saw. Cant—Stephen, the vampire—dropped down out of the sky, carrying another person and with some kind of strange, thick cloth thing covering his head and hands. They landed in the shade of a partially destroyed wall. Stephen set the man aside and pulled the cloth off. The weird cloth shimmered with silver and stood as a shiny, metal person.

He racked his brain for the other two men's names and came up blank. Too many names and faces too fast and in the midst of chaos and crisis left him unable to place both. Paul would've remembered them.

"It's Clive. He's...upset. He has that gun-thing." Waving his hand around, he hoped they didn't need any additional explanation. "So far, he hasn't killed anyone."

The silver one nodded grimly and ran off. Stephen grabbed the other guy before he could follow and took him by the shoulders. "I know you can control yourself while you're in wolf mode, Matthew. I know you can. Believe it. If I can keep my blood lust under control, you can tell your wolf to fuck himself. We don't want to actually hurt anyone, remember that. Hold onto that, brother."

Matthew nodded, took a deep breath, and curled his hands into fists. "I'm in charge. I run this body, not the wolf. I make the decisions."

Uncomfortable with overhearing the conversation, Liam turned away to give them the illusion of privacy. Matthew reminded him of Bobby asserting dominance over his dragons. How many of them had that kind of control problem? More than would admit it, probably.

His parents loved him and would do nearly anything for him, and the same for his sister. Elena held his heart so completely, he had no need to wriggle away from her. None of them offered the same thing that Stephen just promised to Matthew. They couldn't understand it. He couldn't explain it with words and hope for them to help in the ways he needed. Elena would try, but even she'd fall short.

This sense of family they shared, he realized, explained why Bobby fought for them all, why he was so hell-bent on sacrificing himself to save them all, why he willingly stuck his neck out and risked everything, even for the ones he hadn't met yet. If he chose to be honest with himself, recognizing that in Bobby had led Liam to give him the benefit of the doubt in the first place. He remembered calling Bobby "a dangerous man" an eon ago, and although he hadn't fully grasped it at the time, this was exactly what he meant.

Bending down to check on a man with blood staining his uniform, he caught movement out of the corner of his eye and ducked. The silver man sailed through the air and slammed into a wall hard enough to knock a hole through it. Clive must have shot him. That gun had a hell of a punch. He straightened to go check on the silver man when the guy stood up out of the debris and ran back to the fight, unaffected by the impact. Being silver apparently had advantages.

"What happened?" The man with a short length of steel rebar through his thigh groaned and tried to prop himself up on his elbows.

Liam held out a hand to get him to stop moving. If he could keep the soldier from seeing the true severity of his injury, the guy would never know. "Lie down, you took a knock to the head." He grabbed the rebar and yanked it out, doing his best to ignore the soldier's sharp, grunting scream, then put his hand on the leg and healed it. A brand new bloodstain spread on his pants while he clenched his jaws shut to endure the pain.

While he found himself looking off in a random direction, he noticed people stumbling out of one of the partially demolished buildings. They flinched away from the sunshine, moving in a shambling, uncoordinated blob. When he noticed that every last one of them held a sheet up to cover their bodies, his eyes flicked to the building. With a jolt, he recognized it. They'd found Elena in that one.

These people had been the ones on the gurneys.

These people each had a superpower.

These people had to be under Kanik's influence.

His phone chirped with a text. Tearing his eyes away from the sight, he checked the message. It made him want to laugh. Standing this close to a growing mob of potentially hostile people, he didn't dare.

CHAPTER 18

BOBBY

Thick haze drew the swarm from miles away. One regular guy with a funky gun sure did manage to wreck up a ruckus. A plume of dirt or smoke shot into the sky with several large things flying up then falling down again. Jayce, Stephen, and Matthew clearly hadn't been able to stop Clive yet, and they'd had a ten minute head start on him. Violet and Chelsea should arrive with their passengers soon.

Reaching the base, he dropped the swarm down lower to survey the situation. Soldiers moved around, clumping together and checking weapons. That complicated things. He'd been hoping to blow into the base with a distraction timed to provide cover for the evacuation. Of course, he'd been hoping to do this later, after they had a chance to breathe and sketch out a plan. Food would've been nice too.

Moving on, he came across a huge number of people walking around, none of them in uniform. Jayce flew into sight and hit a lamp post, breaking it in half. In the distance, Bobby made out Clive, back to a wall. His face twisted into rage-filled agony, he blasted the gun in every direction, showing off how little time it took to reset between blasts.

Bobby landed where Stephen lurked in the shadows and re-formed.

"What's going on, exactly?"

"Exactly? I can't get involved. I'll burn up. Matthew and Jayce are trying to talk sense to him, but he keeps shooting them for distance with that gun. They can't get close. Ai could probably take it from him, Dan could get him to put it down. I'm sure we'll have plenty of options when the others get here. He wants to kill Privek, so far as I can tell."

"He can get in line," Bobby growled.

"No kidding. I'd like to throw him off a building, personally. Then maybe catch him and do it again a couple of times before I *accidentally* forget to catch him once." Stephen sighed wistfully, and Bobby cleared his throat to get him back from revenge fantasyland. "Liam is off in the aftermath someplace, healing the people Clive hurt already. At this point, Clive's not really harming anyone, so there's no point in making a grand effort to stop him. Contained is good enough until we can get him without much risk."

Nodding his agreement, Bobby watched Jayce and Matthew run in at Clive together and each get tossed for distance before they got close enough to do anything. He opened his mouth to say something when gunfire erupted in the distance. "Heckbiscuits, they found someone to shoot." It could be Liam, so he blew back into the swarm and flew toward the sound.

He found chaos. That bunch of people he saw before had actually been wearing nothing but sheets. Some of them now wore nothing. They swarmed the armed soldiers. Bodies already littered the broken ground. None of this made any sense until he noticed one of the unarmed people had mottled green-brown scales instead of skin. Another glowed all over with red light. A third made sparks shoot from her fingers in a muted, more colorful copy of Lizzie's ability.

No need to break out the formerly homeless test subjects, because they'd escaped on their own. Their powers were all over the map and minor, like Sherrie's and Shane's. He needed to stop this fight. He had no idea how. His dragons couldn't stop this many people without killing them all. Time—he needed more time. With more time, more of his side would show up and could take control of this.

Landing and re-forming, he gave his best shot at some kind of command voice. "Fall back! There's too many of them." He thought it sounded fake and weak. The soldiers bugged out anyway. Either Head Cowboy did a better job than he guessed, or these guys were only too happy to be ordered out of this mess. He caught sight of Liam being stupid by running into the throng to reach the ones bleeding on the ground. Hands and feet and claws got in his way, punching and grabbing and kicking and shoving and stomping.

"Quit it," Bobby snarled. "He's trying to help." Thse nearest him turned to give him the same treatment. It gave him a good view of their faces. Every one had the same slack-jawed expression of empty-eyed, mindless determination. They reminded him of zombies, and he had no clue what to do about it. As the swarm, they couldn't hurt him. Liam, on the other hand, had curled up into a ball while they beat the crap out of him.

One dragon streaked off to get Stephen while the rest of the swarm did what it could to surround Liam and keep them off him. The zombies had to be under Kanik's influence, which meant they had no control over their actions. After all, Sherrie and Shane hadn't acted like this when they woke up. The mutation hadn't caused this.

Leaving a smoke trail behind himself, Stephen zoomed in, grabbed Liam without a word, and fled for the safety of shade. Bobby shifted his attention to trying to corral the zombies, but he'd come too late to the party for that. He watched helplessly as they ran in all directions, some shriek-ing, some yelling, all seemingly out for blood.

Violet and Chelsea arrived, carrying Lizzie and Dan, and landed on top of a nearby building. Why couldn't one of them have brought Andrew? Because they wouldn't be able to fly while carrying him, that's why. Even if Andrew was here, how would that help? It would take a while for him to reach all of these people. Bobby thought there had to be over a hundred of them, maybe as many as two hundred.

He went up to where the four of them stood and re-formed, offering a quick explanation of what he thought was going on. "Best I can think is we need to find Kanik and make him stop."

"That's great, Bobby," Violet said, her Alabama twang making him miss home right now, "but how do we find him?"

Bobby scratched his head and turned to watch zombies streak past, literally and figuratively. Quite a few hadn't bothered keeping a grip on their sheets. "I'm gonna go hunting. See if'n you can help Stephen find a coat or something, and go hang by the entrance to direct traffic when the others get here. Try to keep this contained in the base. If you can, stop any soldiers from killing anybody." His orders delivered, he burst into the swarm again and spread out, looking for any sign of the source of all this madness.

He saw Matthew in his werewolf form, watching Jayce's back with-out rampaging or attacking. Good for him for getting a grip on the wolf. Clive's gun lay on the ground. The poor guy had fallen to his knees, sob-bing and holding onto Jayce like a drowning man about to slip under.

Since he couldn't see Stephen and Liam, Bobby hoped they'd found a hole to hide from the sun and random zombies. Violet had gone off to the front gate with Lizzie. Two cars screeched to a halt, and the newcomers worked on setting up a blockade.

Privek. He found Privek. The man walked through a door as dragons buzzed past it. The person behind him could only be Kanik. Along with them, Hannah, Tony, Javier, and John left the building, following like lost puppies. He'd chosen a weird group to keep for himself. Hannah, he could understand. She could make a force field and had more organizational skills than Bobby could shake a barrel of biscuits at. The rest, though, he didn't get. Tony could turn himself into objects, Javier could climb walls, and John controlled plants. Against Matthew and Jayce, those guys had no chance.

Bobby called the swarm in while Privek swaggered through the zombies threatening Matthew, his entourage in tow. Landing next to Matthew, the dragons flew together until Bobby stood there, hands in his jean pockets, unafraid of whatever might happen next. Privek pulled out a gun, pointed it at Matthew, and fired. The werewolf could heal his injuries, so Bobby didn't even flinch as three shots went straight into Matthew's chest. He took a step back from the impacts and growled.

Bobby lifted an eyebrow. "That the best you got?"

Beside him, the werewolf threw his head back and roared. Whatever control Matthew had, it must have been tenuous, and getting shot broke it. Bobby saw Privek's mouth quirk into a smug smirk. He saw Kanik, the left half of his face covered with queer burn scars, dart forward with a mild limp and grab Matthew's furry arm. Bobby blew out into the swarm and went for Kanik. Take him out, and everybody would be free of his influence. In theory.

The second his dragons touched Kanik, he lost control of them. Kanik laughed maniacally. Bobby had no idea what to do. He still had control of his mind, but the dragons refused to do what he wanted. They launched off of Kanik and went for Jayce, and there Bobby could do nothing about it. He saw out of their eyes and felt the press of them without having the ability to control or direct them. This, here, now, became his new worst thing imaginable: his tiny machines of death under the control of a madman.

Jayce's eyes widened and he grabbed Clive and the gun, then took off running. At least he had enough sense to see what happened. He didn't, though, have enough speed to get ahead of the swarm. Dragons caught up with him in seconds and poured into his mouth, and into Clive's. Bobby's mind screamed out to stop them. They kept going, ripping Clive apart and clanging around inside Jayce's steel innards.

"You can't stop us, Bobby." Privek grinned, stepping up to pat Matthew on the arm. "No one can. Kanik, send the dragons to kill the rest of them. Leave the healer, he's useful. We'll control him this time, though, to avoid any more *incidents*."

A blast of air and dirt and concrete tossed them all back and off their feet. Dragons got tossed for distance, and Bobby's consciousness moved that way, staying in the center of the swarm. Jayce had the fancy future gun in his hands and fired it again. This time, a blue force field sprang into existence, sending all the debris flying around the group of six. Privek got to his feet and dusted himself off in the safety of Hannah's power. The rest of them followed suit.

Yeah, sure, easy fight. With just himself to worry about, Jayce took off running again. He'd have to figure something out, because Bobby couldn't imagine how anything would stop Privek now. Jayce and Stephen were probably the only ones he couldn't kill right now. As soon as the dragons formed back up, they would leave a sea of corpses in their wake.

Again.

CHAPTER 19

LIAM

"Stephen!" Liam turned to find the source of the urgent shout, only to see the shiny metal man charging straight for him and the vampire standing next to him. Stephen had found enough cloth to cover up, and they'd just stepped back out of the building they'd been sheltering in to survey the scene.

He'd never seen so much chaos. People ran all over the place, bouncing around in some demented game of human pinball. Liam clung to the wall, hoping no one noticed and attacked him.

"Bobby's under mind control," Shiny Metal Man called out as he kept running, carrying that big gun Clive brought. "Kanik has to touch you to take control. We need Andrew, can you find him and get him over there?" He stopped next to them and fired the weapon as he panted, tossing people around like ragdolls and kicking up dirt and small things that glinted in the sunlight. "You're faster than me."

"Understood, Jayce." Stephen nodded and flew away from them, toward the front entrance.

"Maybe I should just hide until this is all over," Liam suggested with a gulp.

"Time to grow a pair." Jayce grabbed the front of his shirt and dragged him deeper into the base.

Liam stumbled along behind him, unable to resist such a massive force of steel, and glared at his back. "What do you expect me to do? Heal them into submission?"

Jayce fired the gun again, and Liam noticed more glittery things being forced back. "Privek wants you. He thinks you'll be useful. That means the dragons aren't going to hurt either of us. You need to be up in this."

With more than one reason now to be apprehensive, Liam's eyes went wide and he gulped again. "Are those...*Bobby's dragons* you're targeting with the gun?"

"Yes. I'm slowing some of them down." He kept going, pushing the small clump of dragons back with repeated shots in their direction as they went.

Liam spotted Privek and his entourage as Jayce fired directly at them, knocking the whole group over. Before they had a chance to fully recover, he yanked Liam behind a wall, thumping him into it face first hard enough to make him grunt. They took cover.

His nose felt like it was running, so Liam swiped a hand under it only to have it come away with a small smear of blood. "I don't heal my own injuries."

"Huh. That must suck." Jayce's skin tone shimmered and changed to be the same as the wall, complete with texture. He leaned out only enough to see.

"Yes, thank you, it does."

Jayce leaned back and stared at the gun, his masonry brow furrowed. "I have an idea." The grin Jayce gave him as his expression cleared made

Liam want to get up and walk in some other direction. "Go out there and distract them. Don't let Kanik touch you. I'll circle around and come in from behind."

"I don't really like your ideas." Liam crossed his arms over his chest, perfectly aware of how petulant it made him look. He didn't care.

"You have a better one?"

If only he had a way to smack that look off Jayce's face. From the raised eyebrow to the mild amusement to the challenge, Liam hated Jayce a lot right now. He grunted. "Fine. Just hurry. I doubt I can keep him distracted for long before I become Kanik's new pet." He pointedly did not think about the very real possibility of that actually happening, or what it might be like.

Jayce nodded and jutted his chin out for Liam to get moving, then crept away. Liam stood up with his hands out in surrender. Within seconds, a small flock of dragons swarmed him, landing on his head, shoulders, and arms. It was like...having a bunch of large spiders crawling over him. He shivered at the comparison and brushed a few off.

The dragons chirped angrily at him. A few blew out little puffs of fire. "Okay, okay, I get it," he said, not having to feign a mild panic. "Don't hurt me, I'm ready to talk." He had to force his legs to take him in the direction the dragons obviously wanted him to go, and he noticed himself hyperventilating. Were those awful stuttering, chattering noises really coming from his own mouth? He gibbered in terror, and it was no act. He needed to focus, to think about Elena, safely tucked two thousand miles away from here.

Privek looked sharp in his dark suit. For once, instead of cool detachment, his mouth and jaw below his sunglasses had tightened into impatient annoyance. He held a pistol pointed at the ground. "Liam, how nice of you to stop by." He turned to Kanik. "Send the dragons to find Westbrook."

So much for being a distraction. "I'm sorry I lied to you." Nothing like an apology to break the ice.

Privek's face smoothed over to a cool neutral. "Are you a distraction, then? Kanik, take him. Everyone else, stay alert."

Liam had two choices: stand or run. A true coward at heart, he turned and fled. He managed to get only a few steps away before a blue field formed in front of his nose. Unable to avoid it, he slammed into it and bounced back. Hitting the ground hard with his hip, he groaned and wondered if he'd be able to pass that bruise on to someone else.

Kanik approached, staring intently at Liam and holding his hand out to grab him. In the distance, Liam saw Jayce bounce off a blue barrier.

"Are you a conductor?" Kanik's half-melted face filled Liam's vision.

The burns made Liam pity him, but the mad gleam in his eyes made Liam scramble away. Never mind scrapes and bruises, he needed to not be close to Kanik. Ever. "No. I'm a healer."

Kanik walked beside him, refusing to let him escape. "Can you heal my burns?" His eyes glittered with an alien sort of curiosity, as if he'd never encountered anything quite like Liam before and yearned to dissect him.

"Uh." After what he saw himself do for those soldiers a few weeks ago, he couldn't say for sure. "I, um, maybe? We'd probably have to cut off the affected areas."

Kanik's eyes slid shut and his whole body shivered with some kind of ecstasy for a few seconds. "You could make me whole again."

"I think so, yes." Liam hit debris big enough to stop his backward scuttling. He flinched back as Kanik lunged for him and stopped with his two hands poised an inch away from Liam's face, ready to press them onto his flesh.

"Hurry up," Privek groused.

Kanik's eyes darted all around, then settled on Liam again. "Would you heal me willingly?"

"Of course." Unable to keep himself from doing it, Liam stared at the too-close fingers and braced for the part where he lost control over his mind. "You're one of us."

Kanik's eyes narrowed. The one eye affected by the scarring puckered more than squinted. "Am I?"

Keep him talking.

Liam knew how to keep people talking. He'd once thrown so many words at his mother that she gave in and let him have the keys to the antique Jaguar for a date at the tender age of sixteen. He'd convinced a girl she'd been the one to dump him so they could stay friends and he could still crash her parties. He'd...talked Paul into helping him wake Bobby.

Thinking of Paul and Bobby gave him the angle he needed. One more thing to be grateful to them both for.

"We're brothers. You and me. We had the same mother. Privek is the outsider, the one we can't trust. He's using you, Kanik. He's using all of us."

CHAPTER 20

BOBBY

Bobby watched through the eyes of the dragons as they slipped through the zombie swarm, checking each one to make sure they continued to follow orders. The swarm reached the other side of the throng and his dragons saw everyone, his brothers and sisters. All of them came and they stood together, doing what they could to keep the zombies from escaping and wreaking havoc outside the fence.

His dragons arrayed themselves in a long line and surveyed the assembled superpowered people. He counted and came up short. There should be twenty-two now, plus one if that portal-teleporting girl woke up. He counted eighteen. Four of them had to be up to something. He hoped it turned out to be the right four.

Scanning the crowd, he ticked them off in his head. Stephen's absence stood out. He thought Andrew might also not be there. With luck, everyone understood Andrew's importance and worked to get him in a position to stop Kanik. Either that, or someone would have to kill the guy, and that someone wouldn't be Bobby.

The dragons surged forward, a long cloud of silvery motes winking in the sunshine. Violet figured it out first. She grabbed Andrea, who stood next to her, and flew away. Others turned to look. Chelsea flew off on her own. Heavy pieces of debris jumped out to form a barrier. Ice shot up from the ground. He saw the blurred form of Ai racing around another small group.

Kanik's dragons rushed the defenses. They clawed and burned and scraped at what got in their way. One group stopped in its tracks, probably because of Sam. With horror, he saw one squirm and struggle through a small gap and dive at Lily.

Bricks formed in both her hands, and she smashed them together, crushing the dragon mere inches from her face. Two more followed it through and she caught one before the other burned through her cheek and dove into her mouth, choking her.

If Bobby could've screamed, he would have. He pushed as hard as he could to jump into that dragon so he could stop it. As it wriggled down her throat, he found himself pulled into the dragon. Suddenly, he had a burning need to kill everyone with the icy blue eyes. All of them had to die. He'd been made for this job. He did it without hesitation.

CHAPTER 21

LIAM

Staring intently at Liam, Kanik stopped with his hands still hovering an inch away. "He promised to help me."

"He promised to help me too. But it was a lie." Liam took a deep breath, sure this had to be at least as bad as having a gun pointed at his head. His heart pounded so hard in his chest that he could barely think. "Kanik, he's using you. Look into my eyes and you'll know I'm not lying."

Kanik's eyes bounced back and forth between Liam's. "I just want myself back." He lowered his hands.

"That's what we all want too. Can you stop everyone from fighting and all that? We don't want to hurt anyone, none of us do."

Kanik's face fell, and he rocked back onto his heels. Both men jumped, startled by gunshots. Someone fell onto Kanik, and shoved him into Liam. He gasped, suddenly struck with an overwhelming sensation of drowning. Only a second later, it abruptly cut off.

"You can't kill me with a gun, asshole." The vampire's voice held so much angry darkness, it sounded like he might rip Privek apart with his bare hands.

Kanik's eyes went wide with shock at the same moment that Liam realized Andrew had been the one who crashed into them. Andrew held Kanik's arm with one hand and his own leg with the other. Blood seeped out of the leg to stain his jeans. Privek must have shot Andrew, which Liam had no way to heal.

"Don't kill him," Liam shouted. "Not yet." The fighting had stopped, and everyone in Privek's entourage stood there, disoriented and confused.

The vampire took another shot to the chest before he batted the gun away and grabbed Privek by the front of his suit, then lifted him off the ground. They went twenty feet up and Stephen chose not to bite him or break him in half. At least he responded to orders.

Privek flailed in the air, eyes bugged out and spittle gathering at the corners of his mouth as he shouted. "How? You can't overcome—? This is impossible! You're all mine! Kanik! We can still rule this country, side by side, as the power behind the President!"

Kanik lifted his head. "Who cares about that?"

CHAPTER 22

BOBBY

The dragon burned and bit and scraped. Lily's gurgles and whimpers echoed all around Bobby, the world shaking as she writhed around in reaction. He burst through Lily's chest in a blast of fire, spraying blood and gore everywhere and already looking for his next target. It focused on Anita as she turned to watch Lily fall into Tiana's arms. In that moment when her body went limp and her eyes glazed over, he suddenly got control over his dragons again. They stopped attacking and backed off, all of them confused.

He pulled the swarm together and re-formed on the other side of the barrier between him and her body, unable to do anything but pound on it with one fist. Sam still had control over enough dragons to deny him his other hand and arm up to the elbow. "Let me through, please, Anita! I ain't controlled no more, I swear, let me see her!" Tears stung his eyes. She could still be alive, he had to hold onto that. "I gotta take her to Liam! Help me save her!"

The debris parted and he saw nothing but Lily, lying there, bloody and still. He grabbed her up and ran for it. The swarm broke out and carried her faster than his legs could, and he felt Sam release the rest. She wasn't dead, not yet. He couldn't do anything about Clive, he couldn't do anything about that little girl or her people, but he could save Lily. He *would* save Lily. Somehow.

He flew through the zombies, every one acting confused and disoriented. All of them must have been under Kanik's influence, and now they were free and had no idea what had happened or where they were. But it didn't matter, because he needed to save Lily.

It took far too long to find the smaller group. Stephen held Privek up in the air. Kanik sat on the ground, rocking and holding his head. The swarm set Lily down beside Liam and Bobby re-formed on one knee between them both. He picked up Lily's hand and shoved it into Liam's. "Heal her, you gotta."

Liam looked up at him. As he sadly shook his head no, Bobby heard a thump, a clatter, and a shout. Bobby looked past Liam and saw Stephen on the ground, yanking a dart out of his arm. Privek scrambled to his gun, picked it up, and fired all around, hitting Javier in the arm, Liam in the leg, and Kanik in the back. Bobby jumped up and ran straight at him, taking a bullet in the gut and not caring as he leaped and tackled Privek.

"You did this, all of this," he said, tears rolling down his cheeks. He grabbed two handfuls of Privek's suit and dragged the man to Liam. "Look at what you done, you—" He shoved Privek's face down at the ragged, bloody hole in Lily's chest. "There ain't no words strong enough."

CHAPTER 23

LIAM

Liam knew Bobby didn't mean to shove Privek at him; it was incidental. He had no control over what happened next. The woman Bobby shoved at him—one of their kind—was dead, but so freshly dead he didn't know if healing her lay beyond his ability. All he really knew for sure was that he had no intention of sacrificing himself for someone else, not like that. But more importantly, he hated Privek.

His power swept him up, daring him to try to resist. What would happen clicked in his head, and he let it. A connection formed as he reached out and grabbed Privek. Liam took Lily's death on himself, then passed it to Privek.

The agent gasped and gurgled and goggled. The woman's chest healed over. He collapsed and she drew a breath.

For a moment, Liam stared blankly at what he'd done. It filled him with awe and wonder and horror all at once. As he lay back, fully healed, and stared at the sky, he thought perhaps Privek had gotten off too easy. That bastard deserved something much worse for all he'd done. With that happy thought, he blacked out.

Chapter 24

Camellia

Camellia stayed still, perfectly camouflaged as she leaned against the wall, watching everything happen. Kevin's body heat gave him away, standing beside her. "I'm glad we had orders to stay out of this." She saw Mitchell dive to his knees and shove the now dead body off the now live one, taking her up in his arms and kissing her.

"Me too." Kevin sounded noncommittal. She imagined he leaned there casually, arms crossed and aloof. He spent so much time invisible, she had no idea what sort of mannerisms he really had, and made them up in her head.

"I'm thinking maybe I don't want to be part of the group."

"No? I'm thinking it's pretty incredible how they'll do just about anything for each other. Wouldn't mind having an in to that."

Camellia shrugged, distorting her camouflage. Someone staring at her might notice. "A lot of people die around them. Lots of chaos, destruction. Privek was only the first person who wanted to control us. He won't be the last." She watched the shiny guy and the vampire check on everyone over there.

"Maybe so, but even I know that being invisible only keeps people from seeing me. I'm pretty sure I can be detected. I also have a feeling that if I go off on a crime spree, these guys will be the ones hunting me down. For their own safety, if nothing else."

"I guess you have a point." Camellia shrugged again. "I suppose it won't hurt to give them a try, at least."

"No, I don't think it will."

CHAPTER 25

BOBBY

Bobby got out of the car with Riker, Stephen, and Jayce. Nearly everyone else either needed to rest or had volunteered to deal with all those people. Getting a hundred and fifty formerly homeless folks with minor superpowers across the country without attracting too much attention to the destination presented a complicated problem. Hannah said she'd take care of it, which Bobby appreciated. He didn't have the first clue how to even start on it.

Lily was fine—thank goodness she left Sebastian in the car, so he didn't see much of anything—and so was Liam. He healed up everyone who'd survived, the drugs wore off for Stephen and everyone else, and they had to figure out what to do with Kanik. The guy needed help, and they'd find a way to get it for him. They'd take care of their own, and that was that. Liam said his parents would help financially, and a few of the others had some money too. The farm would be in good shape soon enough, and they might just start their own little town.

The only other loose end besides the one they'd come here to take care of was the wormhole stuff. Bobby felt pretty confident a bright light of publicity combined with some sabotage would slow that down enough to trigger all kinds of bureaucracy. Folks would learn more about Asyllis than the few blurry shots a reporter managed to grab. He had a lot to say still, and nobody could shut him up about any of it.

General Hanstadt had a really nice house with a really nice front yard. Everything was precise and as close to perfect as nature would allow. It felt artificial and sterile, but that didn't matter. Bobby led them all up the front walk. The door opened before he had a chance to ring the bell, which didn't really surprise him. After everything that happened today, they had to be expecting a ten pony circus to ride up to the door and blow it up, or something equally dramatic and destructive.

"Mr. Mitchell." The General answered the door himself, in uniform. "Please, come in."

Bobby gave him the most polite smile he knew how and stepped inside the house. "Everybody calls me Bobby. This here's—"

"I know who your friends are." His interruption sounded less than friendly without turning the corner to ugly. He gestured for them all to use a particular doorway from the well-appointed entry. Inside it, they found unexpected visitors already sitting on the couches and chairs.

The two men in dark suits standing in the corners reminded Bobby too much of ones he'd faced before to be comfortable, but he didn't suppose members of the Secret Service would leave just because he asked nice. Not when the President of the United States was in the room. Though he didn't recognize anyone else in the room, he figured they must be important.

"Is it alright if I call you Bobby too?" The President gave him a perfunctory smile as he stood up and extended his hand to shake with all four of them.

"Yessir, that's fine. You are part of 'everybody' and all." For some reason, he expected the President to be something more than the ordinary man standing before him. He ought to be big, or shiny, or somehow larger than life. The guy was just a man in a suit, really. Taller than him, sure, and probably twice as smart, but not a superhero. Realizing that made it easy to talk to him. "We weren't rightly expecting you, sir, or we mighta dressed up a touch." At least they took the time to clean up all the blood, and Liam sprang for new jeans and shirts. Except for Riker, who insisted upon wearing his Army fatigues.

"Don't worry about it. You've had a rough day." The President sat down and gestured for them to follow suit.

Bobby heard Jayce and Stephen both make little noises and mutter to each other as they stepped around the furniture and sat. A glance back showed him Riker found whatever they said funny too, but he kept it mostly stifled back. The soldier didn't sit with the three of them. Instead, he stood at parade rest behind the couch they took. "That's one way of putting it, I reckon."

"We were expecting William Moore to be with you. Is he alright?"

"Yessir, he's just exhausted. Bunch of us went through a wringer, and the only reason you got this many is on account we figured if no one came, y'all'd get a touch ornery. Sergeant Riker here insisted on coming too."

"Buffalo soldier Sergeant Cory Riker, Sir." Riker saluted. "I want to know how my men and I will be treated after all this."

General Hanstadt stopped a few steps away from him. "You're not going to be arrested, if that's what you mean, Sergeant."

"We'll get to that," the President said with a nod. "First, I want to talk about where we go from here."

Bobby felt everyone turn and stare at him. His eyes dropped to his lap, where one of his hands rested on his leg, and it fell apart into dragons.

The bunch of them turned to watch the President, then all sat obediently in silence. They drew the attention of all those who'd never seen them in person before. It was a kind of power, one Bobby had yet to decide how to feel about.

"You'd be stupid not to be thinking about how you could use us, for the country, for yourself personally, for whatever else, but I'm telling you right here, right now, flat out: ain't gonna happen. You can't control us. Even if you could, we won't let you." As he spoke, he raised his eyes until he met the President's gaze, as serious as he ever got. "If'n you try, we're gonna rain fire and brimstone down on whoever and whatever we gotta to make it stop. We ain't toys. We're people."

"That sounds like a threat," General Hanstadt growled. He seemed coiled and ready to leap over the couch to protect his Commander In Chief. Bobby noticed the Secret Service agents tensing. Stephen stayed calm, draped on the couch like a coat, and Jayce looked thoughtful as he flipped a small piece of steel over in his fingers.

Bobby nodded. "Point is, you deal square with us and we'll deal square with you. You mess with us, and you won't know what hit you."

Now giving Bobby a calculating stare, the President sat back in his seat, a picture of rigid, forced relaxation. "I came here in the hopes we could work something out for mutual benefit, Bobby."

Letting out a light snort, Bobby shook his head. "I ain't stupid. We been abducted, stabbed, shot, poked, prodded, lied to, even killed, all by people what wanted us to 'work something out for mutual benefit.' I got no faith the US government has our best interests at heart, and ain't listening to whatever you got to say all doe-eyed." He stood up, his dragons re-forming his hand again. Stephen floated to his feet and Jayce also stood, shimmering into steel. "Sergeant Riker and his men are under our protection, so're their families and ours. We ain't rightly sure if we all still want to be American citizens anymore. We'll get back to you on that."

The President frowned. "You can't just take American land and declare yourselves sovereign. You do that, and it'll be interpreted as an attempt at secession."

This wasn't exactly how Bobby envisioned this meeting. He had a point to make and he made it, and now it was turning into some kind of pissing contest. "I ain't your enemy, Mr. President. None of us is. Just remember this when you deal with us: we got among us folks what can make fire, disintegrate anything, break a body in half, and fly. You give us a little time, say a month, to bury our dead and set ourselves up, then you send someone out to talk polite-like and we'll listen." He tipped an imaginary hat. "It was nice meeting you, Mr. President."

"That went well." Stephen smirked as the front door closed behind them.

Jayce cracked a grin and chuckled. "You might have told us you were planning on threatening the President of the United States with war."

"Wasn't rightly planning on it."

Stephen clapped him on the shoulder. "That's what I like the best about you, Bobby. Full speed ahead and damn the consequences torpedoes."

Riker snorted. "They're going to try something, just to see if they can get away with it."

"We'll be ready for it."

Sam had ideas about electronic surveillance, and Tiana said something about animal sentries. Even John had thoughts about using the plant life for security.

Bobby opened the front passenger door of the car and climbed in.

Jayce got into the driver's seat and the other two climbed into the back. "Ain't nobody gonna sneak up on us never again."

"Yessir, Head Cowboy." Riker saluted Bobby.

Jayce grinned. "I like 'Spokesdragon' better."

"You would," Stephen said, shaking his head. "Injun."

"Fifty percent," Jayce nodded. "So, technically, I'm a Space Injun."

Riker grinned. "That makes Bobby a Space Cowboy."

"Some might call him the Gangster of Love. Or even Maurice."

"Oh, whatever, just stop someplace so I can get a burger or something." Bobby laughed with them all, happy he could finally settle down and relax for a while. Then they passed a billboard with a woman dressed like a housewife on it, advertising a maid service. The woman looked a lot like his Momma, which made him think of her, and his smile faded.

He thought about it for a few minutes, scratching his chin. He hadn't gone to see her since that one day. Time had been tight. Danger had chased him. He'd worried about getting her mixed up in all of his problems. Now, all that lay behind him. They stopped at a fast food place and got something to eat, and he still thought about it.

Not until he'd polished off his drive-through cheeseburgers did he make a decision. "Guys, I gotta bail."

Jayce took his eyes off the road to glance at him. "Car too slow for you?"

Bobby grinned and shook his head. "Naw, there's something I gotta do."

"I'll go with you," Stephen offered.

Bobby waved the vampire off. "I'm just going home. Ain't no big deal. I'll see y'all back at the farm in a few days. You ask me, I think it's a good idea for folks to take a buddy when we go home to visit, but I think

I'll be okay."

"Head Cowboy only makes the rules," Jayce said with a smirk, "he doesn't follow them."

Rolling his eyes, Bobby pushed the button to roll the window down. "Yeah, whatever. I got someplace to be." He let the dragons peel off and dart out the window. He heard Stephen say something about him cheating, then Bobby streaked up and away from the car.

Chapter 26

Bobby

When he reached his Momma's house, Bobby saw a van from the local news station parked outside, even though it was the middle of the night. National news would probably be here in the morning. That aspect of going public hadn't actually occurred to him until this moment. Since no one else brought it up, he figured no one else thought about it, either.

To avoid attracting attention, he dropped down and re-formed on the back step. The door was locked, of course. He broke in and relocked the door behind himself. He grabbed a banana off the counter in the dark and ate it, then he dropped down on the couch and rubbed his face. How was he supposed to tell her about everything that happened? What would she say about it all? She accepted him for what he was, but that was before...

He saw that girl again. He saw Lily with her chest ripped open. He saw shredded piles of meat. He'd done that, all of it. A hand on his shoulder interrupted his thoughts and made him look up. Momma stood there in her nightdress and slippers, a weary smile visible in dim light coming through the window.

"You look like your Daddy, boy." She sat next to him, putting her arm around his shoulders. "He used to come out here and sit like that sometimes."

Bobby leaned into her, grateful he could still have this, at least for the moment. "There's reporters parked outside."

"They been there since about a half hour after you went on TV. I saw that, by the way. It's all over the place. Some folks are saying it's fake, but I know better."

"I'm sorry I brought that to your doorstep."

Momma tsked at him. "I can take care of myself. Though I will say this house is whole lot quieter with you gone. Empty-like."

What he wouldn't give to be able to waltz right back into his life. Bobby sighed. "Did Daddy ever tell you about the stuff he did as a Marine?"

She squeezed his shoulders. "That's how he stopped having night-mares. He talked about it. He never wanted you to hear any of it, so he'd tell me when he woke up and couldn't sleep, in the middle of the night. Like now."

If that wasn't an invitation, he didn't know what was. Bobby started talking, telling her the whole story, from start to end. Once he started, it came out in a flood of words, and he didn't leave anything out, not a single thing. Through it all, she sat there and listened to him and didn't let go. It was what he needed, more than anything else.

When he stopped, the silence was deep and wide. Momma pulled him into a hug and rocked him like she used to when he was little, until he fell asleep. He woke up later to the smell of bacon and eggs, a pillow under his head, and a glass of orange juice on the coffee table. Sitting up and rub-bing his eyes, he took a long drink of juice. As he stood to take it to the sink, someone knocked on the door.

"Ignore it," Momma called from the kitchen.

He grinned and ambled to her. "You figure they'll get bored and go away?"

She set everything aside and wrapped him in a hug. "I figure my boy's belly is more important than anything they want to know."

Until that moment, he hadn't realized how much he still worried about her acceptance. He hugged her back, reveling in the embrace. "I love you, Momma."

"I love you too, Robert. You're my boy, and that won't never change."

LISTING OF SUPERHEROES

     This listing includes all thirty-five superheroes. Characters without ethnicity notations are nonspecific Caucasian/White.

ROBERT MITCHELL (BOBBY)

Age: 19
Occupation: Appliance delivery
Hometown: A semi-rural suburb of Atlanta, Georgia
Superpower: His entire body is made of tiny robot dragons, which he can separate and re-form at will. The dragons have individual minds that operate on a simplistic level, and are each part of the hive mind that is Bobby. They can all breathe fire and fly.

JAYCE WESTBROOK —NATIVE AMERICAN/YAVAPAI

Age: 22
Occupation: Hotel security guard
Hometown: Las Vegas, NV
Superpower: The ability to change the composition of his body to any material he touches with his hands. He tends to choose steel or similar metals, which give him additional strength along with defenses against most kinds of weapons.

AI DAZAI —JAPANESE

Age: 22

Occupation: Not stated

Hometown: San Diego, CA

Superpower: Speed, 100mph.

ALICE FANG —CHINESE

Age: 21

Occupation: Pre-med student at Stanford

Hometown: San Francisco, CA

Superpower: Creates ice. Her body is immune to the harmful affects of cold.

JASMINE MILANI —IRANIAN

Age: 22

Occupation: Waitress

Superpower: Shapeshifter — squirrel form only. She can also run at unusually high speeds and exercise a mild form of mind control over other squirrels.

HANNAH PARSON

Age: 23

Occupation: Secretary in a real estate office

Hometown: Philadelphia, PA

Superpower: Makes a force field of blue energy that deflects everything she's ever encountered, and can catch or carry people and objects.

Elizabeth Caulfield (Lizzie)

Age: 19

Occupation: None

Hometown: A small town near Little Rock, AR

Superpower: Creates fire. She's immune to fire and suffers no ill effects from exposure to heat.

Daniel Jarvis (Dan)

Age: 19

Occupation: Not stated

Hometown: A small town near Little Rock, AR

Superpower: Body control (others). He can control the physical actions of others as if they were puppets for his mind.

Andrew Roulet

Age: 23

Occupation: Sous-chef in a fancy restaurant

Hometown: Baton Rouge, LA

Superpower: Nullifier. Whoever he's touching is completely incapable of using their own power until he lets go. He also can remove the effects of a mental power from a victim/target.

Stephen Cant

Age: 20

Occupation: College student

Hometown: Dallas, TX

Superpower: Classical vampire. He can fly, has unusual strength, regenerates, and his saliva can overload the senses with pleasure. Unfortunately, he also can only ingest blood and burns in sunlight.

Christopher Gonzales (Chris) —Tejano

Age: 23

Occupation: hairdresser

Hometown: Austin, TX

Superpower: Empathy. He can sense and alter the emotions of others.

Tiana Brown —African-American

Age: 23

Occupation: Zookeeper at the LA Zoo

Hometown: Los Angeles, CA

Superpower: Animal telepathy.

Matthew Garrison

Age: 22

Occupation: Marines veteran/unemployed

Hometown: Los Angeles, CA

Superpower: Werewolf with regeneration. The alternate shape is tied to his PTSD. When in werewolf shape, he's unable to control himself and rampages until stopped.

Lily Thatcher

Age: 20

Occupation: Mom to Sebastian (age 2), employee at her parents' garden center

Hometown: San Jose, CA

Superpower: Creates objects out of a hard white material. She has the most success making weapons and tools, and can create fully functional bullets.

Anita Martinez —Hispanic

Age: 21
Occupation: Casino pit boss
Hometown: Reno, NV
Superpower: Telekinesis.

Kaitlin Tremont

Age: 20
Occupation: Online day trader
Hometown: Shelby, MT
Superpower: Precognition. She sees the future, both on demand and whenever her own safety is in jeopardy.

Andrea Foster

Age: 21
Occupation: Not stated
Hometown: A small town near Indianapolis, IN
Superpower: Disintegration. She can destroy any inanimate object, rendering it to fine dust, but cannot affect living things.

Greg Mezilis

Age: 20
Occupation: Graduate student
Hometown: Madison, WI
Superpower: Gadgeteer. He is a supergenius in the subject of applied science and engineering.

Violet Grace

Age: 21

Occupation: Graduate student (Law school)

Hometown: Mobile, AL

Superpower: Flight, 100mph.

Owen Johnson

Age: 22

Occupation: Garbage collector

Hometown: Denver

Superpower: Sound control. He can manipulate the sound of his own voice in any way imaginable.

John Tseng —Chinese

Age: 21

Occupation: Florist

Hometown: Raleigh, NC

Superpower: Plant control. He can manipulate plants to change their characteristics, supply them with nutrients, and communicate with them.

Javier Ortiz —Hispanic

Age: 19

Occupation: Auto mechanic

Hometown: Los Angeles, CA

Superpower: Wall crawling. He can walk across any surface at any angle, including water.

Maisie Polape —Native Hawaiian

Age: 20

Occupation: Hula dancer

Hometown: Honolulu, HI

Superpower: Portal throwing. She can create a wormhole between any two points, so long as she has a surface to put the portals on. The two portals she can create are person-sized and allow anyone to pass through.

Paul Pearson

Age: 20

Occupation: College student

Hometown: Seattle, WA

Superpower: Telepathy.

William Moore (Liam)

Age: 23

Occupation: MBA student at Harvard

Hometown: Chicago, IL

Superpower: Empathic Healer. He takes the injuries of others onto his own body, then regenerates them himself. Injuries he sustains personally do not regenerate, but can be given to someone else.

Samantha Green (Sam)

Age: 20

Occupation: Webmaster, college student

Hometown: New York City, NY

Superpower: Accesses and controls any type of device that runs an operating system, including peripheral devices, like cameras and microphones.

Antonio Benti —Cubano

Age: 21

Occupation: Not stated

Hometown: Miami, FL

Superpower: Shapeshifter —inanimate objects of a size similar to his own body only.

Lisa Brewer

Age: 23

Occupation: Kindergarten teacher

Hometown: St. Paul, MN

Superpower: Accesses a pocket of extradimensional space with unknown dimensions. She is able to climb into the space herself, and can theoretically stuff something as big as a car inside it.

Camellia Androvitch

Age: 21

Occupation: Customer service call center drone

Hometown: Phoenix, AZ

Superpower: Chameleon. Her body can shift what it looks like to match her surroundings. When she stands still, she's effectively invisible.

Dianna Jackson —African-American

Age: 18

Occupation: None, recent high school graduate with no plans

Hometown: Chicago, IL

Superpower: Controls the movement of air and can propel herself, others, and objects through the air.

CHELSEA O'MALLEY

Age: 18

Occupation: Mental patient (institutionalized)

Hometown: Boston, MA

Superpower: Has two feathery, angel-like wings that allow her to fly.

KEVIN ASTRID

Age: 21

Occupation: Apartment complex security guard

Hometown: Dallas, TX

Superpower: Invisibility.

BRIAN ARRALT

Age: 20

Occupation: College student —marine biology

Hometown: Portland, OR

Superpower: His body can melt into clear water bounded by a transparent membrane as tough as steel.

RAYMOND BELLER (RAY) —AFRICAN-AMERICAN

Age: 23

Occupation: Construction worker

Hometown: New Orleans, LA

Superpower: Creates a physical shield that he cannot be separated from against his will. It can range in size from covering only his fist to a ten foot square, and he can lift it easily no matter the size he chooses. The material is impervious to harm.

KANIK OKPIK —INUIT

Age: 22
Occupation: None
Hometown: Juneau, AK
Superpower: [redacted]

Books by Lee French

The Maze Beset Trilogy
Dragons In Pieces
Dragons In Chains
Dragons In Flight

Fantasy in the Ilauris setting
Damsel In Distress
Shadow & Spice (short story)

The Greatest Sin series
(co-authored with Erik Kort)
The Fallen
Harbinger
Moon Shades

ABOUT THE AUTHOR

Lee French lives in Olympia, WA with two kids, two bicycles, and too much stuff. She is an avid gamer and active member of the Myth-Weavers online RPG community, where she is known for her fondness for Angry Ninja Squirrels of Doom. In addition to spending much time there, she also trains year-round for the one-week of glorious madness that is RAGBRAI, has a nice flower garden with one dragon and absolutely no lawn gnomes, and tries in vain every year to grow vegetables that don't get devoured by neighborhood wildlife.

She is an active member of the Northwest Independent Writers Association, the Pacific Northwest Writers Association, and the Olympia Area Writers Coop, as well as being one of two Municipal Liaisons for the NaNoWriMo Olympia region.

Thanks for reading! If you enjoyed this book, please take a minute to review it on Goodreads and wherever you buy your books.

www.authorleefrench.com

21442499R00154

Made in the USA
Middletown, DE
30 June 2015